The

UNCERTAIN
SEASON

OTHER BOOKS BY ANN HOWARD CREEL

The Magic of Ordinary Days

While You Were Mine

The Whiskey Sea

The

UNCERTAIN
SEASON

ANN HOWARD CREEL

Bestselling author of *The Whiskey Sea*

LAKE UNION
PUBLISHING

Text copyright © 2017 by Ann Howard Creel
All rights reserved.

Published by Lake Union Publishing, Seattle
www.apub.com

Amazon, the Amazon logo, and Lake Union are trademarks of Amazon.com, Inc., or its affiliates.

ISBN-13: 9781477809044
ISBN-10: 147780904X

Cover design by Rachel Adam Rogers
Cover photography by Laura Klynstra

Printed in the United States of America

The

UNCERTAIN
SEASON

PROLOGUE

GRACE

As a child, I believed there were no other places like Galveston, no other islands like mine. But in fact the Gulf Coast is ribbed with barrier islands formed by silt carried from as far away as the Mississippi River. Such islands are transitory places, simple sand spits, and unreliable pieces of earth. God tests us here, every season sending the sea's wrath to shift the ground beneath our feet.

The earliest inhabitants, the native Karankawas, understood this. They visited Galveston Island but never built homes here; in fact, during any given year they never stayed longer than a season.

And yet this island life was all I had lived, and all I had ever wanted.

But it is not the island's story I plan to tell. It's Etta's and mine, Jonathan's and Ira's. And even more so, it's the story of a girl whose name I never knew.

Chapter One

The Girl

When the 1900 Storm hit Galveston, she was aboard a shrimp boat with Harry Gobinet, her brother's best friend and a fisherman's son, a sixteen-year-old sailor who already knew the sea and its signs. Harry sensed something over the shoals, in beds of oysters dug into the sandbars that ribbed the shallows of Galveston Bay, in the rising thick and gray seas, in gulls flying overhead in high spirals, and he felt it in a brisk offshore wind.

The girl and her brother, Anson, often took Saturday-morning boat rides with Harry. Now, as the girl ate oranges and tossed the rinds to imaginary mermaids who swam in their wake, she studied Harry. Normally he was a happy soul, but today he squinted up at the sky and looked around the boat in every direction, as though he were expecting a ghost to blow in. Or maybe he was aggravated that Anson hadn't been able to go out with them today and so he was stuck with her. Something was on Harry's mind, and the girl figured that, at age eleven, she was grown up enough to hear it.

"What's eating at you?" she asked.

Harry, his sun-streaked hair tossing in the wind, only shook his head and kept on watching things he couldn't yet name. The tide was rising, while the winds were blowing against it. High water along with opposing winds was most unusual, but Harry eventually figured out what it was: a storm tide.

Therefore he never put out his net, and he headed not back to the docks on the island's north side, instead tacking the boat across Galveston Bay toward the Texas mainland. He stood braced at the tiller, his eyes glistening with watery apprehension, his tanned face bleak with concern, and at last he explained the storm signs to the girl as he plunged the bow through the beginning chop. The girl, used to the sea's moods and not concerned yet, held on with one hand as they pitched onward, and with her other hand she floated orange wedges on the blustering wind that tousled and twisted her lobster-red hair.

Harry Gobinet knew something huge was blowing in, but even he didn't foresee the magnitude of the storm coming their way. Still, he saw enough to save them.

And that is how the girl came to live through it, even though after the storm swept across Galveston Island, high tides surged ten miles over the Texas mainland, and she and Harry had to scramble from the boat and leave it in the muddies of Buffalo Bayou and run for dry land. Three days later, while they searched for any remains of his father's boat—they found nothing—the girl saw the body of a dead boy caught in a tree, his face the color of horse's teeth and his limbs black, his feet dangling out of the branches like a bird's broken wings.

In a dazed state of fatigue and fear about what had happened on the island, she and Harry made do on the mainland with shelter and help from charities and churches, then returned to Galveston Island eleven days after the storm, when the railroad bridge was finally repaired, and by that time everyone unaccounted for was presumed dead. Boatloads of recovered and mostly unidentifiable corpses were dumped into the gulf or, if they washed back onto the beaches, burned in funeral pyres. The girl saw those fires as she and Harry crossed the bay by train, and from a distance they looked like candles burning golden in the gloom of that dim, gray morning. As they entered the stricken city, however, grim reality set in. Bodies were still washing back onto shore from the gulf, and many still lay in twisted piles. The girl stopped walking and stared. But Harry grabbed her arm and steered her away.

"Don't look," he said and forced her to walk on.

They passed heaps of splintered wood left behind from what had once been houses, bloated corpses of animals, and haggard people wearing threadbare clothing camping out in crumbling schools, churches, hospitals, and the convent. Huge piles of debris lay everywhere. Not even the stench of burning and decaying bodies and stagnant water or the black scum that covered everything had shattered the girl's hopes yet. She imagined finding her family alive and telling them how she had survived.

Their first day back on the island was perfectly still; blades of grass were already sprouting amid the rubble and shining a vibrant green, and as the cloud cover cleared, the sun beamed down yellow light, the sky sweeping and unmarred, altogether cleansed. She and Harry located the street that had been Avenue Q and found it, like most of the city, in shattered ruin. They could not even know for certain where the girl's house had stood.

Realization came to her in one clear and vicious moment. Even in that bright sunlight, she felt the absence of them in her chest, her ribs, and her every breath.

She stood without moving, her hands numb and clenched at her sides.

She and Harry searched for his house, too, but found nothing but wreckage, and then checked at various shelters and camp-out spots, but no signs of either family surfaced. Along with six thousand other islanders, plus thousands of others elsewhere along the coast, their parents and siblings had perished. She and Harry didn't even bother to search for her father's souvenir shack, which had once stood on pilings down on the beach.

The girl opened her mouth to say to Harry, "They're gone," but no sound came. A big, hard stone sat in her middle, making it difficult to breathe. Their families had simply vanished. She drew a tight breath and tried to speak again, but her voice had gone strangely missing, too. She needed to say the words aloud; she needed to say them in a voice bold and big enough so that she would have to believe it.

Harry tried to console and comfort her, but to no avail. And so they wandered more, then came to the steps of City Hall, which was badly damaged but had withstood the storm. They sat side by side, their losses soaking into their cells even as the last of the storm water finally evaporated.

She tried to say those terrible words again, and then she tried to say anything, anything at all, but her mouth refused to work. She could force her lips into the shapes of words, but no sounds ever emerged.

Harry asked, "What is it?" He leaned down close to her face and peered into it. "What's happening to you? Come on and speak up about it. You're safe. And we're going to figure it out together, you and me."

She opened her mouth and tried again. For his sake, for the worry etched into that weary face that no longer looked as if it belonged to a teenager. She wanted to tell him she understood. She was breathing; she was alive. She wasn't knotted in those piles or lost to the deep legions.

God or the heavens or someone had decided that she and Harry should live. But why? The question pulled her air away. If only Anson had come along out on the boat with them that day. He had stayed behind because their father needed help in the souvenir shop. Always generous, always giving.

Anson. Mama. Papa.

"They're gone on to a better place by now," Harry said quietly, as though he could hear her thoughts. He wiped away his tears and then gazed at her haltingly, hands trembling. "That's what people will say."

But all the promises she'd once believed were doubtful now. People did not live, even when you needed them most. Maybe they lived on in eternity, but life after death was nothing she could see or hold in her hands. It could not hug her, tuck her in at night, read her poetry, or run and play with her in the yard. She swallowed several times and then tried to speak once more, for Harry's sake. But she couldn't even hum the beginning of a word, and after that resignation arrived quickly. The hard stone that had settled inside her had absorbed her voice. She could not repeat her father's seaside stories, recite her mother's favorite poems, or confess the antics that she and her brother had engaged in. She could not sing their songs, call to birds, or whistle—something Anson had been trying to teach her.

An emotion previously unknown to her, grief had arrived and taken the form of complete silence.

Chapter Two

GRACE

On June 3, 1903, the day my cousin Etta came to stay with us, my mother had one of her sinking spells and caused a bit of an emergency in our household. Mother had planned to meet the train with me but instead took to her chambers, and therefore I was required to go to the Union Passenger Depot, accompanied only by our carriage driver, Seamus.

And so it was that we generated no fanfare at all for the arrival in Galveston of Miss Etta Rahn, the youngest daughter of my aunt, from Nacogdoches, Texas.

Seamus, my mother's most trusted servant, brought the carriage around to the front of our house on Broadway and awaited me there. My mother had arranged herself on the settee in her private parlor, the exterior shutters having been closed and the louvers adjusted to allow in fresh air, hot as it was. Her favorite maid, Clorinda, was tending to her with damp cloths on her forehead and fanning her with a large paper fan, a gift for herself my mother had purchased on our last trip to the Orient.

Some people might say that Mother was self-indulgent, lying down and allowing herself to be fanned, but in truth she rarely succumbed to feminine frailties. I remembered Clorinda once long ago mumbling, "Too soft for dis here world," but Clorinda, despite her wisdom and constancy, didn't know Mother as well as I did. Normally Mother was as well preened as a show bird, and with her fierce eyes and penchant for wearing her hair high on her head, she often reminded me of a plumed falcon. Mother ran our household and held court over all of our activities just like that bird of prey, searching for sustenance. She had to be in bad sorts to miss Etta's arrival.

I tiptoed into her parlor to tell her I was leaving. She opened her eyes, and then, with a mixed expression of regret and exasperation on her face, she lifted a hand to her forehead. "Dear Grace. What a calamity this is. Do explain to your cousin why I was unable to meet her train with you."

I took her hand and stroked the white skin, as pure and as soft as mine, a lady's hand that had seen little hard work, thanks to my father's family money, made in the slave market before Emancipation. But I had never shared those details with anyone, certainly not during my years at the Ursuline Academy, where I had been a day scholar. In fact, Mother and I never mentioned the original source of our wealth, and now we were partial owners of banks, import-export businesses, and real estate. I held her hand and said, "Calamity might be a bit of an exaggeration, Mother."

She sighed with great heaving movements of her chest and shoulders. "You're still cross with me."

My mother, with her sculpted face and brown hair streaked with silver and raked up with tortoiseshell combs, was an imposing figure, even while ill.

"No," I lied. "I'm certain it isn't my place to know the reason that Cousin Etta's coming. I trust your judgment completely in the matter."

"You're such a jewel. Such a dear, dear treasure to me. But I don't believe a word of it."

I dropped her hand.

"Promise me that you'll be considerate of her. Welcome her. Take her under your wing."

"She's two years older than I am. I hardly think she'll require my guidance, Mother. But of course I will."

My promise lacked sincerity, and my mother knew me too well not to realize that. For the last fourteen years, it had been just the two of us, ever since my father died while he and my mother had been traveling in Louisiana. He had perished in his sleep of some undiagnosed miasma when I was but five years old, and I could barely remember those days when there had been three of us in the Hilliard household instead of just two. All I could evoke of my father were a few hazy scenes and sensations on the other side of clear memory. Of course I recalled with cruel clarity when my mother had told me of his death. She had explained his end to me with pinched eyes and her palms turned upward, as if she held the power to lift him into Heaven.

"Listen to me, Grace," she said now, her eyes boring into mine, pleading.

"I always do."

"Etta hasn't had the privileges you have had. She hasn't grown up within our sort of society. You must be gracious. She will need your assistance."

"I have already agreed."

"You've never experienced living in a new place, either." She shifted her weight on the settee and untied the bow at the neck of her peignoir to let in more air. "Etta hasn't been here since she was eleven years old. Do you remember? We took the carriages for a picnic down on West Beach, and Etta nearly drowned right in our midst. We were all standing at the water's edge, and a large wave simply slammed into the beach and swept her down. You were only nine at the time, but you were the first to reach her and lift her from the surf."

Naturally I remembered the event, especially the sight of Etta's dark eyes, which I recalled as being wide open under a foot or so of foaming water that was drawing back toward the open sea. Pulling her up was instinct, pure and simple, and besides, she was never in true danger. The surf of our island is usually modest, and the slope out to the depths is gentle. But to a young girl like Etta, it must have felt like a storm swell.

I said to Mother, "I do remember the incident. It must have been most distressing to Etta. She and Aunt Junie never came again."

"No," said Mother in a wistful voice. "Not after that episode. They did come once before, however, when the two of you were only three and five, and during that visit you climbed into the attic playroom with a pair of scissors and chopped off each other's hair. Right before Easter." Now she looked slightly amused. "You and Etta together," she said and nodded once. "You were trouble." Her tiny smile vanished. "But this cannot be the case during this visit. You're young ladies now, nineteen and twenty-one. I'll expect you to behave like gentlewomen. No antics or larks. You know how I abhor gossip."

I tried to make my voice sound sweet, not syrupy. "How long do you suppose Cousin Etta will be with us?"

"We've been over this before."

"Any idea? A guess? A hunch?"

"No, and I won't venture a guess. We'll simply have to see."

I said a curt "Very well," then kissed my mother's damp cheek and turned to leave. As I walked away, my footsteps were silent, and my back was held utterly straight, stacked high with my building frustration.

Despite my inquiries, the reason for my cousin's sudden arrival had remained undisclosed. It had started with a flurry of telegrams and letters exchanged between my mother and my aunt Junie, which was most unusual, as they'd never been close. An unfortunate marriage on the part of Aunt Junie to Uncle Ralph had caused much family discord. Mother had once explained to me that her older sister had married far beneath her, to a common "square-head" German who knew nothing but how to repair timepieces. Her words could have come directly out of my grandmother's mouth, as she was the one who had started the dissension before her death.

Now my mother kept alive a multigenerational snobbery I had been forced to endure all of my life. Not only was Etta's father not of our English heritage, he wasn't even an islander but was instead a Houstonian, considered a lesser breed altogether. And on top of all that, he and Aunt Junie had had the audacity to leave Galveston.

Therefore the sudden correspondence between my mother and her older sister was most curious, as was the announcement that my cousin was coming to stay with us for an unspecified period of time and for reasons I was not privy to, all of this occurring during the summer of my engagement, while Galvestonians were also preparing to have their homes, everything in them and around them, including the pecans and magnolias and even the outbuildings and graveyards, lifted while the grade engineering project raised the level of the city right under our very feet.

For my journey to the depot, I donned a navy-blue street suit with a narrowly pleated long skirt and a large hat to shade my face, my hair pinned up except for a few ringlets I'd curled with irons heated and brought to me by my maid, Dolly. I left Mother in Clorinda's care and set off down the main staircase, prepared to face the unconscionable summer heat outside alone.

After crossing the front lawn to the street, I settled myself into the back of the carriage, Seamus cracked the reins, and we headed off toward the station. Our street was lined with the most elegant homes on the island, some of them designed by the renowned architect Nicholas Clayton in the fashionable Italianate design, complete with columns, cornice work, brick, and ironwork. The esplanade running down the center of Broadway made room for old oaks, oleanders, and palms. The greenery was one of the things that made our island so lovely, but much of it was doomed to be ruined during the grade-raising project.

Seamus drew the carriage to a halt before the depot and assisted me out. Seamus's hair and skin were light brown, making those who knew him wonder about his parentage. Some intermingling of the races had obviously taken place in the past, but we didn't discuss these things. What mattered was that he was my mother's favorite. The most private and quiet of the servants, rarely speaking except when spoken to, Seamus was Mother's choice to accompany me on this day.

At the four-story Union Depot building, I waited for my cousin's train on the platform under the shade of a portico and tried to contain my frustration about every aspect of my current circumstances, including lady's fashions that required us to wear corsets and long skirts and cover ourselves almost entirely, with only our faces open to fresh air, even while the heat was so heavy it undulated beneath the ever-present, white-hot sun. A complete lack of wind allowed me to hear the bayside docks—a steam whistle, the rumble of drays, clanging locomotives, and freight cars whacking as they switched from one long pier to another. If I had to be outside in the heat, I'd have much preferred to be near the gulf, where one could at least count on a breeze.

I fanned myself and gazed about. How would Etta view Galveston? How had it changed since her last visit, and how would she see it as an adult? Despite the effects of the storm, rebuilding was reestablishing our island much as it had been before. The deepwater port, protected by jetties that ran over five miles out to sea, was still a major gateway to America.

We hosted a steady stream of foreigners—Russians in their fur hats, the Swiss in their knee breeches, Scots carrying bagpipes, and always the women and children burdened with knapsacks, pots, and pans. Galveston was a great place to depart from, too, and in my lifetime I'd already traveled widely. I'd seen the white sand of Florida, the pink sand of Bermuda, the black sand of the Hawaiian Islands, formed from volcanic rock, but the silver-tan sands of this island were always the sweetest to me.

I did not recognize Etta. After the train arrived and the passengers disembarked, I stood, waiting for her, before realizing with a start that she was already standing before me, eye to eye.

I found her a most striking young woman, with her dark hair dressed up in a cascade of curls and a hat that tilted off to one side. She had high-arched eyebrows, rouged cheeks, red lips, dark eyes, and a jawline that, although not too large, was dominant and determined, giving her an overwhelming impression of vigor, despite the fact that she was petite in stature. The clumsy girl I'd known before had been transformed by womanhood. She possessed a disquieting beauty, different from my own, which was often described as soft and muted, blond and delicate. I was like a greenhouse orchid, whereas Etta was more striking, her looks akin to an Indian paintbrush growing wild along the roadway.

I could scarcely believe this was the same awkward cousin I'd pulled from the water and played with in the sand dunes ten years earlier. Had I changed as drastically?

"Cousin Etta? I'm sorry. I didn't recognize you."

She peered at me appraisingly and held my gaze with razor-sharp scrutiny. "I would've recognized you anywhere." Her voice was bold, a bit husky, like air exhaled through a deeply toned musical instrument.

I said, "What an amazing memory you must have . . . It has been quite a while, after all."

"Please don't worry if you don't remember me. I'm not offended."

We began walking down the platform toward the carriage, while Seamus went to collect Etta's trunk. A pleasant sense of relief came over me. Perhaps I might truly enjoy Etta. It also occurred to me that I'd been given a chance to start anew with my cousin. Etta didn't know me any better than I knew her. We could have a fresh start. She didn't know how often I was described by my acquaintances as *only*, *alone*, and *lonely*. I was an *only* child; my father died and left us *alone*; Grace looks so *lonely*. She had no idea of my life, just as I had no idea of hers. Etta didn't know that when I removed all the layers—the society that surrounded me, my mother's focus, all the exquisite gowns and dresses, and farther still, under my skin, past muscle and bone and into my core—there it lay: something left empty and longing.

I said, "Mother wanted to come, but she's having a bad spell today."

"She's not ill, I hope."

"It's simply the heat. She truly regrets not meeting your train."

Etta waved a hand in the air dismissively, and I led her to the carriage. She walked faster than I did, with clipped steps and a longish stride, her parasol at her side, swinging. Several well-heeled businessmen dressed in nice worsteds and cheviots glanced her way as we passed them.

I said, "Welcome to Galveston, by the way."

And she said, "Thank you."

On the ride to the house, Etta sat next to me in the rear of the carriage. I imagined what I might do with her as the horse's hooves clacked on the cobbled pavement. Over the next few days, I surmised, we could take a short tour of the city, visit the Texas Heroes Monument, The Strand, the opera house, Colonel Walter Gresham's turreted mansion, Woollam's Lake, and of course we could go peek at the ocean over the new seawall under construction. But for now I thought it best to take her straight home and let her get settled. Mother would want to see that she'd arrived safely before we took any excursions.

"How was the train?" I asked.

"Comfortable. I most enjoyed the journey by bridge over the bay. It seemed we were traveling over water forever."

I nodded and held on to the edge of the seat as Seamus made a turn. "When I was younger, crossing that bridge made me think we'd never reach land again. I imagined falling off the Earth."

Etta said, "As the early explorers did. I saw a painting once that depicted such a scene. A tall ship with square white sails was tipping over the edge of a flat world, and at the same time the sea was pouring over the lip into nothingness."

"Well, have no fear. Our island is safe now."

"I must tell you, however, if any hurricane flags are flown, I plan to leave at once." Her face was calm and indiscernible. I couldn't tell if she was masking real nervousness or was relaxed enough to simply make a joke.

"Hurricane season isn't quite upon us yet."

"Favor me with a request, then. Let me know when it arrives."

Back on Broadway, the streetcars, filled with singing and laughing islanders and visitors, clanged as they ran back and forth along the avenue. Residents strolled out onto their porticos, holding glasses of iced tea or lemonade in their hands. Everyone was in search of a cooling breeze, as by now it was midafternoon and the hottest hour of the day.

We had almost arrived. Etta's eyes looked me up and down, and I could almost hear her thoughts, heavy thoughts.

She said it simply: "It was a man."

I wasn't certain I'd heard her correctly. "Pardon?"

"It was a man," she said again and lifted her chin, her dark eyes full of a fiery light that I could see despite the shade of the carriage top. "Surely you're curious to know why I'm here."

I turned, staring straight ahead, and peered over the withers of the horses. My throat had dried. I supposed I could have asked her anything at that moment, but I swallowed my questions, torn between feigning indifference and using the opportunity to learn more. I made my voice light. "Isn't it always a man?"

"I don't know," she said and cleared her throat into her gloved hand. As was typical, dust had worked its way into our compartment. "I've never been involved with a man before. I've also never been disowned before."

I hadn't seen her in ten years, and yet here she was, speaking so candidly. "Are you disowned or simply banished?"

Etta shrugged and half smiled. "My mother needed to do two things—teach me a lesson and get rid of him. Sending me here is supposed to accomplish both."

I almost laughed. "Will it work?"

Etta finally gave me a full smile, which showed off a band of radiant white teeth. "I haven't decided yet."

I became aware of Seamus in front of us and lowered my voice. Seamus was quiet natured, but the biggest gossipers were the house servants. Most of the secrets and stories, both true and untrue, which circulated among our friends from household to household, were spread by them. "Why didn't your mother approve? Did he have warts on his face? Lice in his hair? No teeth?"

"Worse than that," said Etta. "He had no money."

I tried not to laugh, but my cousin was so surprising. "Oh dear," I said. "It is required that we make them proud, isn't it? That we marry better than they did."

"And he worked for the circus."

I coughed into my hand and looked at her hard. "You're jesting me."

"No. He was a flying trapeze artist."

I tried to keep a straight face. "Pardon me, Cousin, but it's no wonder that Aunt Junie disapproved and has sent you our way. We'll be sure to set you back on a better course."

"I'm counting on it."

"How much time do we have to redeem you?"

"My mother won't take me back until I've proven myself contrite and cry daily into my soup for her forgiveness."

Laughter erupted out of me, and Seamus's head jerked up.

I controlled myself and then whispered, "So, you didn't come willingly?"

But even then I sensed that Etta probably did nothing completely against her will, and I was already admiring her cool collectedness and wishing I could absorb some of it.

Etta tugged off her gloves. Even such simple movements of hers had a quality about them, something I couldn't name: a smoothness, a premeditation that made her appear casual but astute, or scheming at every moment.

"I wasn't chained and dragged to the station." She gazed out of the window and then back at me. "I'm considering this stay a vacation, a respite from home and all of its complications."

I had never expected Etta to seem so much older. The gulf between nineteen and twenty-one had never seemed so large. I'd always viewed maturity in terms of worldliness. Now I saw my logic as flawed, and I felt less practiced and mature, and still I couldn't help liking Etta.

Her fingers were long and narrow and unadorned with rings. Only then did I notice that she wore absolutely no jewelry, and the lack of baubles and gems suited her. "Did you love him?"

"Ah, love," she said and gave me a devilish half smile. Then, just as suddenly, she adopted a sober tone. "I'm not sure it was love of the orthodox variety. He made me uneasy, I'll say that."

"Will you see him again?"

Perhaps now I was prying, but Etta seemed unbothered. "I doubt it."

"What happened to him?"

"I suppose I don't know."

I studied her. "What can I do to help you adjust to Galveston?"

Etta gave a short one-shouldered shrug. "Keep me company."

"Of course I will. We'll find much to do. What are your interests?"

"I don't want to be a nuisance. I'll do whatever you do."

"There are so many activities here. Do tell me something of your likes and dislikes."

She paused and laid her gloves in her lap. "Well, let me see. I don't care for books or embroidery or sewing or cooking or, God forbid, prayer."

I spurted out another irrepressible laugh. "Etta!" After composing myself once again, I lowered my voice. "Don't let the driver hear you." And then, "So, what do you enjoy?"

She seemed to consider her response. "Let's just say that I enjoy enjoyment itself."

"Do you like games? Bicycling, croquet, lawn bowling?"

"They can be amusing. But I meant enjoyment of people."

I sat with her answer, so odd an answer.

And then she laughed aloud, a most contagious, throaty laugh.

When Seamus pulled the carriage to a halt before the house, I took the opportunity to ask one last question. Soon the house would swallow us, my mother's presence would overpower us, and close proximity to the other servants would prevent such open talk. "Was he handsome?"

Etta checked her attire in a most casual manner, one hand smoothing down the front of her dress, the other at her waistline. She met my eyes, and for the first time I saw in the corners of her eyes a touch of the sadness this episode must have caused her. "He was the most handsome man I've ever met."

I touched her hand. "I'm so glad you've come. I'm certain to enjoy you."

"Thank you."

My mother would have been so pleased. In less than an hour's time, Etta had captivated my most ardent attention.

After Etta assured me that she wasn't in need of rest yet, I changed my mind about entering the house so soon and said to her, "Allow me to show you around town a bit." It would irk my mother, but I asked Seamus to take us to the ocean. He drove to the beach, while Etta and I chatted longer, making up for much lost time. I told her about Jonathan, informed her that we were recently engaged, and removed my glove to show her my ring. Then, as my mother had instructed, I also told her that we had readied our finest guest room and hoped she would find it satisfactory.

We stepped out of the carriage near Murdoch's Bathhouse, rebuilt after the storm, and then we walked its long pier. The ocean swirled underneath us, the smell of salt and seaweed swept into our nostrils, and an onshore wind pushed against our faces and whipped our skirts around our legs. Our parasols were difficult to manage in the ocean wind.

At the end of the pier, clouds spotted the sea with shadows. Over this deeper water, I searched for any trepidation in Etta, but she maintained the same expression of calm concentration she'd displayed ever since her arrival, and I found myself uncharacteristically chatty. I told Etta that despite the wind and waves she should never fear the Gulf of Mexico waters and assured her they were as warm as bathwater, and the slope of sand made a gentle declivity, almost flat, ideal for surf bathing and wading in our swimming costumes. I told her about sand falls in the ocean, that they were similar to waterfalls, but instead of water pouring off the rims of canyons, these underwater rivers were composed of sand that silently poured off undersea cliffs into deeper water.

She said, "I've never heard of a sand fall."

"As you may have surmised, I love the sea." I then told Etta about the different colors of the gulf—sometimes black, blue, brown, silver, green, or white—and its different moods: sometimes still and silky, other times rolling and swelling, and still other times crashing and exploding.

"Like the human mind," said Etta.

Looking her way, I fought the wind, pulling at strands of hair whipping across my face. "The human mind?"

"Yes," she said. "We're capable of anything, don't you think? Every mood, every act, both good and bad."

I had to let that thought swim around in my mind for a moment. "Etta, you have beguiled me. What interesting ideas you have."

A faint smile formed on her lips.

Turning to face the water again, I inhaled the sea wind. "Yet our minds are not as big as the sea. Human lives are small by comparison."

Etta gazed out, too. "Sometimes my life feels this big."

We stood together then, in silence that was, on my part, full of pleasure and contentedness. How wonderfully our first day was proceeding. How brilliant that secrecy and discord, the banes of our mothers' generation, would not interfere with our relationship.

And so we stood together, two hopeful young women staring at the sea, the sun at our backs and the wind in our faces. In that instant, in that one glittering moment of renewal and new beginning, I imagined Etta and me as marvelous friends, full of potential, free as the birds above, flying beyond the old confines.

Chapter Three

Etta

She remembered Galveston. She remembered a hot wind and a sun like a huge white hole cut out of the sky. She remembered greenish seawater and layers of waves that looked like lace, and then being hit by a wall of water.

Her feet had vanished, the sun and sky disappeared, and she couldn't move. She was lost within a terrifying other realm, where the wall now ran over her face and sucked along her sides. There was little light and no air, and for those long terrifying moments she was paralyzed by shock, surprise, and the sheer speed of it all. *It's a bad dream*, she told herself.

Wake up, wake up.

But when she opened her eyes, there were no bedroom walls around her, no middle-of-the-night darkness, only murkiness, a weak light coming through a thick fog, a burning in her eyes. She was underwater, taken.

Instinct had told her not to breathe.

In Etta's memory, no one lifted her from the water. Gasping for air and coughing and choking, she had groped her way to her feet on her own. Etta recalled only that she was responsible for her own rescue. And even more alarming was that surrounding her, as she made her way out of the rushing water to safety, were the people who were supposed to take care of her, namely her mother and aunt, both of whom had done nothing. They were rushing toward her now, but it was too late. Their cries and questions were hollow and after the fact.

Etta looked at them hard as she shivered, held herself, and lifted her feet out of the wet, heavy sand. She let them wrap her in a shawl and console her, but for the first time she saw those adults for what they really were. Why, they were nothing but larger versions of children, no more able to control the world around them, and in no way able to keep her safe in the world. She decided in that moment that she would never again let down her guard.

Etta remembered little else about Galveston beyond that incident on the beach. Perhaps the terror, no matter how momentary, had caused her to forget the rest of the visit, and therefore she arrived on the island again after ten years with an open mind and few preconceived notions.

During that first carriage ride in Galveston with Grace, the city streamed before her with new sounds, smells, and sights. After Grace had taken her for a walk on the pier, they took a quick tour of the city.

The beach side of the island was all sand and sweltering salt breezes. Wealthy people strolled down the sand, and children frolicked in the shallow waves. Tourists made sand castles, searched for shells, and wandered in and out of souvenir shops. People came there for pleasure.

The bay side, however, was a place of work. The port was a chaotic scene of fishermen, oystermen, buyers, and sellers milling about. Fresh fish in lines, docks stacked with bales of cotton ready for export, and the sounds of clinking knives against oyster shells were everywhere. The red-faced sailors and wrinkled, squinty-eyed pirate look-alikes were even more weathered than the lifelong farmers Etta had known, and their wives bore the scars of waiting, the skin of their faces cut sharply with lines.

Before they pulled up to the house for the second time that day, Grace asked her, "What do you think so far?"

"It feels dangerous."

Grace put a hand on Etta's arm. "I promise it's not. Please don't be—"

"You misunderstand. I'm not frightened. I like that it feels dangerous."

Grace looked puzzled.

"In the middle of Texas, it's just land and farms. Some brown rivers that occasionally overflow their banks. We hear of twisters, but I've never seen one. Being out here on an island surrounded by water, well . . . it's akin to taking chances, don't you think?"

"I've never thought of it that way."

"Because you're accustomed to it."

"It's my home," Grace said, giving her a smile that appeared to be utterly genuine. "And I'm so enjoying viewing it again through a newcomer's eyes."

"Thank you for your most gracious welcome. I fear I've been too outspoken. I probably shouldn't have blurted out . . ."

"Have no fear, Cousin. Your secret is safe with me."

If Etta had thought her cousin's welcome was gracious, she was soon overcome by the house, her living quarters, the servants, and meals. She hadn't expected her stay to be totally unpleasant. On the contrary, the photographs of her aunt Bernadette she'd found among her grandmother's things revealed a most striking and elegant woman, who despite her stateliness had a warmth to the way she held her mouth and the way her hands were folded in a loose knot on her lap.

Nothing, however, could have prepared Etta for the different world into which she walked that day in June of 1903. Her mother had said nothing, had not readied her at all for the Hilliard household. Etta's only clue had come from her grandmother, dead two years by then, but who, upon her last visit to Nacogdoches, had dropped little occasional comments to indicate that the youngest of her three daughters,

Bernadette, had done well for herself. The middle sister, Memphis, had succumbed to infection and fluid in the lungs when she was but seventeen years old, and Etta's grandmother reserved comment about how Junie, Etta's mother, had done; she held herself in check around Etta.

So until then Etta hadn't known that such disparity existed between her mother and her aunt. Her mother and father had a comfortable life in a modest house, no better or worse than many others surrounding them in Nacogdoches, but her aunt turned out to live at a highly elevated place as one of the wealthiest people on what turned out to be a very wealthy island.

The following day, when her aunt Bernadette had recovered from her heatstroke, they dined in the formal dining room on fresh fish and beef, vegetables in sauces, select fruits, and just-baked bread. Her aunt tasted everything first to ensure the food was excellent and then passed on her compliments to the kitchen. Her only suggestion, given with a smile, was for more salt in one of the sauces.

Before retiring for the night, Etta was told that she could ask the servants for her breakfast to be served in her room if she preferred. Never having been doted upon in such a way before, she now had assistance in dressing, bathing, hairstyling, and even lacing her shoes. During the day, Grace took her for carriage rides to show her more of the city.

Etta soon learned that her new territory ran between Twelfth and Nineteenth Streets on the north side of Broadway and several blocks to the north; this was where the most prominent islanders lived and played, in mansions that spoke of the dividends of the island's commerce. Everywhere surrounding Etta in those first whirlwind days were wealthy people who lived in huge houses and held influential positions. In fact, within the circle she had entered, except for the servants there were no ordinary people.

Even more interesting were all the young men who appeared to be unattached among the well-to-do islanders. Now Etta understood why her mother had been so determined to end her tryst with the circus man. She could almost hear her mother sending silent messages she would never spell out in words: *See what might have happened to me if I'd made wiser choices.* So whenever her aunt or cousin suggested an activity, Etta did it. She watched her cousin and followed her lead in manners and speech, but never let anyone notice that she was carefully studying every step along the way.

One evening, after her first week had come to an end, the three ladies of Hilliard House were sharing a late dinner in the small dining room used only by family when Aunt Bernadette asked, "How are you enjoying our city, Etta?"

"It's charming," Etta could answer honestly, but she didn't want to reveal everything, especially how different it was for her.

"Is it what you'd hoped?" continued her aunt.

Etta lifted her napkin and touched it to her lips just slightly, the way she had learned by observing her aunt's and cousin's every move. "I'm finding everything so very interesting. Such a change from the countryside."

"I hope both of you will live it up this summer." Bernadette sighed and sipped her chilled vermouth, which she had proclaimed the perfect drink for a hot day. After glancing first at Grace and then at Etta, she asked, "Do you have specific plans?"

Grace answered, "We're planning on spontaneity."

Bernadette's mouth tilted downward at its corners. "Spontaneity could be an excuse for laziness, my dear."

"Not in the least," said Grace.

"Mark my words," Bernadette retorted, "time is a fleeting thing. Youth is a fleeting thing. You are allowed to do as you please, but I advise going for greatness."

"What does that mean?" asked Grace, while Etta observed this strange interaction between mother and daughter.

"It means that you live your life like a body of water. You cover everything you can. You make a beautiful surface life and also a deeper one that lies underneath and feeds the surface. You are in constant movement and change."

Grace stared at her mother as if baffled and a bit dazed at her words, but Etta said, "I couldn't agree more."

Aunt Bernadette seemed pleased and leaned back a notch in her chair. "Please let us know if there is anything we can do to make your stay more pleasant, Etta."

"But I've never been so pampered in my life." Etta let a little smile curl her lips. "Promise not to spoil me."

Bernadette laughed and passed a hand through the air. "I'll promise no such thing." She turned to the servant standing behind her and said, "Dessert, please."

Etta knew for certain then that she had gained her aunt's favor, that she had passed some mysterious and unspoken first test.

Within a week, Galveston's grid of streets, its mixture of multistory mansions and beachside shacks, busy docks and quiet gardens, raised houses and sagging tenements, had worked their way into Etta's heart. Many of the buildings and houses were built on stilts like matchsticks. Some were rebuilt, optimistically, upon the sandy soil. Warehouses, schools, and churches were scattered everywhere, and many small businesses were run out of homes. The look of the city suited Etta. Things weren't completely settled here yet. There was still room for her.

She no longer cared that she represented her mother's chance at redemption via her daughter. Etta's older sister, Rachel, had married a farmer, leaving Etta as her mother's last great hope, and the ploy to dispatch her here had worked. She had been sent here to learn something; so what? It was a valuable lesson. So far, however, she had encountered her aunt and cousin's social circle only in small doses. Introductions had been made when Grace or Bernadette ran into acquaintances while the three women were shopping or luncheoning, but Etta had not yet been presented to this new society. Her aunt had planned a party in Etta's honor for that, and Etta was counting the days.

In between accompanying her aunt and cousin for various short soirees, she was idle. Hours of letting the days drift by piled up, and often she found herself pacing the front portico, holding a glass of iced sweet tea that dripped with condensation.

On her second Saturday in the city, she was watching the trolleys go by and trying to convince herself to write a letter to her mother when a fine carriage pulled up and a young man stepped out. *Ah yes.* Grace's fiancé was expected today. Jonathan had recently completed his annuals at Yale for the year and had returned to the island for the summer, but she had yet to meet him.

She watched as a tall man with dark hair glazed away from his face came forward. He was lean but built well and appeared strong and energetic.

"You must be Miss Rahn," he said with a warm smile, his blue eyes piercing. His nose was as straight as a drawn line and connected thick eyebrows to the smoothly shaven skin of his upper lip, which was almost crimson in color. "I'm Mr. Ellis."

As he climbed the front steps to the portico, Etta extended her hand and then regretted it. Jonathan's face showed confusion. It was too casual a greeting for a first meeting. She wasn't even wearing gloves.

But to her surprise he took her hand in his and lightly touched her fingers with his lips. As he straightened he said, "But please call me Jonathan."

"Only if you agree to call me Etta."

He smiled. "Etta it is, then."

They exchanged pleasantries; then he looked toward the door and asked, "Is Grace at home?"

"Yes," answered Etta. "I believe she's resting. It's the heat, of course."

"Of course."

He gestured at the settees and chairs strung along the portico. "Shall we sit together and wait for her?"

"Certainly," Etta said. "I'll call for some refreshments."

Jonathan shook his head. "Don't bother on my account. I see you already have a beverage." They took seats next to each other a respectable distance apart. "I dislike asking the servants to attend to my every need, especially at this, the hottest time of day. They need some rest, too, don't you think? Or perhaps they're already making preparations for dinner. I'm always amazed by what they manage to do."

Etta's family had been able to afford only a half-day maid, but Etta said, "I agree." Jonathan's demeanor put Etta at ease. He carried himself with such effortlessness and lack of awareness of his social superiority that, had it not been for his aristocratic looks and attire—a fine black lightweight suit—she would not have been able to gauge his background.

Bernadette had already informed Etta that Grace had captivated quite the catch. Jonathan's father, Mr. Parker Ellis, owned the Galveston Building and Loan Company and also served on the Deep Water Committee, responsible for dredging and constructing jetties. His mother was one of the founders of the Wednesday Club. Together his parents had driven the first automobile onto the island, a 1902 Oldsmobile.

"Have you been away?" asked Etta.

"Yes, I had only been home from Yale for two days before my mother whisked me away to New Orleans for fittings at a tailor she favors. It seems I must have a most elegant and stylish summer wardrobe, since it is the summer of my engagement."

"So I've heard. My best wishes to you and my dear cousin. Please don't allow my presence here to interfere with any plans the two of you have made."

"No need to worry about that. Grace and I will pass most of our evenings together. As for the days, my father has required that I spend time at the seawall this summer."

"Oh my. For what purpose?"

He plopped his chin down onto his chest and managed to appear absurdly stoic, then said in a baritone, obviously imitating his father, "To learn, my dear."

Etta smiled. "Learn what, pray tell? I've been told you're studying science."

He sucked in a deep breath and then lifted his eyebrows, which arched nicely and appeared to have been combed. "He tells me that the wall will be an engineering miracle and that I shouldn't miss the opportunity to observe and learn about modern construction marvels. He wants me to be familiar with just about everything. But the truth is, he simply wants to keep me occupied and out of trouble."

He then slumped back with his legs stretched out on the painted planks in front of him. To her surprise, Etta saw that Grace's betrothed was a bit of a rogue. A dutiful son who did not mind mocking his father behind his back. Still, his small acts of rebellion were not without their charms.

She said, "At least you'll be outdoors in the fresh air down by the sea."

"It is still blasted hot," he said, running a finger around his collar, releasing its hold on his neck. "And truth be told, I know little of construction. For the most part, I'm just in the way."

Etta said, "I'm sorry you're feeling in the way."

"Don't be. I try to avoid watching the actual work as much as possible. Instead, I spend most of my time in talk, protecting those who are doing the real work from those who have come down to ogle the spectacle."

"Are you tripping over yourselves?"

"Every day someone new comes to reassure themselves that all is going well, that Galveston has a secure future. I show them around the wall, and they leave feeling better. Have no fear," he said. "After the wall and grade-raising are completed, the city will never be ravaged by a hurricane again."

So far Etta had managed to put storm risks out of her mind. It was the beginning of hurricane season, but the street on which the Hilliards lived ran along the high point of the island, about nine feet above sea level, so many who lived on the street, along with their servants, had survived the 1900 Storm.

Etta cocked her head and said, "Can you give me a guarantee?"

He laughed, and she caught herself batting her eyelashes, then stopped.

"Sorry. No guarantees from me. But I will say that the wall is an impressive structure." He gazed out at the front lawn and its gardens, but Etta caught him stealing a halting glance her way. It was a look of thinly veiled reexamination, as if she was not what he had expected either. Grace had likely not spoken well of Etta before her arrival, but how could her cousin have known how much ten years would change a person?

Etta gazed away from Jonathan, but not before noticing him reach up and touch the pox scar on his left cheek, the only imperfection on his velvety skin.

Out in the garden, the air was heady with pollen, and flowers were listing from the day's heat. Jonathan sat up and removed his suit coat. "I hope you don't mind," he said.

"Of course not."

As he folded his coat and laid it over the armrest, he stole another one of those inquisitive little glances at Etta. "What are your plans for your time here?"

She sighed. "To do what my aunt asks of me."

"Oh dear. Why, that sounds so . . . obedient."

Etta laughed. "If so, then it's the first time in my life that I've been obedient."

His eyes sparkled. "That sounds as if it would make for some interesting stories."

Looking down at her lap, she smiled wryly. "Perhaps."

He grinned. "But a gentleman would never ask you to elaborate."

Etta kept her eyes averted. She couldn't trust herself not to flirt with such a handsome and charismatic young man. But she replied pleasantly, "No, he would not."

He leaned closer. "I suppose I'll have to be obedient myself, then."

Despite her best efforts, Etta could feel her face flush and hoped that Jonathan would not notice. "I'll mind myself at all times. I mustn't shame my mother."

"Of course not."

She thought of home and, inevitably, of her circus man. "You have no idea."

"In that you would be wrong. We have more in common than you think. All of us are terrified, if you must know, of displeasing our parents."

"How very . . . ordinary."

He laughed and settled back into the chair again. "Quite. Well said."

It was almost dusk by the time Grace appeared on the portico, dressed for dinner and fully prepared by her maid. Lovely, naturally. "I'm so pleased you've met!" Grace exclaimed as Jonathan rose to greet her, kissed her hand, and led her to a chair. "How long have you two been chatting?"

"Hours," answered Etta.

"And yet they have passed as mere minutes," Jonathan added.

Grace beamed and gazed at Jonathan adoringly. "I'm so happy you've returned. How are you?"

Jonathan answered, "I've already listed my complaints about seawall duty to your poor cousin. I'll not bore you with more."

"Nothing you say is boring." She gave Jonathan her hand again, and he grasped it, gave it what looked like a gentle squeeze, and then let go. "I'm sorry to hear you've been peevish."

"More like feverish," Jonathan said and mimicked wiping his brow. "You young ladies may stand under a parasol, whereas we men must endure the blasted sun in its full force beating down on our brows and backs."

"I'm sorry for you."

He held her gaze and smiled. "Please don't be."

As the sun slowly sank, turning blood orange, the three of them lingered and chatted on the portico, giving Etta an opportunity to assess her cousin's relationship with Jonathan. They were kind and soft-spoken toward each other, even deferential to the other, but she found something missing. Their sweetness seemed about as valuable as penny candy. Clearly they were fond of each other, but she sensed no passion, no unspoken undercurrents, and no undying love. More troubling than that was the fact that Jonathan continued to send probing and admiring glances her way.

This could not happen. She had done nothing! Etta hadn't come here to cause any trouble. She'd had enough of that back in Nacogdoches. Had those glances been actual advances or simply the way the well-off entertained themselves? Either way, she would have to keep her distance from handsome, spoken-for Jonathan. On the other hand, befriending him might have its benefits.

A brilliant idea flamed to life inside her head. Surely he knew other rich and eligible young men on the island, and if she had dazzled him, she could dazzle others. She would be ever so cautious around Jonathan, but she had learned a valuable lesson on this day: she was capable of infatuating a man who seemed to have it all.

Soon they were summoned inside for dinner.

Etta took one last look at the garden before going indoors. She had always loved the entrance of evening; she had always been entranced by the spread of shadows and the shifting light as each new moment took a step closer toward moonlit night. The grass had turned silver, sparkling with dewdrops, fireflies winked against the violet light, and other garden insects were tuning their instruments, beginning the night's song with a low hum—a perfect sound to announce the opening notes of Etta's new life.

Chapter Four

THE GIRL

As the girl and Harry roamed the ruined city, he cried hard—something a sixteen-year-old boy wasn't supposed to do—but after he got it out of his system, he had to consider his options. His family boat was gone; he had no place to sleep and stay out of the elements. He could find a sailor friend to bunk with, but it would be no place for the girl. Some of the girl's other relations had lived on the island—a cousin and a spinster aunt, he thought—but he could find no sign of them, either.

And the girl was but a girl, who needed a woman's care.

His first idea was to take her to St. Mary's Orphan Asylum. But it was located on the far western edge of the city, almost on the beach, and later he heard that disaster had struck there as well. His choices were limited. He eventually took the girl to the headquarters of the American Red Cross. Volunteers had turned it into a goods distribution center, a kitchen, an orphanage, a dormitory for Red Cross workers, and Clara Barton's headquarters. Thinking he was doing the best he could under the circumstances, he left her there in the care of those kind-looking women, at least until he could come up with a better plan.

◆ ◆ ◆

The girl watched Harry leave. She already knew staying here without him was a mistake, and she wished again that she could get words to come out of her mouth, at least enough to say, *Don't leave me here.* But instead she was led to the room upstairs set aside for orphaned girls. She was questioned, and when she couldn't speak, the volunteers assisting her assumed she suffered from shock, from the effects of what she'd seen on this besieged island.

But as the day turned into more days, then weeks, and the girl remained mute and strangely detached from everyone, the workers began to wonder. One, who wore a tight bun and a stiff collar with a cameo pinned at her neck, stood at the foot of the girl's bed and said, "She's soft in the head, she is."

"I'll say," said a second woman, who was tall and broad and just as stern of face as the first.

But a third woman, who had a kind look about her eyes, only said, "Perhaps."

"No one left for her, either," said the first woman. "No one has come to claim her. That tells you something."

The girl wanted to shout, *That's not true.* Harry had returned on many occasions.

But the second worker said it for her: "That teenaged boy has come."

The first woman stiffened her back and harrumphed. "Fine chance we'd let the girl go with the likes of him."

"He gave us names of other family members, but they all seem to have perished. We haven't been able to locate a single living relative," said the second woman, shaking her head. "So sad."

"The boy's staying with a local family now and wants her back for the time being. He says he'll look after her until a better home can be found, but it would be most improper to hand her over to him."

No, no! It wouldn't be improper! the girl wanted to scream, if only she could. But instead she slipped silently under the bedcovers, as if sinking underwater. There, under the sheets, bathed in a filtered bluish-white light, she imagined she was under the sea, under the swells, in that gentle, easy part of the ocean, that dreamlike place of soft, surging waters that drifted to and fro, over the sandbars, where the tiny, almost-invisible fish chose to live.

"But what are we to do with her, then?" asked the kind woman, but no one answered. She approached the girl, sat on the edge of the bed with her ankles crossed, and pulled away the covers. "Talk to me. Please. Tell us what we are to do with you."

The girl searched the kind woman's blue eyes for something, some bit of understanding.

The woman cocked her head to one side. "Anything? Anything at all?"

The girl made the motions of writing, and when the women guessed what she meant, they brought her a salvaged piece of chalkboard and a stub of chalk. The girl wrote, *stone in my middle*.

The women glanced at each other. One of the mean ones said, "Definitely soft in the head."

The kind one asked her to write something else, but it was no use. Every effort to communicate overwhelmed her. They were already speaking for her, already deciding for her, but everything about them and their words was wrong. The girl shook her head and gazed away. The kind woman stood again and then rejoined the others at the foot of the bed. Apparently resigned, she said to the taller one, "She'll have to remain here until we figure it out, I suppose."

By October, Harry still hadn't found anyone to take her in on more than a temporary basis. Therefore the girl was still living with about twenty other orphans on the second floor of the warehouse, which had been furnished with salvaged items from the damaged Galveston Orphans Home. Harry had come by many times and explained that she'd spoken normally before her family disappeared. Others were beginning to doubt the truth of that, however.

So after a few more weeks, during which the girl remained silent, the volunteers at the Red Cross, fearing her either inferior from birth or permanently damaged by her losses, decided her fate. They shook their heads over the unfortunate child. The events of the 1900 Storm, the grisly experience, had turned her into a simpleton, or perhaps she had always been that way, even though Harry Gobinet denied it. It mattered little now. They had no choice but to recommend placement in an asylum. They spoke about it in her presence as if she were also unable to hear, and the girl knew that word. Asylum. A place for crazy people; a place to hide the crazy people out of sight; a place with cages.

She watched them listlessly as they mailed the necessary papers, as they awaited a response from an asylum and made the plans to send her. Adoptive homes, however, were found for the other remaining orphans, most of them removed to Houston.

Harry offered once again to try to find a place for the girl, but as a single young man, he was not deemed appropriate as a guardian, and Reena, the girl's former housemaid, who had been found alive, was also turned down, because a colored woman was out of the question as an adoptive parent to someone white.

The girl understood what was happening; she listened to everything discussed around her, particularly those comments uttered by people who thought her deaf. And then she stared out of the white-framed rectangle of the second-story window, watched oleander branches swaying in the night breeze, then followed thin, fast-moving clouds as they threaded across the moon's face, and she decided, in one moment, not to wait any longer, not to leave her fate in the hands of others.

When all was quiet, the girl slipped out the window, slid down the outside trellis like a drop of oil, and then crept down the city streets. She imagined it a game and not so terribly real as she held her body close to walls and tried not to be scared. She slipped into shadows when people drew near. Finally she reached the city's alleys, where the Negroes worked and many of them lived in backhouses.

Only then did she realize that she'd been formulating this plan for some time. She didn't know where Harry was staying. And even if she could find him, the shelter volunteers would *also* be able to find him, and she'd never be allowed to stay. She had heard it discussed and dismissed many a time.

Reena had visited her once and had told the girl she was now working in a bigger, fancier house. She lived in an alley house behind the mansion. So the idea came to the girl. Even at her age, she knew that life in the alleys was difficult and often unruly—Reena had told her about it once—but a person could be left alone there. This was her new life, her new plan. In the alleys, she could hide quietly, eat and breathe and live out in the open, and few others would again be bothered by the small matter of her.

Chapter Five

Grace

After Etta had been with us for almost two weeks, Mother and I hosted an evening party on the large back lawn to introduce Etta to choice friends and acquaintances. I wore an ecru tea gown with a high choker collar and Renaissance sleeves. Before any guests arrived, I asked Seamus to set up my easel on an open spot on the back portico overlooking the open lawn, where the men and many of the women so inclined would later play croquet during the cooling hour as the sun went down.

I had excelled in art at the Ursuline Academy and then had continued my studies with lessons from the court painter of Austria-Hungary, and later still from the American artist William Merritt Chase, who had instructed me in the latest methods. I particularly liked the new fast-brush technique, which was bolder, quicker, and more self-assured. Some people would say that art was an extravagant hobby, but for me it was a necessity. In front of the easel, I was confident, full of ideas and floating color and wise thoughts. Even the old empty feeling inside me was eased when I made the perfect stroke on my canvas.

Mother's guests included the entire Sidney Sherman Chapter of the Daughters of the Republic of Texas, and I in turn felt obligated to include the members of the Girls' Musical and Literary Club. All of the ladies were invited to bring a gentleman guest to ensure that the party would be balanced with a near-equal number of men and women. I finalized the list with Jonathan, of course, his family, and my closest friends, Viola Waverly and Larke McKay, both of whom I'd known since my first year of studies at Ursuline. In addition, I sent an invitation to Larke's brother, Wallace, who, with his curious nature and gregarious ways, could always be counted on to add verve to a party.

Under my mother's guidance, the preparations had been under way for days, and on the morning of the party our cook, May, brought over her cousins and nieces to help. They clucked and fussed over the main entrée slated for dinner, a roasted pig with an apple in its mouth, which they were cooking long and slow in a big brick oven in the outdoor kitchen. In between peeling cucumbers and potatoes, frosting cakes, and whipping meringue, they checked on the pig and polished everything, from silverware to floors, gave even the stair railing a final dusting, and arranged all the flowers.

Jonathan arrived ahead of the other guests and suavely offered his assistance to my mother, deferring to her directions since he was well used to seeking her favor by now. Dressed in a suit with a printed oxford vest underneath, he watched over the tables being set up on the back portico as the maids carried out the flower arrangements and left room for deviled crab, dishes of salted almonds, and other tidbits to entice us before we would be served dinner later indoors. Many of our guests had responded favorably to their invitations, despite this being the season for much overseas travel among our set; therefore, the maids had to arrange a third long table in the large dining hall to accommodate everyone.

I watched all of this out of the corner of my eye, and after he apparently determined that all was proceeding well, Jonathan found me on the portico in the shade as I was readying my oils. He came up behind me, took me by the shoulders, and spun me around.

"My dearest," he breathed out. He kissed my cheek, and then after looking around to make sure we were alone, he planted a softer, longer kiss on my lips. Jonathan's kisses were urgent enough to assure me of his desire but not so heady that either of us would abandon our senses or cross any lines. "You're ravishing as usual."

Playfully pushing him away, I said, "Jonathan, you cad!"

He growled and grinned, then grabbed me again. "I get so little time with you alone now."

After I allowed him to hold me for a few more moments, I stepped back. "If my dress is in disarray, Mother will notice at once and admonish us. And I do hope this party goes well, especially for Etta."

"Ah, yes, Cousin Etta." His voice hinted at annoyance. "Why must she always be around during our precious evenings together?"

He valued our private moments, and I loved that. "If all goes well tonight, she'll receive so many invitations that she'll be much too occupied to spend time with us."

Jonathan put his hands together and gazed up. "And so I pray."

I swatted at him.

Jonathan appeared hesitant and then asked, "When will she come down?"

I hadn't seen Etta yet that afternoon, so I could only assume she was still dressing. "She'll come when she pleases."

"That didn't sound like my usual generous Grace," said Jonathan. "You're not fond of her?"

"On the contrary. When we were girls, I wasn't impressed by her, but now I think highly of her."

Only that morning Etta had joined me in my room for coffee, and together we had perused my jewelry chest. She had selected some earrings and a matching pendant necklace to wear to the party tonight, and only then did I understand that she usually wore no jewelry because she didn't own any. Her dresses were inferior, too, but Mother was quickly remedying that situation.

Bright sunlight had poured in through my bedroom windows, and we had complained about the heat. Etta told me that she often dreamed of seeing snow. She placed a triple-strand bracelet on her wrist and was holding it in front of her, examining it. I didn't tell her that I had seen snow—many times, in fact.

Bringing me back from my reverie, Jonathan said now, "What have you found to like?"

His eyes were genuinely inquisitive, but there was something else, too, something that looked like shame. Had he spoken ill of her to our friends? I doubted that. "Did you not enjoy the evenings we've spent conversing with her? The night you first met her, you told us the hours had passed like minutes."

Jonathan rubbed his chin. "Oh, that. I did say that." His face was flushing. "I was being polite."

I gave him a glare. "She surprises me. And she's mysterious."

"Well, you know her much better than I do. Shall I prepare myself for a surprising evening? Do I need any special directions or warnings?"

"I'm sure you'll be your usual fascinating self."

"Very well." Jonathan reached into his pocket. "See what I've managed." Cupped in his palm were some salted almonds. He selected one and brought it to my lips. "May I?"

He slipped the treat onto my tongue and fed himself two or three at a time. Then, simply to amuse me, he tossed the last one high in the air and managed to catch it in his mouth. A funny thought came to me, of Etta's circus man. Was he more handsome than Jonathan?

I turned back to my painting, a landscape inspired by the lawn in front of me, a montage of greenery and flowers. On my palette I had placed smears of molten gold, sage green, and jewel blue that I would use to add touches of color tonight.

But there was something missing, something unsatisfactory. I couldn't name it, however, nor could I point to a particular area and say for certain what it lacked. Often the more I thought about my art, the less I could see what I was trying to accomplish. Jonathan was sitting now and whistling softly, a habit he exhibited when he was feeling rested and pleased.

I couldn't remember the first time I met Jonathan. Our parents had traveled in the same social circles and were better friends than most; therefore, Jonathan had always been a part of my past. Even from a young age he had a habit of whistling some little tune while we played together under the supervision of our mothers or the servants, and because he was three years older than me, as we grew older and began to venture out on our own a bit more he took on the role of older brother and protector.

"Jonathan," I said. "My painting. Something is wrong."

He laughed. "Here you go again, you and your self-criticism."

"I'm serious. I'm imprisoned by this piece. I can't escape it. Perhaps I should stop painting."

"Well, let me see . . ." He pushed back his hair. "After all the years to improve your technique, all the study. Yes, definitely, you should give it up."

"It's not as simple as that. The work consumes me."

"Yet it is you who have created the work. If you don't like it, put this one aside and begin another. It's your choice."

I shrugged. How to explain? Jonathan and I had much in common, and he appreciated the arts, but he didn't understand my need for self-enrichment through art. But I had decided that one need not understand one's companions entirely, and vice versa.

When I was fifteen and he was eighteen and it was his last year in Galveston before going off to Yale, Viola suggested him to me as a suitor. She said that we were already such good friends it would be a natural course of events to become more than that. She must have made the same suggestion to Jonathan, because one day soon after he changed in his attitude toward me, and I knew his intentions had transformed, too. He asked me to the Garten Verein at Avenue

O and Twenty-Seventh, a place known to incite romance, with its octagonal dance pavilion complete with pilasters, balustrades, and a cupola. Under the flags of all the nations, we ate a supper of cold meats, salads, and ice cream, with lemonade to drink, all served to us by rotund, mustached German waiters, and then we strolled the landscaped park, past the bowling greens and tennis courts.

Jonathan was clearly nervous; he had stopped whistling. Finally, as we walked on and had no place else to go, Jonathan took my hand in his, turned me to face him, and then kissed me. The old, sibling-like feelings flew away and what was left was a natural love, like a love of life, as essential as breathing.

From that moment on we were a pair. And after a few weeks, when he started to whistle around me again, I knew he had become comfortable with the idea.

I said to him now, "I'm not satisfied." Again I looked back at my painting. Yes, something was definitely ill placed or absent altogether. "I'm simply not satisfied."

Jonathan sighed.

Etta didn't make her appearance until after all of the guests had arrived, until all were nibbling off plates held high in their gloved hands and sipping on iced tea seasoned with mint leaves. I had just excused myself to go check on her when I saw her coming down the main staircase. She was dressed in the most colorful costume I've ever seen, a square-neck gown of a bright-red color made of organza and trimmed with shirred ribbon. My mother had funded a trip to a local seamstress who could produce gowns quickly but had left the choices up to Etta. The gown looked outdated, even though it was new, and I chastised myself for not thinking, for not realizing that of course she didn't know how to order a gown of the latest style inspired by European designs. The seamstress should have advised her, too. Etta and I were both petite ladies, near the same size. She probably could've worn one of my gowns, or I should've accompanied her to the seamstress.

But a glance at her face, which was radiant and relaxed and expectant, let me know that Etta would be fine. On anyone else the color would have been too flamboyant, but she entered the party looking like a package under the Christmas tree arrived early in June.

I looped my arm through hers and made the rounds, introducing her to many and enjoying the shocked silences and raised eyebrows by those of my mother's set, whereas my friends were clearly taken with her daring attire. She flowed among them all with ease, and despite conversations about receptions in the Artillery Hall, voyages to Liverpool, itineraries on the Hamburg America Line, she never faltered.

Soon I left her to her own devices, and later, comments made their way back to me, such as "clever," "bold," and "fascinating."

Mother worked her way to my side. She whispered almost indiscernibly to me, her smile focused ahead on nothing in particular, "You haven't introduced Etta to all of the guests yet."

"I think Etta is doing quite well on her own."

A long pause, and then, "Make sure of it."

I gave my mother a look and then went about as I pleased. There were some advantages to being an only child; I never lacked attention. But in my mother's eyes I always needed a fair amount of direction, too.

Later, when the sun was dipping behind us in the west and evening was finally easing the heat of the day, Etta joined the croquet game on the lawn, whereas I went back to my painting. Soon the game was in full swing, while I settled in to entertain those who preferred the shade of the portico.

Wallace McKay was peering over my shoulder. Often I received this kind of attention as I painted, and rather than finding it annoying, as some artists did, I enjoyed it. Praise and awareness of others had always improved my technique.

"Which style do you prefer?" asked Wallace as he perused my work with a practiced eye. He was a student of architecture and could always be counted on to make meaningful comments. If not exactly handsome, he was pleasant looking, with his oval-shaped face, wavy hair, cherubic cheeks, freckles, and hazel eyes. He reminded me of a grown-up toddler.

"I suppose I would be called an Impressionist." I didn't want to paint exactly what my eye saw; instead, I only wanted to capture the best parts of it, the best of what whirled around me. Colors and lines shifted, lightened, brightened, and blurred to surreal softness. Illusion.

"Claude Monet. Or better yet, Vincent van Gogh, only watch your ear," he said with a wink.

"Not to worry. I'll avoid the compulsion to torture myself."

"He never admired his own work."

"Yes, I know," I said sadly.

Wallace put his right hand into his pocket, gazed back toward the lawn, and then turned again to me. "You don't exactly look tortured, but you do appear discouraged."

"Well, not quite," I said and took a step back to assess the wisps of gold I'd just added to the undersides of clouds in my painted sky. "It's just that artists don't generally like to be categorized. I'm not certain that I'm an Impressionist. Classifying artists affronts our sense of singularity."

"Dear me," said Wallace with arched eyebrows.

I smiled and went on adding my touches here and there. Soon I realized that Wallace had left me and that no one had taken his place at my side. Often during our parties a small circle enveloped me as I worked.

And then I saw that all eyes were on the croquet, and in particular on Etta, who obviously had a natural affinity for the game. She didn't hesitate to swing her mallet with more force than I'd ever seen demonstrated by a woman. She slammed the ball with a loud thwack and sent it straight through the wickets with pure purpose. People who weren't normally interested in the game had stopped to watch. She became the focus, the river running before the evening's eyes and ears, the current propelling the conversations. And Etta took it all in with reserved enthusiasm, with grace.

Later I overheard snippets of Etta's conversation with Larke, my black-haired, exotic-looking friend, who despite her partial Greek heritage paled next to Etta. I heard talk of a train excursion they might take together to Dickinson, and then a discussion of proposed shopping on Market Street, where Larke was saying she had just seen a new bolt of purple fabric displayed in her local seamstress's collection. Although most of Larke's wardrobe came from Parisian designers, this fabric had caught her eye.

"I do believe you're the only person I know who could wear that color," Larke said to Etta. My friend was lively on this night, animated and enthusiastic. She acted as if she'd been waiting for this meeting with Etta all her life. "I'd thought of having a street suit made for myself, but it would be more splendid on you."

Etta said, "Thank you, but we'll see about that. Perhaps you can wear the color, perhaps not. We should go together for a look, and I'll promise you an honest opinion. We must make the decision together as to whom it suits."

Later my friend Viola came to stand beside me, but by then I had put aside my oils in favor of viewing the interactions nearby. Viola glanced several times in my direction.

Viola was a plain, brown-haired, brown-eyed girl with an unfortunate chin that made a sharp V on its end. Once I was trying to comfort her about it and said that it gave her face the shape of a heart, but in reality it drew the eyes downward and gave her an overall appearance of prudishness, which would only worsen with age.

Viola made up for her lack of attractiveness, however, with intelligence, not only of the bookish type, but also of the social type, and she could converse on any subject, from the most serious to the most inane. She called my mother "the Queen" behind her back, and she called Wallace McKay "the choirboy," often to his face. More than with my other friends, I trusted Viola's judgment.

As she stood beside me and watched Etta mingle, her face darkened. "There is something of need about her, isn't there? Something yearning."

I thought of saying that Etta had not been brought up with money and privilege as we had, so perhaps that accounted for the yearning. But I didn't want to reveal anything about Etta's past. "She's new here, so I'm certain she's yearning for friends."

"Hmm," murmured Viola. "No, it's more than that. There's something feral about her."

I laughed. And then I recognized the undertone in Viola's comment. She meant "sexual," though she wouldn't dare actually say that.

After the sun disappeared and pale moths and mosquitoes filled the night, we retired indoors to the dinner tables, set with porcelain, cut crystal, and silver. The ladies in their shining dresses bedecked with jewels swarmed around with the brightness of shimmering fish, the men were dark currents in their austere clothing, and Etta was the central whirl.

She ladled gravy onto her plate and dipped each bite of pork and even vegetables into it for extra flavor. I'd already noticed this about her during shared dinners with my mother. She always added extra seasoning and pepper, too, as if unadorned food was simply not good enough for her. Things needed embellishment.

People sensed this. They shared extraordinary but true stories about the 1900 Storm, about houses twisting and rolling off their

49

foundations during the high water. They described the line of wreckage left afterward, which had stretched for miles, and told her of the winds that had exploded roofs and wagons and trees as if they were made of straw. Although our area of town sat on a high spot and we'd mostly been spared, several of my friends had lost someone—a cousin, a favorite maid, or a former classmate. Mother had lost an old friend. Others had been trapped in their homes, terrified, left with horrible memories, and some still suffered from nightmares. No one had been left unscathed.

Etta's captivating eyes were open and unblinking as she listened. She asked questions with a piercing look and a lilting voice. "Why didn't people leave? Why was there no warning?"

Wallace launched into the story of Isaac Cline, the meteorologist who tried to warn Galvestonians but didn't predict the ferocity of the storm, and Etta acted as if she had never heard the tale before, although I was certain she had.

"So what is he, then?" she asked to all within earshot. "Is he an unsung hero, or the scapegoat, or the real failure in this matter?" On her face was rapt attention as she waited for a response. Every opinion seemed important to her.

"Scapegoat," answered Wallace.

Larke disagreed. She shook her head, and her dark hair, left down against convention, swam about her shoulders. "Failure. He neglected his vocation."

"No one could have forecast such a storm. Only a prophet," said Jonathan.

"A prophet of doom," said Etta thoughtfully, and that silenced everyone.

Viola finally spoke. "He's an unsung hero. No one took him seriously, even when he did warn them. He flew the hurricane flags, but people kept on working and going about their business. They even remained on the beach, of all places."

"On the beach?" said Etta, her eyebrows lifted even higher, her fork poised in the air.

"Apparently the waves were something to see," said Wallace by way of explanation.

"Cline lost members of his family, too," said Jonathan.

"What a tragedy," said Etta, shaking her head. "But it ends well, does it not? The storm heralded the advances that Galveston needs, did it not?"

Everyone was in agreement about that. They nodded and explained and even complained about all of the upcoming changes, as necessary as they were. Mother and I had been traveling when the storm hit, and the house had suffered only minor damage, so we had been mostly untouched. But I said nothing. No need to flaunt our good fortune. By then it was obvious that my friends and even my mother's friends were quite taken with my cousin. Among our guests, curiosity about her had made the dinner scrumptious. Her newness was just so new. She stared at people, a trait that was normally frowned upon and considered unladylike, but coming from Etta it was fetching. The men were mesmerized though a bit uneasy, and then I remembered what she had told me in the carriage on the day of her arrival: that her circus man had made her uneasy. And that was the effect she was having on many of the young men, including, to my surprise, Jonathan.

After the guests had left and Jonathan and I were taking a final stroll together out on the lawn, now lit with lanterns, he recalled many of her comments and antics. She had openly admitted to coming from the "sticks" of East Texas, and she had made the comment as if it were a novelty rather than a shortcoming. She claimed to need our assistance in adjusting to her new surroundings.

"I was certain everyone would like her," I said to Jonathan.

"Why, she was delightful, a natural at a party," he said, and then an expression of regret crossed his face. "Not as delightful as you, my dear, but nevertheless a charming addition to our little group for the summer. Since I am forced to spend long, dreary days observing a wall being built, I'll look forward to any and all moments of frivolity."

But only earlier today he had said he wanted to spend most of his spare time with me alone. "You're taken with her," I said, my ire rising. Why, even my Jonathan was enamored. Heat climbed up my face, and my eyes burned.

Jonathan's smile faded as he stopped walking and turned to me. He grasped my upper arms in his hands and peered deeply into my eyes. I was having a hard time meeting his eyes. "Sweetheart, you're jealous. But you needn't be. Let me tell you what I think will happen this summer: Etta is like a new young actress who walks onto the stage of our lives and brightens it for a while. But someday she will become a familiar face. I find her amusing, but you have nothing to fear. I'm flattered that you would feel jealous, but no concern is warranted. I'll always be true to you."

I watched his chest rise and fall. I'd never expected this, and I thought I might cry. Then Jonathan took me into his arms, holding me solidly and tightly, and finally I breathed. He held me until my taut muscles relaxed and my hands no longer trembled.

When I pulled back, I said, "I wish her only well. I'm happy every-one enjoyed her." And then he kissed me in a way that made most—but not all—of my worries sail away.

Later still, before we retired to bed that night, my mother summoned me into her private parlor, as she too wanted to recount the evening. I sat on the foot of her settee while she at first recalled some interesting comments made by and about our houseguest, then some humorous incidents I hadn't even noticed, followed by a favorable critique of the food. But then, as she went on amusing herself, I found myself growing more and more annoyed, because a picture of me emerged that I took exception to, one of me as withdrawn and without humor.

She said, "You are my finest accomplishment, Grace. It disappoints me when you are not at your best."

Cold fingers gripped my spine. "Oh," I said. "And how did I disappoint tonight?"

With her lips pursed, Mother appraised me for a long moment. She looked at me as if I were a stranger and then crossed her arms. "You were distanced and moody." Her wand-like fingers fluttered against her skin.

"Moody?"

"Perhaps sullen even."

"I was not."

She sighed. "Now, you know I rarely take my eyes off you for long. You simply weren't up to your usual inviting self. You neglected our guest. But not to worry. We all have an evening or two when we aren't as amiable as usual."

She could be so hard. And even now, at the end of a long day, her appearance was polished. Not one hair fell out of place, and if it ever did, my mother would quickly press it back into order. Which is exactly what she was doing to me now.

I said, "Sorry to dissatisfy."

"Come now," said Mother. "You're not above reproach, even though you're engaged to the perfect man, are you?"

"It has nothing to do—"

"Never mind that. The evening is over. Etta fared well enough. She told me so herself, although she did mention that you didn't introduce her to the Hardys."

The Hardys were close friends of my mother's, not mine, and they had just returned from sailing around Italy and Greece. They had talked about it the entire evening. "I was sparing her their travelogue. Etta hasn't been anywhere, has she? I thought she'd feel uncomfortable."

"Give her more credit, Grace. It seems to me she can handle anything. I made the introductions myself, and Etta conversed with them famously." She reached forward and gave me two short pats on my knee. "Not to worry. We'll do better next time."

Later in my room I rolled her comments around in my head like dirty coins. How could anyone view me as lonely when my mother kept me occupied and under constant scrutiny? All my life I'd been the focus of something my mother was carefully crafting and shaping, like a centerpiece.

And yet tonight her concern had been for Etta, and I had borne her scorn, which crusted inside me like rust. And why would Etta mention the Hardys to my mother? Was Viola correct in her assessment of Etta as a human variation of a feral cat? Had I just suffered the first tiny scratch from one of her claws?

But I quickly dismissed the notion. Etta had been nothing but open and honest with me. She had shown not one ounce of ill will. Unless her complaint to Mother had indeed been intended to slight me. I simply didn't know . . .

I looked out beyond my window. Hilliards before us had lived on Galveston Island for three generations. But my father's parents had died early, and my father had been an only child, so I had no family on my paternal side. I remembered little of my father beyond big hands, a soft laugh, and smiles that came at unexpected times. In my blurred memories, I sensed his gentleness. And a vague recall of his charms—he would get down and frolic on the lawn with me as if he were a playmate.

But my mother? She was normally a most perceptive person, but concerning the party this evening she had been incorrect in her assessment of my behavior. I had been gracious, observant, and certainly not negligent. Yes, I had been a bit undone by Etta's charms and her attractiveness, and Jonathan had indeed hurt my feelings. But I had still wanted Etta to mingle well, and it had been a perfectly glorious evening.

So why did I feel like I needed a good cry? Why did I suddenly feel like hurling something across my room?

A tiny idea came to me then, just the tiniest idea.

After my maid, Dolly, helped me out of my party attire, I asked her to help me comb out my hair. And as I sat before my dressing table, letting her bring the comb all the way to the ends, the tiny idea I'd had earlier took shape and form, color and dimension. I could envision lips moving. I could hear the whispers. And although she was Clorinda's oldest daughter and a fine and steadfast employee of ours, Dolly didn't own one ounce of the discretion that her mother did.

I made a foolish decision that would change everything. "Etta had a good evening, I think."

"Yes'm."

"After what she has been through . . ." I shook my head. "She deserves a little enjoyment."

Enjoyment. How ironic that I had managed to use Etta's very own word.

"Yes'm."

I lifted my chin and fixed my eyes on Dolly's reflection in the mirror. "Have you ever known anyone who worked for the circus?"

Dolly's eyes widened, but she never looked up from my hair. I admired her restraint. "No'm. Cain't say as I have."

"It's a wonder Etta met him at all."

That was all I had to say. Dolly knew all the servants everywhere.

Chapter Six

Etta

After her introductory party at the Hilliard home, Etta attended the opera, a party aboard a ship in port, and numerous day excursions, mostly in the company of Grace and her closest friends, among them a black-haired girl named Larke, who had an annoying habit of giggling, and a smarter one named Viola, who was, unfortunately, ugly.

Many evenings came and went in the company of Grace and Jonathan. After his graduation, Etta could imagine that he and Grace would have a most auspicious life ahead of them. Jonathan's daddy would most likely pay for him to continue his studies in science or engineering or set him up in some type of business with offices downtown or on The Strand.

But Etta would do nothing to try to sever the ties between Grace and her fiancé, as that would doom her here, and despite the fact that Jonathan undoubtedly found her attractive, he wasn't complex enough for her. Too much complaining about duties forced upon him by his father, without any evidence he'd ever stood up to him or anyone else. He had tried to portray himself as a little on the wild side, but there was no evidence he had a truly rebellious streak. No, Etta thought. Someone more interesting would crop up.

She found it ever so easy to get invitations, and more importantly, she could effortlessly amuse the crowd into which she'd fallen. Many members of the circle, including some of the younger ones, were so stiff Etta thought that if she talked or laughed too loud, they might blow over like walls made of paper. They were friendly but not particularly amusing or exciting. She found them blue-blooded and thin-skinned. But surprisingly, they seemed to admire her contrasting characteristics. Etta found that when she let little select pieces of her differences show, they found her even more enticing, and her invitations piled up.

Every day brought something new. Etta went roller skating and was learning to play tennis. She visited the racetrack and the velodrome, went to card parties, and took strolls at the Garten Verein. She attended a ballet and a debutante ball organized by the Artillery Company.

And it was only the beginning. Etta was told that winter would bring the bona fide social season. Until then, Galveston lay in wait, shuddering under the heat, steaming. If only she could draw out this stay. She would have to make sure to be no bother to her hosts, and perhaps even endear herself to them.

One afternoon, Grace's friends took her on a ride up and down Postoffice Street to see the red-light district, with its gambling houses, saloons, and prostitutes, as if this forbidden drive would demonstrate their defiance and free spirits. If Bernadette had known, she would've been mortified. Her aunt directed the behavior of others like an orchestra conductor. She inspected the servants' white gloves to ensure they were spotless and made unexpected checks of the kitchen for cleanliness. Frequently she told Grace, "Hold your shoulders back, please," and "Please don't clack the silverware," and so on.

◆ ◆ ◆

One Saturday, they took a picnic to a place that islanders called the Three Trees. Grace and Jonathan had organized the excursion down West Beach, and in the morning Jonathan showed up in his father's automobile, explaining that his father had taught him to drive the day before. He offered to show their little group the advantages of automobile transportation. Before they left, Bernadette looked over the car and asked about its safety and reliability prior to giving her permission for Grace and Etta to ride. Larke and her brother, Wallace, were coming along, too, so the group would also have to take a carriage and take turns in the motorcar.

When it was Etta's turn in the Oldsmobile, she sighed but made no comment. She supposed she should be impressed, and she had to admit that the automobile did provide a more comfortable journey. Travel was faster and more sanitary, too, without the smell of horses, without nearly so many flies and mosquitoes buzzing about, but she simply sat quietly and let Jonathan ramble on about the interior comforts and the sophistication of the machinery.

He drove out of the city on a deserted dirt road, explaining that it was an old stage route that once connected Galveston and the port of Velasco. A long strip of sand with small dunes lay on one side of the road, and low grass-covered flats lay on the other, and as the time passed, Etta realized that much of West Beach would no doubt be the same way—nearly flat, dry except in low, marshy spots spiked with cattails, grasses, and weeds, and utterly treeless. Away from the city the island looked like prairie.

She remembered the tart smell of yellow pine, the feel of wet pine needles and decaying leaves underfoot. As a girl, she had often searched the woods for the darkest, most secret place to hide and then remained there until hunger called her home. Etta missed her familiar hometown and the gently rolling, sharecropped fields rowed out with cotton plants. But she missed them for only a moment.

◆ ◆ ◆

The west end of the island was only about a mile or two wide, but they would've had to drive for hours along its length to reach San Luis Pass at its end. Etta began to doubt that any clump of trees existed on these salt marshes and tidal flats.

She closed her eyes. Jonathan was explaining the reason for this excursion: In Cabeza de Vaca's diary he had written of an Indian camp beside a grove of trees on a high point of the island. Indians had once fought a battle in the same spot with Jean Lafitte's pirates, and rumor had it that Lafitte had buried his treasure beneath the trees before he left the island for the last time. But what Etta found most interesting was the description of the legendary Lafitte himself, said to be over six feet tall, dark, handsome, with long side whiskers and deep-set hazel eyes.

Jonathan was saying, "People have been digging for years, searching for the gold. At one point there was so much digging they formed a trench." Jonathan looked over at her then, and she flinched. His attention was subtle, but it could be noticeable.

Etta found the long journey hardly worthwhile for such folly as digging for treasure. But she knew better than to show it. She needed to use each day as an opportunity to fit in and further endear herself. Her stance for this day was to be intrepid and interested but veiled. Now she pretended to be entertained. "Has anything been recovered?"

Jonathan answered, "Only a few coppers and doubloons, but nothing of value."

She gazed to her left and spotted the white curls of waves and glittering sand. "Might we stop at the beach for a few moments?"

He shrugged. "I don't see why not." He turned toward the gulf, and those in the carriage behind followed.

At the beach, after it was explained that Etta had wanted to walk, everyone paced about, the young ladies under their parasols, the gentlemen helping them walk in the soft sand. Some seemed a bit annoyed about the detour, but Etta suddenly felt unrestrained for the first time since she'd arrived. While the others stood about and looked at the sea, she tore off her shoes and stockings, swept up her skirt, and strode to the water's edge. When the surf chuffed in, she pulled back from the surging seawater and then ran farther away from the group. She cared not a whit if running down the beach barefoot was considered unladylike.

Finally she could breathe for a few moments. With her back to them and the empty beach in front of her, she slowed down to a brisk walk but knew she shouldn't go far. Even so, in this tiny moment she could let down her guard; she could be herself. She deeply breathed in the moment and then let it go.

She didn't want to annoy anyone further and soon returned to the group, her cheeks flushed from her run, her chest heaving, and her mouth smiling. Her little escape had been worth it. She could carry on with the outing now. It couldn't hurt that she'd had a chance to show off a little leg while running, too.

Her female companions appeared confused, and Larke asked her, "Aren't you afraid of hurting your feet?"

Etta shook her head.

The other women looked at her a bit disapprovingly, and Grace's face showed dismay, but the two men—why, they seemed positively mesmerized.

Back on course and at the ten-mile road, Jonathan turned toward the bay. They rode onto a ranch that was privately owned, but Jonathan explained that he knew the owners and therefore didn't hesitate to trespass. He stopped the motorcar near a fence. Beyond it, a small, murky pond and a grove of old oaks could be seen.

"What did I tell you?" exclaimed Jonathan and pointed. "We come to the trees." But Etta had to force a smile.

Wallace and Jonathan carried the picnic baskets, packed by the maids at the Hilliard house, and then the young men helped the women over the fence. Jonathan wove his fingers together to make a hand step, and when Etta put her foot there, she could have sworn that he blushed.

Soon they had walked around the pond and were standing in the middle of a grove of about fifteen oaks with gnarled, rough-barked limbs and glossy dark-green leaves that shimmered in the sunlight. For a moment, Etta remembered her hometown, where on Mound Street a single oak tree grew out of a mound said to be an ancient Caddo Indian burial site.

Grace said, "I thought we were to expect only three trees."

Jonathan answered, "The others are probably offshoots from the originals."

As Etta watched the exchange between her cousin and her fiancé, she once again had that same feeling about them. There was no friction to light the match. No fire there.

Turning to the others, Jonathan asked, "Shall we eat first or dig?"

Grace seemed pleased, but Etta considered it a silly notion, this digging. If treasure were to be had here, someone else, someone hungrier than the members of this bunch, would have found it by now. The ground was pockmarked with holes dug by many other foolish boys. Everyone except for Etta sniffed around for a bit, but she stood her ground and waited. The contrast between this almost-barren land and the finery of the clothes around her was somewhat disturbing.

The group agreed to eat first. Grace unfolded a quilt and spread it on the dry ground between two of the largest trees. They ate finger sandwiches, pickled eggs, Spanish olives, peaches, and plums, and then drank cold tea poured from a crockery jug. The talk was all very typical, but what were those little glances shot between Grace and Viola?

They sat for an hour to let their meals settle, and then Jonathan jumped back over the fence and returned with two shovels. After he handed one to Wallace, Jonathan rolled up his shirtsleeves, letting the ladies see his arms, then began digging.

The men dug for nearly an hour for something that would not be there. As they pitched dirt, Etta sent cursory glances their way from time to time but didn't relish the sight of their reddened faces, foreheads and upper lips glistening with sweat in this, the hottest hour of the day.

With bemused eyes, Wallace said, "Etta won't watch."

She sniggered. "I always leave the dirty work to the men."

Everyone else laughed, but Wallace stood his ground, leaning on the shovel handle, smiling down at her, a quizzical look in his eyes, his round cheeks already reddened from heat and effort. "I frequently have the feeling that you are far away from us, Etta, lost in thoughts you won't share."

Grace caught Etta's eye and then darted her eyes askance. Odd.

"Hmm," murmured Etta. "Yes, my mind is full of weighty things."

"You confound us, that's all. What are you thinking?"

Etta shrugged. Her plan was to keep them guessing. But Wallace was more impressive than she had imagined. Yes, he had a good future before him as an architect here in Galveston, but that wasn't all that Etta saw in him. He would take his time. He would be persistent.

Wallace jammed the shovel into the ground again. "I'll make it simple. Let's start with some easy questions. Which do you prefer, night or day? Sunrise or sunset?"

Grace answered instead. "I would choose the sunrise."

And then Larke, "The sunset."

"And you, Etta?" Wallace insisted.

She paused for a minute. He would wait until she answered. She gazed up at him now. She did not find him handsome, but there was an interesting look about him, and at least he could hold a conversation that held her interest momentarily. Of course, his appeal had much to do with wealth and the fact that his life had prepared him to do just about anything he wanted.

The sun was behind him; she couldn't quite read his face anymore. Finally she answered, "I couldn't choose. How to prefer one to the other? It makes no sense. The beginning of light, and the beginning of darkness. Both must exist."

"Ah," said Wallace. "A good answer. I would have expected no less."

"But so biblical," said Jonathan.

Etta stiffened. "I didn't mean for it to be."

Larke, the silly creature, giggled and twisted her hair. She didn't have the intelligence of her brother. But Wallace, apparently satisfied for now, went back to digging.

Then Jonathan piped in with a question he addressed to everyone. "Which would you choose—a grand love or a deep faith?"

"Love," answered Grace after only brief consideration, and Etta wasn't surprised.

Larke answered, "But love can be fleeting, whereas faith has the facility to sustain a person through adversity."

Jonathan turned to Etta. "As usual, Etta, you haven't answered."

"Well," she said, picking at a loose thread in the fabric of her skirt, "why only those two choices? You haven't offered me the option of power, or adventure, or unusual talent."

"All right then," said Wallace, looking even more impressed. "Of all those mentioned, which would you choose?"

Etta smoothed her skirt against her lap. "Ah yes, let's see if I can remember them all." She counted on her long, outstretched fingers. "We have love and faith, then power, adventure, and talent. But I still can't choose. I'm afraid the question is far too limiting, because I would take some of them all."

"Another good answer," said Wallace, now glowing from the heat, or was it from admiration?

"Yes, I'd take everything," Etta said.

"And why not?" asked Larke, her question hanging in the air unanswered.

Wallace dug again and then stopped. "What would you do with the treasure, Etta, should we find it?"

She gazed at him from beneath her eyelashes and tried to smile. "I would give it to a museum."

"Ah, for posterity, for the enjoyment of the masses."

"Something such as that."

"Are you a philanthropist?"

Etta said, "No."

"A reformer?"

"No again."

The heat was horrendous. Etta found herself growing anxious and even a bit nauseous. The waistband of her dress was digging into her, and she was beginning to sweat. On the verge of fainting, she didn't hear Wallace's next question or anyone's answers. She blinked hard and took a few deep breaths, until her head cleared.

Then she felt Wallace's eyes on her, and the light in them had changed. "Are we boring you, Etta?" he asked.

"Are you all right?" asked Grace.

"I'm fine." Etta fanned herself and hated how her entire body was becoming damp. How did these other young women do it? Did they have no sweat glands? "It's just that the day is growing long. This is a fruitless endeavor." She was surprised by the venom in her voice. The heat was wearing away her façade.

Wallace was still peering at her. "So, I guess we *are* boring you."

Now he was getting on her frayed nerves. She looked at him, meeting his now-piercing stare. "You said it, not I."

Obviously irritated, he pursed his lips, while the others remained silent. His face reddened even more. "We came out here to entertain you. Most of us have been here before."

Why would he not let this drop? She glared at him. "Perhaps you might have consulted me first."

Anger flashed brightly in his eyes, matching the burn in hers. He said curtly, "Perhaps you might have been more entertained by a ring full of elephants and tigers. Perhaps we should have taken you to . . ."

Etta's head jerked back, and she stared even harder. Wallace stood without moving and paled, an expression on his face: instant realization, then almost horror, and certain fear.

Things had suddenly become much more interesting. Immediately, her composure returned. Etta focused on Wallace. "To . . . ?" she asked with her head cocked to one side like an inquisitive bird. "To what?" He didn't answer.

"What, dear Wallace? Where could we go? Don't be shy now. Don't hesitate to finish what you've started."

Wallace glanced at Grace, who appeared aghast. She stared back at him in obvious dismay, and then she looked down into her lap, her forehead creased like pleated fabric.

This was clearly an awkward moment for everyone present. No one smiled, and Wallace made what seemed like an involuntary grimace. Jonathan scratched that unfortunate scar on his cheek.

"I was going to say . . ." Wallace gulped, "that we could take you to the circus." He glanced at Grace and then said, "Sorry. I forgot myself . . ."

Grace gave no reply, and Etta watched as four sets of averted eyes and halting movements affirmed Wallace's grievous slip.

But Etta almost laughed aloud. Obviously her cousin wasn't able to keep private information to herself, and the smart gentleman with the big mouth had opened his mouth one too many times. Etta smiled in Grace's direction, letting her know this disclosure wasn't the harbinger of death, but Grace wouldn't meet her eyes, and her eyelashes were batting about like butterflies.

"No need to be sorry," said Etta as she gazed back at Wallace. "I find people from all walks of life to be interesting and entertaining. And sometimes people who excel at odd things do so because they have little else to live for. There's power in such desperation. One shouldn't make the mistake of discounting it. As for me," she said, smiling, "I plan to experience everything I can."

"Oh," said Wallace, who remained unmoving in that same awkward pose. His mistake hung over them, and Etta didn't know how they would work themselves out from under it. Yes, things were definitely becoming more interesting.

Then Wallace simply went back to shoveling.

Grace began repacking the picnic baskets. Larke sat very still. Finally she cleared her throat with a sound like a frog's croak, but when Etta's glance met Larke's eyes, she saw something like admiration in those depths, which were almost as dark as her own. Or was it fear? Then she looked at Jonathan, expecting some type of glaring look. Well, he did have a glaring expression on his face, but it was aimed not at Etta but at Grace.

Grace, focused on repacking, didn't even see it.

Chapter Seven

GRACE

At first, I tried pretending as if nothing had happened. But over the next two days I could see that Etta was avoiding me, waving off my attempts at conversation and keeping her nose inside a novel she said was riveting. When I invited her into my room to chat, she said, "I'm busy at the moment," and when I found her on the front portico staring into the street, she claimed some reason to go inside.

An apology was certainly in order, but what was I to say? That during a foolish moment I'd said something I immediately regretted? I *had* suffered a foolish moment, but it hadn't been an accident, and how could I explain that away? Etta had been nothing but kind and pleasant to me ever since her arrival. If only I could take back what I'd done.

I remained in a state of heightened awareness, watching Mother swoop about the house, ordering servants about, hosting private visits with friends, and then looking harshly upon me while the three of us were dining, speaking primarily to Etta. I dreaded an answer to my question, but the question remained: Had my mother found out?

I spent most of my time in my room. Three days came and went, and I started to believe I had been spared. I didn't deserve it, but I was relieved nevertheless. And I vowed to myself never to do something so impulsive again.

Immediately after arriving home from an outing one evening, Mother ushered me into her private parlor in a way that startled even me. Her movements were fevered, and her lips pursed. "Close the door behind you, please," she ordered.

In front of her settee, she positioned herself like a marble monument and said, "I know what you've done."

So the gossip circuit had assured that my mother was informed but had not served to warn me. Not even Dolly had given me time to equip myself.

Fire in her eyes, Mother said, "I'm ashamed of you."

Then she paced the floor. "You've done something spiteful to stain your cousin's reputation. Did Etta tell you about her past? Obviously she did, which surprises me, but it is evidence of her trusting nature. She put her faith in you! You, on the other hand, have shown yourself to be untrustworthy. I assume she told you in confidence, and you've broken that kind confidence. Her time here was unfolding so well, and now you've ruined it. Her reputation will never be the same. Do you comprehend that? I'm sure you do, which makes it all the more shocking that you would make such a poor decision."

Mother was answering her own questions, so I simply stood and listened, fighting off the smart in my eyes. What my mother said was mostly true. And still her admonishment hurt.

Skirts swishing, she continued: "Grace, I have tried to raise you right. I've done all I could in the absence of a husband to help, and now I feel as though you've betrayed me as well. I'm truly and deeply disturbed that you would behave in such a way."

"It was wrong of me."

She stopped pacing. "So much more than simply *wrong*. Frankly I'm surprised. I've always thought you good-natured at heart, but I've been blinded by a mother's love. Now I learn that you are ill-tempered, inconsiderate, and indiscreet."

"What I did was out of character."

"Out of character indeed." Her face rigid, she demanded, "What else do you have to say for yourself?"

"Only that . . . I'm sorry. I was thoughtless."

"Not only thoughtless but reckless," she fumed, "and small. The only explanation for your conduct is vanity and jealousy. Petty, silly, girlish reactions. I had thought you beyond such things, and . . . now . . . you must learn the error of your ways. You will do as I say."

"I'll apologize. I'll make it up to Etta."

Mother shot me through with her arrow-like eyes. I was made of nothing. Nothing.

"Don't even dare to believe you would get off that easily. Oh no. I've been arranging a much more suitable occupation for you in hopes that it will make you reconsider your ways."

My heart stopped beating. *Suitable occupation?*

"You'll be doing some benevolent work; I've arranged this with the help of the church. A minister who has recently arrived in town has been recommended to me. He's working among the alley dwellers, helping out with various deeds and goods, and you will be sent to act as his assistant and perhaps to work firsthand with some decent poor whites."

The slightest breeze could've blown through me. "The alleys?"

"You heard me correctly."

"The alleys? Why? B-but they could be dangerous."

"I've been assured that you will be in good hands."

I inhaled and exhaled deeply in an attempt to calm a rising panic. "Mother, I understand I've committed a grievous mistake. But what you're doling out is too severe. I will make it up to Etta in my own way. I'll think of something that will soon result in making my error of little consequence. People will forget about it, and besides, I've seen no evidence that anyone holds her past against her. Her invitations are still pouring in."

"You indeed may make it up, as you say, to Etta. But you will also do this charitable work."

"May I ask a question?"

"If you must."

"What am I to do with myself down there?"

"You'll do as you're instructed by the Reverend."

"What will he want me to do? What if it's something *awful*?"

Mother clasped her hands in front of her. "I've been told he's a sensible man. I doubt he would ask you to do anything unreasonable."

A choking sensation was rising in my throat. Feigning contriteness, I said, "May I ask another question, please?"

She nodded curtly once.

"How will my doing what you've outlined help Etta?"

"It's not to help Etta. This service will be for your benefit, Grace."

Panic and disbelief were crumbling my façade. "Benefit? It's clearly punishment! I've already said I'm sorry."

"That is simply not enough."

"My father—he would not have done this to me."

Her already drawn face fell even more. "Your father was a fine man who would've been appalled by you." She pointed at me with a lace-gloved hand. "You are attempting to change the topic of this conversation, and I'll not have it. Your punishment is light. I could've sent you away for the summer."

"Now you're being cruel."

"How dare you! What *you* did to Etta was cruel."

The pulse in her neck was throbbing. She had never been this angry with me before. Trying a different tactic, I said, "What will people say?"

Mother crossed her arms. "You should've thought about that before, my dear. After all, you initiated everything that has led to this."

"I can't believe it. Listen to reason, Mother. I'll hold a special party for Etta. I'll introduce her to more friends. I'll spend more time with her, grooming her, coaching her."

"She hardly needs *your* help."

That stung hard. "You mustn't mean all that you say."

"You would be wise to start believing that I do."

I had only four days to prepare.

The evening before my sentence began, Jonathan and I took our evening iced tea out on the front portico to escape Mother and Etta, but we found no privacy even there, because nosy strollers couldn't keep their eyes off me. It was amazing what people thought was their business.

"Dear Grace," Jonathan said as he lowered his eyes. "You're to begin tomorrow?"

I gave a nod and gazed out across the esplanade. The sunset was nearly complete, and only a faint orange glow remained in the west. I breathed in the smell of night-blooming jasmine in our gardens.

"There is one advantage," I said to Jonathan.

"What's that?"

"At least no one will know me there. I can become invisible for a while."

He looked my way, and there was sorrow in his eyes. "You'll never be invisible," he said, forcing a smile. "You're too sweet and pretty."

I couldn't thank him for the compliment. In fact, I almost winced at his words—they were undeserved. We'd endured a long separation during the previous academic year, which for me had dragged by. I had looked forward to his company for the summer. I had imagined becoming familiar again, but a plot had been hatched against us. First his father demanded his time at the seawall, and now my mother was sending me into the alleys, all of this in addition to my continued concerns that he was a bit charmed by Etta.

Jonathan fidgeted and then said, "May I ask a question?"

"Of course."

"Did you accidentally let the information slip about Etta, or was it purposeful?"

I lifted one shoulder. There was no use in hiding anything from Jonathan. "It was purposeful."

He seemed surprised and even a bit undone. But he gazed straight ahead. "For what reason?"

I sighed. "I was angry at Mother."

I was used to disappointment from my mother, but Jonathan's displeasure felt like fire on my skin. "I know," I said and gulped. "It was vile of me. Why propel my anger toward Mother onto Etta?"

He nodded.

I had to pull in some air. "I know it makes little sense, but that's what I did."

He glanced my way. "And I must not have been paying you enough attention."

I shrugged, although Mother hated it when I did that. "There's no one to blame but myself."

"I just never thought you would've . . . What I mean to say is . . . you've simply never struck me as one who would act maliciously."

"Maliciously?" That word seemed particularly harsh, but I supposed it was true. "I didn't think it through at the time. My anger overcame my usual judgment."

"Were you angry only at your mother?"

"Yes." Then I rethought my answer. "Etta was garnering so much attention. So perhaps I was a little jealous."

Jonathan paused. "Thank you for telling me. Anything else?" He looked askance at me.

Now it was my turn to be surprised. He doubted me now. I had thought there wouldn't be even a moment's uncertainly between us. "We're betrothed. I'll always be truthful to you, Jonathan. That I can always promise."

He gazed down, studying the polish on his shoes. Finally he said with a loud sigh, "Dear Grace" once again. "It's sure to be dreadful."

"Yes," I said. "I know."

Chapter Eight

Etta

Etta heard the news from Dolly. Apparently the circus man gossip had made its way back to Bernadette, including the fact that it had been leaked by Grace, and her aunt therefore had decided on a most stern punishment for her daughter indeed. Grace would be doing work organized by the ministry of the First Methodist Church, the Hilliards' regular place of worship.

Every conversation between her aunt and her cousin had been relayed among the house servants. But it was never mentioned while Bernadette, Grace, and Etta were together. They all walked around holding close this unspeakable knowledge. Though Etta had once fallen for a circus man, even worse was the fact that Grace had revealed it to all. A few days after the incident at the Three Trees, Grace appeared at the supper table, the skin on her face so pale it appeared bleached, her eyes rimmed with delicate red flesh. She did not eat.

Etta observed this turn of events with silent astonishment. Finally someone had surprised her, truly surprised her. Everyone else on the island gave her the impression of being all too visible, but dimly visible instead of bright, with no unforeseen hidden corners. Grace had revealed herself—most notably, she had exposed her flaws—and Etta could only barely hate her for it. In fact, she thought very little about Grace, especially since she'd been hiding out in her room for most of the past few days. Etta's attentions had turned elsewhere.

The most remarkable person in Galveston was Etta's aunt, a lady who obviously maintained a tremendous sense of right and wrong, who meted out punishment even to those she normally protected, who could command the servants with grace and even inspire their dedication, who didn't succumb to flurrying or flustering or hesitation or feminine spells (except for the occasional melting from the heat), who could organize perfectly tuned events in a number of days, and who seemed elegant and at ease in every situation, much like royalty.

Everywhere in the house Etta stole glimpses of Bernadette, who was often found standing perfectly still on the landing of the main staircase and listening for anything out of order, or perusing the glass doors of the china cabinets for smudges, or checking the polish on the floors. Her presence was powerful and dominant, but she never left a lip print on a piece of crystal or a fingerprint on the furniture.

When Grace disappeared the next day to begin her penance in the alleys, Bernadette took Etta shopping on Mechanic Street for Etta's winter wardrobe. They selected new fabric for the tailor, along with various hats, adornments, and accessories, and Etta found her aunt's taste much as she had expected it to be—immaculate, understated for the most part, but with touches here and there of things that might seem a bit daring. Bernadette referred to the male shopkeepers as "dear lambs," the females who helped them as "sweet dolls." They smiled and blushed in return. Clearly they adored her.

As they scrutinized the goods, Bernadette would make comments to Etta, such as "You could get away with this color," or "I'd like to see you in this." Once her aunt told her "You have an untouchable beauty," and Etta didn't know whether this was a compliment or not.

Bernadette never asked the price of anything, and once, when she pointed out a sapphire silk woven with gold flowers and insisted that Etta look it over, Etta lowered her voice and said, "It's lovely, but . . ."

"But what?" her aunt insisted.

Etta regretted the momentary slip, the obvious reminder that she wasn't like them here. Not only was she of a different class and status, a silent pain still ravaged her, too. She had successfully hidden all evidence of her wretched, fractured heart thus far. No one could know that when she thought of Philo—a poor man so very far removed from this life—her eyes and throat and even her lips ached.

"Go on," said her aunt.

"Isn't it costly?"

Her aunt harrumphed and straightened. "Living is costly. At the very least, we should be able to go through it in style."

Etta couldn't have said it better herself.

In the end, the disclosure about Etta's tainted past did little to harm her. In fact, Grace's punishment seemed, in retrospect, much too severe and uncalled for, although Etta would never say such a thing. It wasn't her place to do so. In fact, she and her aunt never discussed the subject, and the matter ended up having the most remarkable effect. Among the crowd that Grace favored, the rumors only enhanced Etta's already expanding intrigue and appeal, and her circle of friends grew.

And still Etta told herself to rein herself in—don't go too far; don't do anything to risk your opportunities here—and so she never dropped her outward offhand attitude. During the day Etta's emotions flowed through her like water, sometimes softly coursing and other times churning like a wave, but her face remained unchanged no matter how the currents were moving under her surface. At night she reexperienced the seascape, the busy sounds, and pungent smells of this new and wealthy city in vivid dreams. All blurring and flowing and yet reachable, touchable. Hers for the taking. She had never dreamed a life like this would ever be made available to her. Even a love like she'd felt for Philo could come, and the men she encountered here were wealthy. Things were finally turning in her direction, and she would do everything to stay on course. She had lost the luminous glow of Philo's love, but she would not lose the starry prospects that now lay before her.

She would do whatever it took. She would grasp and hold the extravagant island in her fists and never let go.

Chapter Nine

· The Girl

The Negroes and poor white workers of the alleys took her in with little speculation and with occasional kindnesses, too, and unexpectedly, she was even looked over and worried about by two kind souls. She had located Reena, her family's former housekeeper, who now cooked for her and patched clothes and acted as a mother of sorts.

Back in her earliest years, when the girl was small enough to still sleep in a crib, she had awakened to Reena's liquid black eyes staring back at her through the slats. Reena's real name was Moreena, but when the girl was only a toddler, just learning to speak, she could only manage Reena, and the name had stuck. Even the white family she worked for now called her Reena, and everyone in the alleys had also picked it up, except for her boys, who simply called her Mama.

A big woman, Reena had a love for buttered biscuits and brown gravy that kept her as stout as a stove, but her arms were muscled and tireless. Only the skin of her belly was like jellyfish. Reena was the most eye-twinkling person the girl had ever known, and better to be around than everyone else, maybe even Harry, because after all she was a mama. Every day the girl was thankful that on the day of the storm, her mother had sent Reena to her own home, thankful that Reena had made her way back to Ward Five, where she had lived at the time with her own family, where she and so many others had taken shelter in the Union Passenger Depot, a big brick building that had withstood the hurricane.

Not long after the girl had located Reena, the woman had shaken her head and said, "We got to get you back in school somehow."

They were sitting on the stoop of the backhouse, facing the alley, which was normally quiet during the day.

In the rears, those back sides of properties, the privileged people of Galveston kept their servants' quarters, working kitchens, privies, woodpiles, chicken coops, gardens, and such, and the girl could keep company with mostly Negro washerwomen, housemaids, and gardeners. Many dockworkers, draymen, and laborers lived in the alleys, too. In the rears, she could move about nearly unnoted. Individual human existence was almost invisible here, but all these nearly invisible lives threaded together to form a mesh that could hold her.

The winter of 1900–1901 was on the way, and a cold wind was blowing. The girl hugged her sides and shook her head. She had made a place for herself here, and she had no want of changing it.

"You gonna grow up with no schooling. That ain't good."

The girl lifted her hands, palm up, as if saying, *How could I possibly go to school?* She had learned to communicate with gestures, and Reena could read her well.

Reena faced forward, and her chest heaved once. "I know what you saying. I done pondered this every night. I can't take you to the colored school, and I suppose I can't take you to the white school, neither. People is bound to ask questions, and people is searching for you anyways. But I do has me one idea. What if we dye your hair and cut it off so you don't look like yourself no more? I could sew you some new school clothes. Then Harry there, he takes you and registers you as his sister. That might work."

The girl shook her head again adamantly. Then she pointed to her mouth.

"I know, I know," Reena said with the beginnings of resignation. "They bound to get all upset, cuz you ain't speaking. I don't know what to do about that. But maybe you start speaking again. Could you try that for me? Could you try that for me, baby girl? And then after that we can try to get you back in school. You always did like school. I remember. Will you try for me?"

The girl *had* tried. She had tried and tried. But as surely as the storm had taken away her parents, most of the city, and six thousand souls, it had planted that stone of silence in her middle, and now it felt lodged there for life.

Soon she gave up even trying.

The girl had also befriended Madu, the old voodoo man, who scolded her and fussed about her almost constantly but scared others away who might have bothered her. Madu was a hunched-down raisin of a soul with long fingernails at the ends of long fingers, and he had yellow eyes that appeared as if rubbed with cornstarch. Madu didn't reckon the girl much of a young lady, as was obvious by his silence and his scornful glances and the way he breathed out like a snake hissing at prey while in her presence. But he looked after her, often fed her, and gave her some old clothes that had belonged to his daughter.

One day, they sat on his sagging porch facing an alley busier than Reena's, and he produced a book he'd obviously borrowed, a scratched and scarred copy of *The Baby's Opera*. He handed it to the girl, and she took it, although she had already read the book. Still, she ran her hands over it, savoring its feel.

Madu said, "Me, I never done learnt how to read."

The girl listened.

He started peeling potatoes, then sighed. "It shore would be nice if some good-for-nothing girl would read that there book to me."

The girl looked down at her hands, at her dirty fingernails and freckled skin, and her eyes began to burn. If she could have, of course she would have read aloud to Madu. Didn't anyone understand that this silence was not her choice? She put the book down next to Madu, jumped to her feet, and took off.

As she ran away, the old man called out, "Now you knows I didn't mean you no harm. Where's you going? You come on back now." And then, almost out of earshot, she heard him call, "Just go on then!"

But he forgave her, and she ended up reading *The Baby's Opera* so many times to herself, she could recite many of the rhymes by heart in her head.

For the next three years, she lived in the alleys, in the shadows of back-facing houses and businesses. She ran around neighborhood corner stores, charcoal shops, rows of white-painted servants' quarters, commissary houses built identically right after the storm, and older back-houses with narrow-slatted wood fences enclosing miniature yards, pawnshops, and cluttered porches, clotheslines strung across sandy, grass-spiked yards, the ropes hung with bleached linens, and yards littered with crates.

She pilfered bread and cast-off clothing and accepted pies and pails of unwanted fish given to her as she ran the oyster-shell and sand-covered alleys and ventured out on the city boardwalks and the docks from time to time. She moved often, always dodging police and relief workers and society types, who would have her caught and locked away. She slept in back kitchens, abandoned sheds, on splintered wood porches, and under houses.

According to Harry, after her disappearance the Red Cross workers, convinced that he knew of her whereabouts, had hounded him. He sent word to her at Reena's to stay away for a while. She had to avoid all people in positions of authority and even those who might have helped her, because she couldn't tell the difference between them. Once, two men chased her, but she escaped through a small hole in a crosshatched fence, where they couldn't follow.

Another time a pack of older boys gave her a long chase, even using their dogs to terrify her with their barking, but the dogs weren't the kind that could follow her scent. And still another close call came when four women from the Trinity Episcopal Church set out to find her, combing every backstreet and alley, offering pennies to anyone who would give them information, but she had foiled them, too.

The girl grew and thrived and developed into a young lady, while keeping her existence as quiet as possible. With eyes her father had once said were the same gray blue as seawater on overcast days and long bright hair, she had gone from a pretty girl to a striking young lady. And when her shape changed, the manner in which people, particularly men, observed her changed, too.

Once she was chased by two police officers all over the ward and finally down an alley, where she was forced to stop. Ahead, the alley was blocked by a wagon loaded with crates. No longer as slight as she had been only a few months before, she couldn't slip to either side of it.

As she backed up against the wagon, her chest heaving, the two policemen, holding clubs in their hands, approached her step by step. So utterly exhausted, so tired, so consumed with the struggle to stay free, she considered giving in to it. Giving up. Let them do as they wanted with her. Hiding was too much work.

As she softened, so did one of the policemen. She looked him squarely in the face and saw that he was young, only a boy, probably about eighteen years old, probably still in training. He had sandy-colored hair, brown eyebrows, and a face as open and filled with tender-heartedness as her brother Anson's had once been. He set his club down on the ground without a sound and then gave her a nod that seemed to say he meant her no harm.

The other officer—the older one—said, "It's time to quit your running now. Let us help you," and took a step closer.

The young one said nothing but simply held her gaze. There was a peaceful air about him and something inviting about simply going with him. Surrender had a certain draw, a certain serenity, like the depths of the ocean. She came close in that moment, so close. She heard herself take a long deep breath and let it out.

But then the older policeman stepped forward. It seemed he knew he was nearing his goal; he had won. He had succeeded where others had failed, and the slightest of smiles played on his lips. "We'll take you into the station, but only for a little stay. We have food. Lemonade."

The young officer's eyes pleaded with her to listen.

The other one said, "We'll find a place for you. Don't you worry."

A place for her?

In that instant, the girl's hands balled into fists. The spell broke. Her determination returned, and she grabbed it tightly and held it inside her closed hands.

No telling where they might take her. She had to be able to run and swim and move about at will. None of them, not even this tender-hearted young officer, could promise her that.

Within a split second she was gone. Slithering under the wagon against the gritty ground was not easy, but on the other side sang freedom.

After that she started wearing boy's knickers and shirts and tucking her distinctive red hair up under an old straw hat so that people who didn't know any better assumed her to be a poor urchin boy slipping in and out of the shadows of Galveston, as elusive as smoke.

But at fourteen she was old enough to begin thinking about the future. Life was good for now, but as she got older, what would become of her? Harry Gobinet had found work along the docks and in the warehouses, but only men worked there. Sometimes she and Harry sat on the edge of a pier and watched the sunset after he got off work, and she could tell he was worried about her future, too.

"You cain't go on running and hiding," he had said once a couple of years earlier.

The girl had shrugged.

"If I ever get a boat again, I might go away from here."

She grabbed his arm and peered pleadingly into his eyes.

He looked away, squinted into the sun bleeding across the horizon, then glanced back at her. "You could always go with me. How does that sound?"

Adamantly the girl shook her head.

"That so? You don't want to leave here ever?"

She shook her head again.

"Ever?"

Again she shook her head.

Harry gazed back toward the sun and sighed. "It's no matter anyhow. I'm saving, but don't look like I'll have boat money for a long, long time."

That day, he gave her some coins and bought her an ice cream, but there was nothing else he could do. His eyes showed worry, but there was nothing to be done about that, either.

She had hours to lie awake at night and ponder her possibilities. And during those quiet endless nights, she allowed herself to daydream. Not since before the storm had she done so. Fear had kept her too occupied, but now that was easing. Since the police episode several months earlier, no one had snooped around in a while. Perhaps they had finally given up.

She drifted along on currents of daydreams that involved a kindred spirit: an imagined teenaged boy who also could not speak in words. He would be cute and kind. It mattered not if he was Negro or white, only that they would understand each other, and he would be loved by Reena, Madu, and Harry—her new family. Maybe someday she and the boy would get their own place together. Maybe Reena would teach her how to cook. Maybe Harry would teach the boy about the seas. Maybe they would love each other in the way that her mother and father had loved each other. Maybe she and the boy would bestow upon each other voices that only the other could hear.

Chapter Ten

GRACE

I thought I had arisen early, but by the time I finished eating breakfast in the small dining hall by myself and instructed the maids to have Seamus bring around a carriage, the clock in the main floor hallway was already chiming the nine-o'clock hour, my appointed time to meet with the Reverend Ira Price, the exactor of my punishment, handpicked by my mother. By all accounts, he was a stern man, but I was determined not to appear ashamed, overwrought, or downtrodden. I would do as my mother pleased, because in truth I had no choice in the matter.

I gathered my parasol and hat, picked up my skirt, and almost ran out of the house, not caring whom I disturbed, or about the curiosity I would arouse in those who might be happening by on Broadway. Everyone in our circle knew the story anyway, and I no longer cared. I had done a stupid thing simply out of spite, and now the boom had come down on me. The last thing I wanted was sympathy, even from Jonathan.

Immediately after my mother had informed me of my penance, I began asking around and thus had already learned many things about Ira

Price. He was a Yankee, from Philadelphia, who had come in search of a needy community. He believed that the upcoming grade-raising project would be hardest on the poor, most of whom would likely have no place to go while their homes were lifted and the land was filled in. This would particularly hurt the Negroes of our alleys, who lived such threadbare existences anyway; therefore, he had set up a headquarters down in the worst of it, in Ward Five; he was, in particular, seeking to help those who lived in Fat Alley and Tin Can Alley. Friends of mine who'd met Ira Price assured me that he was a nice enough gentleman, but Larke, who had attended a lecture of his, told me that he'd made reference to the virtue of promptness several times while speaking, all to the embarrassment of two young men who had come in late.

And now I was going to be tardy on the first day of my servitude. In the carriage, I said to Seamus, "Please, let's take our leave. You know where I am to go?"

Seamus cracked the reins. He drove the carriage up to the front door of a small building facing Avenue D, past intrigued and amazed faces, eyes studying the carriage, peering for a look inside the windows. After I told Seamus there was no need to assist me further, I stepped out on my own.

And then the sights and smells assaulted me. On the corner was a two-story grocery store, including a meat market on the front, and down the street sat a cobbler's shop and a wood-sawing shop, a lime warehouse, and an old hotel. Canopies extended over the walkways, under which people stood and watched the happenings on the street. I could smell rotting bananas and bad fish, raw meat, horse manure, and overwhelmingly, the odor of people who lived in too close of proximity to each other.

I'd never given much thought to the poor before. In truth I'd simply pretended that poverty didn't exist. In my art I sought only to re-create the lovely and sublime. Now poverty and ugliness were screaming in my face. Attempting to squelch my nausea and to quiet the flipping fish in my stomach, I entered the one-story building to find Ira Price.

No one had told me that he was still on the younger side, probably only about thirty years old. I had imagined a tall, frail, gray-haired gentleman, stern of face, with glasses pushed down on his nose, with whom I might share heated discussions about Darwinism that affronted his sense of the religious truth. Mother and I attended church regularly and adhered to the doctrine, but I'd read *The Origin of Species*, although it was forbidden in school, and it fascinated me. I didn't know if I completely believed Darwin's theories. But what I most liked about the idea of evolution was the proposal that all life had emerged from the sea, fins and flippers becoming the precursors of arms and legs that allowed a creature to crawl up onto the soil. As always, life is never satisfied with what it has and longs to expand.

Instead of matching my preconceptions, however, the Reverend Price was a bit on the heavy side, built solidly, like an overstuffed leather chair. Dressed in tweeds, he had some orange-smelling pomade combed into wavy, unassuming brown hair, and his beard was curled along the chin line. His cheeks were round and shaved and looked sunburned. He wore spectacles trimmed in gold wire, round discs set directly over the eyes, reflecting the light, making it difficult to catch his gaze directly.

I could tell from the way Ira Price greeted me that I was not what he had expected, either. There was first a sense of surprise and then a touch of wariness about his eyes, as if I had taken him aback. Did he have any idea I had been forced into this duty?

After the introductions, I said, "I do apologize for my tardiness."

"There's no need, I assure you," he said in a voice that was low, soft, and kind. "I hadn't noticed the time. Besides, I'm so pleased you've decided to assist me."

So much for Larke's warnings and Mother's revenge.

But then he said, "There's much work to be done here, as you soon shall see. Later I'll show you about." He fussed around the small dusty room that held a scratched desk stacked with papers, and against the walls, crates stacked with firewood, sacks of flour, sugar, cornmeal, and fruit. A place of confinement, with dark, dusty wood, curtains made of mattress ticking, and a water-stained rug of an indeterminate hue. Ira Price seemed nervous in my presence and yet comfortable in the space, and I detected no hint of apology for the conditions. He could easily have obtained cleaning services from those around him, but apparently he hadn't requested such help.

"I have been given some direction from your mother," he said. "Of course we shall want you to avoid the blocks north of Avenue E."

I knew the area he meant, the so-called District, with its disrespectable saloons, boardinghouses, gambling halls, and brothels, where once I'd clip-clopped by in our carriage with my friends for fun. "I understand."

"And you are to find some deserving whites who need your help. Not Negroes."

"Of course."

He looked up with a baffled expression on his face. "And why would you agree so easily?"

"I agree to most everything my mother tells me, Reverend Price."

He appeared to blanch at that, and I felt myself momentarily dismissed. "I see."

"Is that your mission as well? To help the poor whites?"

He glanced up. "Why no, I don't believe our Savior makes distinctions based on skin color."

So he believed in equality among the races. "Aren't there altruistic needs where you come from, Reverend?"

"There are. But I didn't find them as grave as they are here, Miss Hilliard. I go where the greatest need exists."

He acted as if suddenly remembering other things to do or something else he'd set aside and forgotten.

"For now, would you take a letter, please? I need to respond to an offer of support from the First Baptist Church, and then . . ." He gestured to the crates that littered the floor. "We can begin to distribute this food."

"I'm at your service, Reverend. And where might I find paper, ink, and pen?"

He opened a drawer and pointed to the supplies, then removed his glasses, and with his large square-shaped hands, hair on his knuckles, he wiped each lens using a cloth. I then had my first clear glimpse of his eyes, which were soft around the edges and green, a dusky opaque green, like pond water.

He replaced the spectacles back on his face, wrapping the ear-pieces around each ear, and then he began to dictate a formal letter, using business-mannered proper English, but his sentences were filled with kindness and sentiment, true appreciation for the offers he'd been given. Obviously the Reverend believed in his work, but he lacked the usual pomposity of a zealot. In his letters, he claimed no private pathway to God.

After I penned his letters, we took a walk down the alleys. Along the passageways were various small, unpainted one-story houses, stables, sheds, two-story up and downs, and on corners, some tiny businesses. The people were mostly Negroes, with a smattering of white families here and there.

As we walked, I smelled raw sewage. Every inch of my skin became hypersensitive, taut, and overstretched. I walked cautiously, hesitantly, not the graceful flowing vision I'd always been told I was. I felt a strong sense of pity for those around me but also for myself.

The Reverend didn't seem to notice the smells or the change in me, or at least he didn't let on that he noticed. He kept close by my side, and I wondered if my mother had warned him to make sure nothing happened to me, or if he was staying close of his own accord. No matter the reason, I appreciated that he seemed to have at least some awareness about just how difficult this was for me.

He handed out food with soothing words, greeting toothless women and old consumptive men as skinny as the stray dogs running about, made jokes, and doled out gentle teasing compliments to the children, explaining to me that most of the broad-shouldered young men were away all day, working on the docks or in the cotton warehouses.

He greeted them all, but although he did no preaching then, not all of the alley residents were receptive to him. I was surprised that pockets of people refused our charity, and others avoided us altogether.

We came upon an old, snakeskin-faced man wearing an undershirt and suspenders. Ira introduced him to me, then said, "Charles, this is Miss Hilliard. She's going to be assisting me."

He met my eyes and smiled, showing off a surprising white strap of teeth. His eyes were sparkling black beads recessed into his face. "Well. So she is. Howdy-do, pretty lady?" Then he winked.

I didn't move. So crass to wink at a lady, and one he didn't know at that. I was surprised by how heavily this disrespect lay on my chest. I wondered whether to leave or not. But Ira gave a short laugh and patted the man on the back.

Then Charles retrieved a crumpled envelope out of his pants pocket and sat on the stoop of a dwelling little better than a shack, which must have been his home.

The man looked up at me. "I was only meaning to pay you a compliment."

I tried hard not to show my offense, but it didn't take long before it simply slipped away on its own. I didn't exactly soften, but I could see that the man meant me no disrespect, crass as he was. Instead, he seemed like a happy soul who had no knowledge of good manners.

Ira took the letter from him. Gesturing at it, Charles said to me by way of explanation, "My grandson be learning how to read now. First one in the family. But he's done gone until later. He's in school, making himself good marks."

Ira smiled and then commented, "Soon you can ask him to read your letters."

"Maybe some, but not this one," scoffed Charles.

"And why not?" asked Ira as he opened the envelope and sat down. I remained standing.

The old man let out a big laugh, a sound that erupted from his chest like a hacking cough. "This letter here be personal," he said and gestured toward it again. He laughed once more, and this time it sounded almost like choking. I wondered if he was ill.

I also wondered about his letter. Had it come from a lady friend? I didn't ask, looking away. What could such a letter possibly contain? Ira sat down on the stoop next to the man and read the letter to him in private. I kept my distance and my eyes averted so I wouldn't accidentally overhear.

A boy about eight years old with chocolate-brown skin and closely cropped hair ran up to us. Charles's face opened up like a full moon. "This here be my grandson Isiah." The boy launched onto his grandfather's lap and received a hug. Charles patted his head. "Isiah here, he be sharp as a nail. Gonna end up out of these alleys someday, shore is."

Isiah sprang out of his grandfather's arms as quickly as he had arrived there, stood before me, and extended his hand to me in greeting. "How do, miss?" he said.

Such nice manners and a delightful smile. After Ira introduced me, I told Isiah I was pleased to meet him, and then he ran inside the tiny house.

"He gotta change out of them school clothes before he can go playing," explained Charles.

When we eventually walked away from Charles, Ira said, "I regret any embarrassment he may have caused you with that wink. He's really a good man, Charles is. One of my favorites. A widower. He works nights at a warehouse, despite his age, so he can look after his daughter's boy. Doesn't drink."

I was shocked that Ira knew such details of the man's life. Ira was not only a do-gooder, he clearly meant to make everyone his friend.

"What happened to his daughter?"

Ira paused and then said, "No one knows."

"What do you mean?"

"She disappeared."

I stopped walking. "How does one simply disappear?"

"You might not be aware of it, Miss Hilliard, but people who live hard lives sometimes do just that."

Later we took a carriage ride to deliver the letters he had dictated to me, and then we walked to the Colored Free School. There, during the heat of the afternoon, we gathered together a large group of children and took them to the beach for wading. I was already violating my mother's request that I spend my time among deserving whites. So be it. The Reverend didn't mention it, either.

The sea breeze was warm and dry for a change and smelled fresh. The children splashed and kicked in the shallows and shook their hair, their faces wide with happiness, cheeks shining and lustrous like my paintings before they dry, and foamy droplets pouring off their bodies. They played with abandon, and I envied their lack of restraint, their unselfconsciousness.

Reverend Price and I stood together under the shade of my parasol and peered into that dazzling light reflected off the ocean. We received odd stares and looks. It was unusual to see white people and colored people out together. The Negroes were our servants and our workers, and that was all. I hadn't thought much beyond it. Perhaps my mother intended to humiliate me by sending me to do such humble work down here, but so far it wasn't working. Perhaps my best approach would be to enjoy it. Ira didn't seem disturbed by the glances, and so I determined not to be, either. We counted children and watched to make certain no one ventured out too far. I was fairly sure none of these children had ever been taught to swim.

Ira said to me, "Leisure time is good for the soul, especially a child's."

I couldn't think of a response.

He said, "Don't you agree?"

"Yes, Reverend."

"Please call me Ira."

The Reverend was obviously determined to make this a friendly relationship, and that would certainly make my penance more bearable. "Only if you will drop 'Miss Hilliard' and call me Grace."

"Grace it is. And what a lovely name. It suits you well."

I glanced his way, then back to the sea and the children. We watched the mass of jumping, cavorting children, and soon the sunlight lulled me into a fatigued thoughtfulness.

One boy was hanging back on the beach away from the others, chewing his fingers. He had dark skin, a crown of glossy hair like feathers on the wing of a raven, and enormous eyes. But I saw fear there. I remembered when Etta had been swept under. The boy was probably the same age as she had been, about ten or eleven, and perhaps he'd had a similar experience. The waves were high that day with Etta, as they were now.

I waited to see if Ira would go to him, but he looked flushed with the heat, so I left Ira with my parasol and searched the damp sand. I found a nice piece of a white-chambered shell, broken in half to display the intricate compartments inside, and I took it to the boy.

"Do you know what this odd thing is?"

He had a lovely smile. "That's a shell, ma'am."

I put the shell in his hand. "A shell? You must tell me what that is."

"It comes from out dere," he said, pointing to the ocean. "If you finds a big one and puts it up to your ear, you can hear the ocean."

"Have you ever found a big one?"

He looked down. "Nah." It was obvious that he felt bad about not being out there with the other children. Perhaps they teased him about it.

"You don't like the water?"

He shook his head. "My sister drowned."

A stab in my gut. I shouldn't have asked personal questions. "I-I'm sorry."

He didn't say anything else but instead seemed to be studying the sand under our feet.

"You know what?" I said, leaning closer. "I don't like to go in the water, either. I love to gaze out at the ocean, but it scares me to think of being surrounded by it."

The boy shrugged.

"Do you want to stand with Reverend Price and me?"

He shook his head. I left him alone for a while, but later I brought him a small piece of bleached driftwood shaped long and narrow like a shoe, with a hollowed-out center perfect for setting a candle. He clearly loved it. He curled his sandy fingers around the wood and held on tight, his eyes spilling light.

He thanked me, and I asked his name.

"It's Joseph, ma'am."

"I'm Miss Hilliard, but if we're to be friends, you may call me Miss Grace."

He beamed, and I returned to stand with Ira. I didn't want to single out Joseph too much; the others might tease him for that, too.

Ira said, "After they cool off, they can help us pack and deliver crates."

Just then a large wave crashed into the shallows, exploding the sand, and stirring up foam. The children splashed closer toward us, shouting and squealing until the water flattened out and slid away.

I said to Ira, "You're going to make the children work?"

"I won't force them, of course."

"Of course."

"But as you'll soon see, they want to join in."

"Most are such sociable people," I said.

"Yes," he agreed.

At the end of the day, he praised my work. In just one day I'd seen people with skin diseases, crippled animals, and stinking privies, and still I was standing. What had my mother thought would happen to me? Did she have any idea what she'd sent me into? Except for an occasional gawking, none of us in our social circle ever saw this side of the island. Now I had, and I hadn't collapsed under the strain. There was a little bit of pride in that.

"I see that you're not undone by your first day," Ira said. "Your face does not change when you look at those less fortunate than you. You seem to be at ease, and therefore you put others at ease. You'll do well here, Grace."

"Thank you, Reverend—ah, excuse me, Ira." I smiled for a moment. I couldn't accept the compliment, however, even though after my mother's harsh admonishments I was so in need of kind words. "But I have to confess that I've misled you. I'm sorry to say that I'm not the charitable sort." Tears threatened again. What was wrong with me lately?

He appeared confused.

"I think primarily of myself. I always have."

A line made its way down the center of his forehead. "Then why are you here?"

I let my breath out slowly. "It was not my doing."

A look of realization flashed across his face. "I see. But don't discount your contribution nonetheless. I believe one achieves goodness by doing good things."

I stood still.

"It is most important what we do in life, not necessarily how our deeds began."

I glanced down. It would've been easy to agree, but after my mother's words to me, Jonathan's disappointment, and with the aftermath of my actions regarding Etta still reverberating through my life, it was difficult to believe Ira's words. But I decided to place a moratorium on my self-loathing for the time being.

My voice softened. "You put up a powerful argument, Ira, but I'm sorry to tell you I'm not sure I agree. It seems to me that if we do good things in an effort to better our view of ourselves, then perhaps that might be the most fundamental act of selfishness."

"Fine point. But some very wise people believe that humans are always fundamentally selfish, so why not put that selfishness, that need for inner reward, toward causes that aid others?"

"Perhaps it is more honest to openly accept one's selfishness."

"Perhaps more honest, yes, but not as beneficial. Channeling our human frailties in a way that helps others—perhaps that is the better way to embrace our humanity."

"We are to sacrifice our way to a loftier realm?"

"One could put it that way."

I shrugged, because I couldn't think of a reply. It was unlike me to have so little to say. My confession must have seemed pitiable to Ira. But for some reason I didn't feel as poorly as I had earlier; I wasn't sure why, but perhaps confession was good for the soul after all.

He offered me his hand, shook it as he would another man's, and said simply, "Welcome."

During the carriage ride home, my thoughts drifted to Jonathan. This was the summer that was supposed to bring us closer. We had corresponded with long letters throughout his academic years and then had recouped lost time in the summers. This year, as his education was only a year away from being completed, he had come home with a ring, a sapphire surrounded by diamonds, which he gave me to launch the season of our engagement. This summer should have been the best one of all. Instead, I had disappointed him with my behavior, and now we were going to lose valuable time together.

Our formal engagement party would be held at the end of the summer, before his return to the university. The event was already being planned by both of our mothers to be the handsomest party of the season. I would be wearing a dress designed in pink satin, and the flowers would coordinate. There would be pink Killarney roses, white hyacinths, and pink azaleas. We would have an orchestra for dancing, and the food would be lavish as usual, but I ended up leaving the details and arrangements to Mother, because my life had taken a strange and altogether different turn, and I had little time to think of such things now.

My second day of service with Ira Price began with rain. It came down as a steady drizzle and filled the air with such a wet I couldn't find enough air to fill my lungs. Despite the rain it was still hot, and the air in the office smelled of mildewed books.

The bad weather provided the Reverend with a good opportunity to catch up on his correspondence, and we worked inside throughout the morning hours. Again he dictated while I penned the letters, mainly notes of thanks for some kindness or donation toward the charitable work the Reverend was conducting there in Ward Five.

In the afternoon, the sun peeked out from beneath clouds as big as my thoughts, and we stepped outside into a cool breeze that trailed the rain. Low-slung roofs framed the sky, and the blue of it was so sweet it looked like hope. Even the alleys appeared washed clean and shiny in that emerging sunlight. Ira and I made our rounds. This time we had bolts of fabric to give out to the women and bags of clothes for the children, all of it donated.

On that day I first saw the girl, during that tiny flicker in time everything changed.

I was in the yard of an old colored man named Madu. I'd already heard about the man, a practitioner of so-called black magic. Short, slumped, and wrinkled, he looked exactly as he had been described. Ira told me that he was quite harmless, that he kept to himself for the most part, and that he concocted all manner of potions and cast spells that few people believed in anymore. He inspired no fear in me whatsoever.

Joseph, who had apparently taken a liking to me, and another boy had led me into the voodoo man's yard. They had taunted me onward with promises of something funny, and I had let them. They took my hand, and the three of us sneaked under the man's window. Joseph's eyes were wide and gleaming. Fighting laughter, he put a dusty finger up to his lips and whispered, "Just listen."

Soon I heard what they found so amusing. The voodoo man was snoring. It began with deep breathing, which became louder and louder, building in volume and depth, and then finally those sounds stopped, replaced by a few loud coughs and snorts, then some indiscernible mumblings, and finally a brief silence. Then the whole process began again.

What we were doing was really the most absurd thing, truly a ridiculous activity, but not all that unusual when one considers the lengths boys will go to in order to create nonsense. Joseph was doubled over, laughing silently to keep from awakening the old man. As we walked away, he whispered to me, "It always go that way. Every time."

I returned to Ira's side, as we had much work to do, but when I looked up, there she was, in the yard we had just exited, a striking young white girl, about thirteen or fourteen, I guessed, dressed in ragged clothes that appeared to be castoffs from boys. But what struck me most were her pale-bluish eyes, perhaps the palest eyes I'd ever seen. She had coppery-red hair that appeared uncombed and windswept. Together the eyes and hair lent her the appearance of a wild creature. But I had to wonder why a white girl, no matter how poor, was here in the worst part of the District, which housed the poorest of the poor, where even water and sewer services had still not arrived, where outhouse content was stored in barrels and then collected overnight in horse-drawn carts and later dumped into the gulf.

I peered at her, and she stared back with eyes that were intense and piercing, her body tense as if she were ready to flee in an instant. I couldn't shake the image of an animal, something untamed and feline.

I turned to ask Ira a question. "Who is the girl?"

"Beg your pardon?" he replied.

But when I turned back to point her out, she was no longer there. I saw only the rutted shell road she must have followed, though the dust did not appear disturbed, and on either side of the road the shacks and sheds were so tightly spaced they left room for only some odd shapes of blue sky above and patches of grass and woodpiles.

I was dizzy with the feeling that I'd lost something. As though something I'd wanted badly had slipped through my outstretched hands. I went on to describe the girl to Ira, and he answered, "I know the one. They tell me she's an imbecile. She can't speak."

"What is her name?"

Ira stroked his bearded chin. "I don't know. I've only heard her called 'the girl'; nothing else, I'm afraid."

"That's abominable."

"Yes. I've asked, but everyone denies knowing her name. Even those I'm sure are aware."

"I wonder why?"

"They seem to be protecting her."

"From what?"

"I don't know. There's an air of secrecy about it all."

"Do you know where she came from? How she happens to be here?"

"No. I'm sorry. I'm not in the habit of asking a great deal of questions."

"Do you think she's an imbecile?"

"I've no idea. I tried to speak to her once. She ran away from me. But in that instant, while I had her attention, I saw something in her eyes. Intelligence, something sharp beneath the fear."

I looked back to where I'd seen the girl in hopes she might reappear. "I wonder . . ."

"Go on."

"I wonder if I might be able to help her."

Ira gazed over at me. "I suppose there could be no harm in trying. But for the most part I think we should focus our efforts on those who want help. God knows there are enough of them who welcome our charity, and I've been told she shuns any offers of help."

So she was elusive. That made her even more intriguing. I'd always lived my life under such scrutiny, and I imagined that her life could not have been more the opposite. What would it be like to live in the shadows, in the places where few eyes could see? But there was something else inside me besides curiosity and intrigue, something compassionate. I did want to help her.

I still tell myself that.

I said, "Perhaps she's simply frightened."

He paused. "Your mother wants you to work with needy whites. We would not be violating her directions."

I didn't say that I no longer cared about my mother's directions.

He paused again. "I'll relent," he said. "Go ahead. See what you can do with her."

That evening, Jonathan and I met after dinner on the portico. He told me he'd been forced to dine with his aunt, uncle, and parents to celebrate his uncle's birthday, which made his humor sour. Jonathan was even more displeased with his work at the seawall, and he also voiced his unhappiness over my punishment, which left me too exhausted to do much beyond share a glass of iced tea and a half hour or so of conversation at the end of the day.

"How awful is it down in the alleys?" he asked me when all was quiet. Mother and Etta had left us alone.

"The living conditions are awful."

"How are you coping?"

I shrugged. "It's not as bad as I had thought."

"Tell me about it," he said, pulling my chair closer to his.

But I found myself as mute as the girl I'd seen that day was purported to be. How to describe so many people, smells, sights, and sensations? It was too much, and I ended up shaking my head, while those annoying tears threatened again.

Jonathan took my hand and searched deeply into my eyes. "That bad?"

I had to glance away.

And he said, "I'm so sorry, Grace."

Later I slipped into bed to find the linens unusually cool from the rain of the day. I let them warm against my body, my eyes still open, exhaustion taking me under its grip. But sleep wouldn't come, despite my fatigue. The walls creaked and moaned. I turned and found another section of bed that remained cool. The sights and sounds of the day tumbled through my mind, then more questions and finally sleep. But my last thought was *Who is she?*

Chapter Eleven

ETTA

The most interesting things in Nacogdoches were under the ground. Even as a child, the Caddo burial mounds had intrigued Etta. She had imagined treasures and riches hidden in the earth and was painfully disappointed when a site was excavated and nothing but old tools and dirt-encrusted bones were found. The Caddo had been a poor transient tribe, and thereafter Etta's belief in hidden wealth and surprises virtually vanished, and her belief in herself, in the value of making her own way, soared even higher.

Her parents shook their heads and worried over her. When she was about thirteen, she took a walk in the woods one warm, humid day. Overhead the trees were green and lustrous under the heat, and the vegetation below her was soft and inviting. She had intended to lie down for only a few minutes but instead fell into a deep sleep as if under a spell. She ended up staying for hours, stretched out faceup in the tangle of greenery, alone but for the company of insects and birds.

They found her well after dusk. Her parents had organized a search party with neighbors and friends, and when they came upon her in the depths of the woods, asleep, caring not at all for whom she had worried, she explained, "I took a nap."

She had never understood what all the fuss had been about. After the incident, people looked at her with a sort of confounded wariness, as if they found her difficult to take seriously, and in her parents' eyes she saw disappointment, and even a fair amount of embarrassment. There had always been something in her—an unconventionality—that evoked their glances of disapproval. She saw it from teachers, ministers, and classmates, too.

She came away from that event with a profound sense of being misunderstood, underestimated, and it didn't take long for a desire for some kind of reckoning, even revenge, to follow. How glorious it would be to succeed in her own way and prove them all wrong. After that there was a wildness in her actions, a lack of appropriateness, an impulsivity, and other parents found her worrisome, a child to be avoided, a less-than-desirable playmate.

Despite disapproving parents, she had always had a fair number of friends, and when she reached courting age, her looks triumphed over any doubts in the minds of young men. By the age of twenty-one, she had been turning away suitors for years, all to the distress of her mother, who, although she wanted her daughter to marry well, didn't want her to wait so long that she ended up without a husband at all. It was clear that her mother wanted her off and married, often saying, "You can't live here forever."

At the time, Etta disliked the idea of marriage—it was too much like being owned, like becoming another piece of property belonging to a man. Etta had observed her mother's constant unhappiness with having to do menial but hard work and having to be subservient to her husband, her frustration often taken out on Etta. A strong woman who'd once worked for suffrage had turned silent and cold, distant from everyone. Etta could not end up like that.

She had thought about applying to the teachers college in Nacogdoches but never got around to doing so. After years of "lolling around," as her mother put it, she was finally attempting to do something, to secure a post as a bank teller's assistant.

She met the circus man a few days later. A long line of ancient-looking wagons pulled by shaggy-coated beasts had passed through town and then stopped in a cleared cotton field on the outskirts of the city. There, strangely dressed men set up tents, pens, and stands.

Etta had heard the nightly show they were putting on was worthwhile, so she and a friend decided to take in the performance one Friday night. They were early to arrive and found seats in the front row.

After the animal acts, clowns, cannons, stunts, and men on stilts, Philo was the last act of the evening. He strutted out under the lights, and Etta sat back in her seat. This was the first time she'd seen a man so scantily clad, in form-fitting clothing that was thinner than any undergarments she'd ever seen before. They showed off every muscle in stark outline. He strode around the ring, arms outstretched, basking in admiration before he'd even done a thing, and as he scanned the audience, Etta could have sworn that his eyes landed on her. She could also have sworn that a knowing smile played on his lips, also directed at her.

He had deep-set eyes, dark features, well-shaped lips, and blue-black hair that curled like filigree. He was statuesque but fluid, his body like a dancer's. As Etta watched the way he triumphed over the room, something inside her did a cartwheel.

The announcer introduced Philo as the Flying Greek and went on to say that the Flying Greek normally did his act with a net underneath him for safety, but sometimes he would do the act without one. The announcer, with much dramatic flair, then turned to Philo for a decision about that night's performance.

Philo waited for a pregnant pause to go by, the audience hushed and expectant, and then, Etta could swear, he looked at her again. He turned, walked back toward the announcer, and nodded yes, he would do the act tonight without a net. Only later did Etta learn that this was a part of the act; he always performed without a net as a "matter of honor."

The tension built while the circus workers disassembled the net and Philo climbed what appeared to be hundreds of steps straight up the tall center pole and then perched on a platform no bigger than the stoop behind a poor farmhouse. The other trapeze artist, the man who would catch Philo, was already swinging on the opposite trapeze, his arms dangling in loose arcs, his muscles flexing. Etta waited, each breath like a bullet lodged in her chest.

Philo's act included swinging gracefully and flipping and completing somersaults in the air before being caught by the other man. Etta and the rest of the audience sat in a state of hushed trepidation, and the moments when Philo flew loose in the air were the longest moments of her life. When it was done, he descended the hundreds of steps again, all to a roar of applause and the crowd's shouts of approval.

While the cheers and clapping went on, Etta sat in shocked stillness. To do such a thing, to take such a chance with his life, he had to be the most fully alive person she'd ever seen. How did it feel to touch death and then fool it? How did it feel to be free and flying out in the treacherous open air, nothing beneath you, and then turn in a split second's time and grab on to life again?

After the show, she and her friend parted, and Etta asked around for him and was eventually led to his wagon. Hoisting her skirts, she went up the steps and knocked. He said for her to enter, and when she opened the door, his back was turned to her, his shoulders huge, round and shiny like overturned polished bowls. Then he swiveled her way. He was wiping his face with a small towel, and the sight of his bare arms, ridged with veins, gave her a pleasing jolt. He smiled and gestured her closer.

"The lovely girl in the front row," he said with an amused expression on his face.

"Thank you."

"And what brings you here?"

She found his voice softer than she had expected. He hadn't the booming baritone of the circus announcer, and his demeanor was softer than she had expected, too. But he was even lovelier up close. His hair was black satin, and his dark eyes were rimmed with lashes like tightly woven nests. He was still scantily dressed, and Etta couldn't help herself; her eyes drifted downward.

He noticed. "But you are a good girl," he said.

Etta lifted her chin. "I am not."

And then he laughed.

He amazed her with stories about the Greek gods that his parents had told him, about sailors captured by mermaids, and sunken treasure in the straits between the Greek isles. Then he told her his life story, how he had learned his stunts as a child from his father, then was orphaned in his teens, and how he later joined the fighting in the Philippines, where he ran gunboats up the Rio Grande and survived being ambushed by the Filipinos in the bush.

He had traveled first by jumping trains and then with the circus. He'd seen automobile races run on the Merrick road from Springfield, Illinois, to Babylon, twenty-five miles out and back. He'd seen New York's Central Park, where rich boys sailed miniature yachts on the lakes and girls sat with sketch pads on their laps at Lily Pond. He'd seen the razor-stubble deserts and mountains of Arizona, where the Apaches were still fighting for their freedom. He described Washington, DC, as the cleanest city he'd ever seen, most of its electric-light wires, telegraph, and telephone lines underground. And he'd sat on the balcony at the famous Cliff House, in San Francisco, which hung out over the ocean on a cliff at Point Lobos, where sea lions played below.

He moved his hands as he spoke, shaping and sizing and directing his stories. He was the only person she knew who was perfectly content with his life, who didn't constantly try to rewrite his history and better his part in it.

He told stories about far-distant places, and she could almost hear the click-clack of the trains, the roar of steamships, the horse's hooves padding along roads.

They met in secret, and being in the bunk of his small wagon, closed away from the outside world, was not unlike being in the berth of a ship bound for other lands. Until he had finished the evening show and she could see him again, Etta could do little else except busy herself with trivialities. The smell of a man's hair oil similar to his was enough to make her heady and anxious beyond reason. She drifted through her days and waited, just waited, until she could unfold against his pliable body under the candlelight again.

When the circus left town two weeks later, she and Philo corresponded with letters. Etta found his penmanship almost unreadable; he was nearly illiterate, his English grammar and punctuation indicating he'd had little schooling, but she cared not a whit. As soon as he'd made his way back to a nearby town, Etta took the train to meet him.

Neither of them mentioned plans for the future, which told Etta more than she wanted to know. Of course there could be no future; the circus was poor, and she couldn't go with him, but in the moment she swam in powerful feelings she didn't know she was capable of. Once she'd thought of herself as too mature and wise to let anything so overwhelmingly sweep her away. Once she'd thought of love as a mere decision to make along the way, but every time she remembered him back then she experienced a simplemindedness that knocked everything else away, a clutching feeling in the pit of her stomach, and a warm weakness that spread from neck to knees against her will.

Throughout her day, the huge swelling passion it had come to be overwhelmed her, and finally she saw love as the power behind all human movement and decisions, and she was stunned by this loving, this loving Philo.

Her mother discovered them. Etta never knew how her mother learned that she was seeing Philo in secret, and it no longer mattered. Once the plans for her banishment to Galveston were announced, Etta put up only a weak fight. Philo had mentioned nothing about the future, and despite her dreamy tendencies, Etta was a realist. Circus life was hard, and hardship might ruin her looks and thus the love they had. Besides, Philo didn't even ask her, perhaps aware that he had little to offer. So she packed her best belongings, said good-bye to friends, and stepped off the edge of the world as she knew it. No one knew that she was taking a newly fractured heart along with her. No one knew that she had left behind a love that had meant everything to her.

In Galveston, there were so many things to occupy her. She went to luncheons, dinners, parties, and exhibits, and pushed Philo out of her mind as best she could. She had always maintained the ability to improvise. Only at night, when she was out under the open sky, alone, a warm wind breathing on her cheeks, did she let herself remember his kiss and yearn for it so powerfully that her chest compressed.

But life was so delicious here, so edible. Her aunt would settle for no less than freshly squeezed orange juice every morning. They ate imported cheeses and sampled wines from Italy. Etta put on weight. Her breasts became heavier, her hips more curvaceous, and she'd never felt so womanly, so bountiful. Her body was a finely honed instrument to advance her opportunities, and every day she tested, observed, and learned more about how she should appear.

She began to question the love she'd had for Philo. Perhaps the secrecy, the forbidden nature, and the hopelessness of their ever having a life together had given it much of its passion. But one thing still haunted her: she had never said good-bye. In an act of cowardice, she had failed to answer his last letter before leaving Nacogdoches, the only place he knew where to find her.

Throughout wakeful, cavernous nights, finding no comfortable spot on her mattress, she fought through her grief, and before long she stopped tangling the covers. After three weeks in Galveston, all that was left of Philo in her heart was a vague sense of loss.

Grace began returning home from her charitable work later and later in the day, leaving Etta more time with Bernadette. During Grace's second week of duty, she did not appear until after the appointed dinnertime. Etta sat with Bernadette at the table and watched her aunt become angry and irritated, maybe even a little afraid, as they waited for Grace to arrive.

The servants were doing everything they could to keep the dinner dishes warm.

Finally Grace appeared, and Bernadette said simply, "You're late."

"Yes, Mother, I know. I was detained. I'll be back down as soon as I can. But I must change my dress first." Grace's face was rosier than ever. *Well, well,* thought Etta. It appeared as if her cousin's punishment agreed with her. Or maybe it was just the heat.

Bernadette said, "I'll send Dolly to assist you."

"No," said Grace quickly from the bottom of the staircase. "I can manage on my own."

And so they sat. And waited yet more. Etta recognized relief on her aunt's face, but she was still showing signs of irritation, too.

It was obvious that Bernadette was forcing a smile. She said, "I was looking at the calendar today and was surprised to realize that you've already been with us for a month."

Etta's heart froze. Was her aunt ready to send her back?

Instead, she said, "I'm proud of you, Etta. You've adjusted well. Everyone adores you."

"Thank you."

A devilish expression came over Bernadette's face. "And I have a feeling that you won't be leaving Galveston any time soon."

Etta's heart leapt joyously, but she managed a sweet smile.

"In fact, I've written to my sister and asked that she allow you to stay as long as you wish."

Etta had to contain her elation. "I confess, dear aunt, that I was hoping you would do just that."

Bernadette leaned forward a notch and lowered her voice. "Surely you know that you're of a marriageable age."

The mention of marriage temporarily stilled Etta. In Nacogdoches, her prospects for a husband had been limited to farmers, workers, and perhaps salesmen. But here the outlook was entirely different, and the idea of marriage to a wealthy Galvestonian turned her mind and heart. If marriage here meant a life of luxury, she would be crazy to avoid it. Her pleasure was so huge that Etta let down her guard. "But all the young gentlemen I've met are so much more . . . prosperous. I venture they think they know but really have no clue about my humble background."

"There is no need for disclosure at this point. You're living with me. And besides, the right gentleman, once he's fallen for you, won't care about your so-called humble background."

"I do hope you're right."

"Of course I'm right," stated Bernadette. "Oh, it shall be so much of an adventure to help you find the right match. Grace and Jonathan were destined since childhood, so there was never a need for me to guide her, to enjoy the courtships she might have experienced. It would be ever so pleasing to help you."

Etta sat completely still. She'd had no idea that Grace's marriage had been carefully designed, and she doubted Grace knew it, either. If Bernadette had orchestrated that auspicious union, and in secrecy from her daughter no less, what could she do for Etta? She could scarcely believe how well things were going. Aunt Bernadette was more like a mother than Etta's true mother was. Bernadette guided, listened, advised, and included. She had pulled Etta under the broad warmth of her wings. "Oh, thank you, Auntie! You have no idea how much this means to me . . ."

At that moment, Grace appeared in a clean dress and took her chair, and the conversation at the table came to a fast stop. No one spoke as they ate delicately like proper ladies, until Bernadette excused herself before dessert.

Even Etta was astonished by how fumingly her aunt could act toward her only child. Etta knew then never to cross her.

Grace stared after her mother and then turned to Etta. "She's still angry with me."

Etta said nothing as the dessert plates were delivered. "Give it time. It has been only a couple of weeks."

Grace picked up her fork and looked at the fruit tart piled high with whipped cream before her but didn't start eating. "I'm terribly sorry for what I did. I should've apologized right away, but I sensed you weren't ready to hear me out."

They had yet to speak about it, and Etta thought it would be one of those things that was simply never again addressed. She almost admired her cousin's courage. Etta said, "I'm sorry your punishment is so extreme. Is it terrible?"

"No," said Grace, then seemed determined to change the subject. "How are you faring overall? It had been my intention to be your companion."

"I'm doing well. Many of your friends are showing me about. And then there's your mother . . . I'm rarely alone."

"I'm happy for you."

Etta studied her cousin and was stunned to realize that Grace was not the least bit disingenuous. Her open face and clear eyes suggested she was telling the truth.

Grace asked, "What have you found the most enjoyable?"

After a moment, Etta answered, "Automobiles."

"Not people?"

"Some people."

"Whom do you like best?"

A loud laugh escaped Etta. "Dear cousin, I'm a forgiving person, but you don't expect me to confide in you now, do you?"

Grace's eyes immediately reddened and grew glassy. She sat in apparent stunned silence for what felt like long minutes, while Etta took a taste of the whipped cream. A funny memory suddenly came to her. During her first visit to this house, Etta had admired her aunt's cherished china figurines. Bernadette kept those treasures displayed on the mahogany tables in the main parlor, and the young Etta had mistaken them for objects of play. Grace had to tell her that children were not allowed to touch the poised faces and graceful limbs of those painted ladies. Grace had been very kind to her back in those days. Perhaps Etta should search for more kindness inside herself now. She didn't really hate her cousin.

Grace's voice was weak and shaky when she said, "Memories fade. Maybe in time . . ."

But Etta only shrugged. True, she didn't hate Grace, but she also wasn't ready to let her off the hook yet. "Give me one good reason why I should tell you anything," she said in a falsely sweet tone.

Apparently Grace wasn't going to give up easily. "I'll give you two."

"Fire away."

"We're cousins. Blood kin."

Etta was unimpressed. Grace's words could have been annoying clatter coming from the kitchen.

"And second, we could begin again."

Etta shook her head. "I'm in the business of forgetting my beginnings."

Grace sat frozen while Etta dug into the tart. It was peach. Wonderful. Without looking up, she said, "Once someone has betrayed my trust, it's never to be regained."

She had almost finished the tart by the time Grace spoke again. Her words were little more than whispers, breathy and soft. "I had hoped for genuine affection between us. I suppose I ruined that possibility."

Etta took her last bite and licked the spoon. Her cousin's obvious remorse moderated her a bit. "Maybe it will all turn out for the best. Look at it this way. Now you don't have to endure your mother's supervision all day. I'm doing that for you."

The next day, Grace was late coming home again, even though Jonathan was joining the three of them for dinner. Etta had welcomed him after he arrived and was now waiting with him in the front parlor, whereas Bernadette had decided not to come downstairs until after her daughter arrived.

Sitting alone with Jonathan was decidedly awkward. Etta looked at the flowers placed throughout the room instead of at Grace's fiancé. Bernadette spared no expense in filling the house with vases of fresh flowers in each of the occupied rooms and also the foyer, the main parlor, and the dining hall.

Finally she had to let her gaze fall on Jonathan, or she would be considered rude. His dewy eyes said it all. He was enamored of her, under her spell, captivated yet clearly torn, because of course he had to have known that he shouldn't have any of those feelings for any lady other than his fiancée.

"Another long day among the poor for Grace, I presume," Etta said.

He sat tall in his chair and wouldn't allow himself to slouch, as he often did on the portico. He glanced away and murmured, "I presume."

She made her voice just the slightest bit vulnerable. Men liked vulnerability; they liked any perceived weakness in a woman, even if it wasn't real. "Are you angry with me?"

He held her gaze a moment longer before glancing away again. "No. Why should I be? You haven't wronged me, have you?"

"No, but it's on my behalf that Grace is being punished. If I hadn't come here, the two of you would be spending much of your summer together. But now she hardly has time."

He took a moment before answering.

He was lonely, Etta could see that, and vulnerable, too. He had a malleable mouth that gave too much of him away. She could have him if she wanted. All it would take would be a little more play and then a snap of her fingers. But it wouldn't serve her purposes. She felt no desire for him anyway. Etta wanted passionate love, along with prosperity. Being in Galveston and becoming a part of its high society had made the idea of marriage palatable, even desirous, but she didn't want to sacrifice love. There was no reason she couldn't find a wealthy man who could also ignite her passions. She was becoming greedy; she wanted it all.

Jonathan said in a sorrowful tone, "Grace accepts the blame. She accepts her punishment. She knows she was wrong."

"Yes, I realize that. It's honorable of her."

He appeared weary. "Yes. Honorable."

A long uncomfortable silence. Even Etta had no clue what to say next. Then he gave her that appraising hungry look again that spoke of anything but honor.

She no longer cared if she behaved rudely. She said in a heated manner, "What are you thinking when you give me those looks?"

Jonathan glanced down, took a deep breath, and then gazed back at her. "What looks?"

"Oh please. Don't deny it. You look at me like a dog circling a bitch in heat."

Looking stunned, he shook his head. "I hadn't thought it was noticeable."

"Noticeable? It's downright blatant."

He grasped his hands between his knees.

"So, go ahead. Let there be no secrets between us. What are you thinking when you give me those looks?"

"I'm wondering what you think of me."

"I think that you are Grace's," Etta snapped. "That's what I think."

His face trembled a touch, and he grasped his hands so tightly they were blanching. But his eyes did not leave Etta's. "I barely see her now."

Poor, poor, lonely rich boy. "You're feeling neglected."

"Perhaps," he said. "So go ahead. Say it. What? What *do* you think of me?"

"My God, Jonathan. You don't want me to tell you what I really think. Truly you don't."

"Yes, I do."

Now Etta shook her head. "You must trust me on this."

"I want to hear it. Say anything."

"Very well," Etta said and then, "What I think is that Grace is too good for you."

Chapter Twelve

The Girl

A Saturday in June, and the girl found her present living situation to be a shed on Madu's property. That morning she'd already visited old Gwendolyn, a hickory twig of a woman who sold the best tamales and stuffed crabs on the island and often gave her a handout; then she found Harry down at the docks and shared the food with him, sitting beside him on the wharf, where they listened to an old man playing the harmonica until it got too hot in the sun and Harry needed to scrounge for work anyway.

Back in Madu's small yard that faced the alley, the girl drew water from the cistern and washed her hands before creeping back toward the old shed.

Madu had a supernatural kind of knowing, not unlike a witch's, and he knew when the girl had been thinking about the sea, when she'd been dreaming of it. He could see its motion in the way she moved. She swayed on her feet, wavelike, and he knew her feet were inclined to go running there. He heard her dreams in the night wind that rattled his cracked windows. But in the summer the beaches were full of tourists and city folk taking strolls and eating out of their wicker picnic baskets.

The beach was not a good place for the girl to spend her days. Too easy for her to be noticed.

Madu's crinkled face, so black it was almost indigo, thrust out past the screen door. He bared his stubby yellow teeth. "You ain't aiming to go down there today, is you?"

The girl looked up and gave a shake of her head.

Madu shuffled out beyond the door and nudged a stray tabby cat that had balled herself up in the shade of his porch. Then he straightened up and rubbed at the small of his back. "I be making my magic black candles with monkey blood today. You best stay around here and help me."

The girl stood still. The truth was she *had* been planning on heading to the beaches later, when old Madu took his second nap of the day. Today the air was unusually still, quiet as the clothes hanging on lines, and hotter than the blue part of a flame. The beach was the only place to go on a day such as this. It was still June, but the air was already suffocatingly hot and heavy, drifting up sultry out of the Tropics. The only thing to do was get wet.

When she'd been barely old enough to walk, her father had introduced her to the ocean; he had used his life savings to build a souvenir shop down on the sand. The store stood six feet off the beach on pilings he sunk himself, and board by board he was putting it together, always with his son and daughter there for company. One day he paused from his work, held the girl up high in his rough, big-fingered hands, and together they looked out to the sea. The girl remembered how deeply her father had breathed, and she sucked it in, too, the smell of freshly cut lumber, the sweet dustiness of wood chips and shavings all around them, mingled with the wet and salt of the sea. She held on to his shoulders while he told her just how vast that world of water was. "We're seeing nary a drop of it," he said.

That was the first time she could remember finding her favorite spot, that place far away on the water where the sea was a calm and quiet shelf of palest silver, and then beyond it, where it took the curve into nothingness or maybe the first reaches of Heaven. She tried to find the exact spot where bright sunlight floated away into sky and then disappeared. In her nightly dreams, the girl lay on her back, arms outstretched, and drifted all the way to that distant watery band.

Her father worked inside the shop every day, selling his shells and trinkets to tourists, and the girl would play down below on the beach, jumping in and out of the gentle breakers, searching for shells, and chasing sand crabs. The pull of the ocean was especially strong in her legs, a swirling sensation around the long bones that sucked her feet into the foam. Eventually her father taught her to swim.

Madu snapped, "You stay put, you hear?" He terrified others, but the girl knew better. He was all bark and no bite. Overhead a flock of laughing gulls circled and let out their hoarse screeches. More than speech, the girl missed laughing. She would've laughed at him along with the gulls if she could, but Madu craned his neck upward and shouted, "Quiet!" He looked at her then, his gaze piercing her skin.

"There's a white woman been sniffing around," he said solemnly.

The girl let out a sigh, because she'd seen her, too. Several times.

"She been helping out that white preacher man."

Yes, the girl had seen her passing out sacks of flour and baskets of fruit, calico cloth, buttons, notions, and worn but clean shoes and coats. The woman was only an inch or so taller than the girl, small boned with golden hair and pink cheeks, and she always wore such finery—netted or flowered hats and white gloves, and on her feet polished, buttoned shoes. She was so pretty; the girl wished she could grow up to look like her.

But wealthy white women had no business in the alleys. Instinct had already convinced the girl to keep out of her sight. Reena had more than once proclaimed that white folks, even the ones who occasionally came offering goods and kindnesses, would probably find it upsetting that a white girl was living amongst the Negroes. They would want to take her away, and images of cages had never left her fearful thoughts.

The girl smirked, as if to say to Madu that it was no matter, but in truth she was concerned. The young rich woman had spotted her, and instantly her interest had been piqued; the girl could feel it in the way the other woman's eyes landed on her heavily, and she could see it in her changed stance, which became more upright and alert.

Avoidance became the girl's plan, although the rich lady was everywhere now, walking the alleys, talking with the people of the neighborhood. The girl ducked away as soon as she caught sight of her, but she had trouble evading her. She came quietly, peered curiously, and many times the girl wasn't fast enough, letting the young woman get too clear and too long of a glimpse.

Gazing at Madu, she lifted her palms upward with an inquisitive expression on her face. He said, "I don't know who she be. Some church lady or something. People say she nice. She some kinda artist or something. She give a drawing or two to some people."

The girl frowned. An artist?

"Maybe she want to paint you and your red hair."

She shook her head fiercely.

"I knows. You best be staying clear of her. Either she's wanting to take you away somewheres or paint you so everybody knows who you is, and ain't neither one of them things good."

After she nodded, Madu worked his way back indoors. She slipped away again, then combed the marsh for scallops and flounder, always on the lookout for rattlers. A flock of brown pelicans—there must have been fifty of them floating on the flat waters—entertained her for a while, and then she ended up on the beach near Fort Crockett for the sunset, admiring the changing colors as the polished copper light took leave.

Again that nagging question: What was to become of her? How long before the authorities took interest again and someone caught her?

The young white woman was fraying the girl's nerves. The girl had no answers yet, but she knew for sure that she could never leave this island; it held her best memories, and in the early days after the storm the girl had found things from her house all over, scattered from one shore to the next. Stuck in the mud way over on the high side, a scrap of fabric that looked like their old kitchen curtains; later a shoe that might have been her mother's. And once she found a painted shell she recognized from her father's shop.

Now she picked up a stick and started absentmindedly drawing in the sand. Small scratches that made no sense. She stared at them in confusion. Then she smoothed the patch of sand in front of her until it was flat and unmarked, and she drew a wave. Then another wave and another wave. Layers of waves. She sat back and studied her work. Not bad. When she was in school, she had been told that she drew well.

Above the waves, she drew a big sun and then some clouds. She sat back on her heels and thought hard. Maybe she would become an artist. You didn't need to speak to be an artist. You just had to see things and then re-create them on a flat surface while making them look anything but flat.

As the last rays of the sun finally beamed away and the darkness lifted out of the ground, she began to like her idea even more. Once she was too old for the authorities to bother her anymore, she could make drawings or paintings down by the sea and sell them to tourists. Her father had sold some local artwork out of his souvenir shack.

It was a good idea, one that meant she could take care of herself in the future. Though the girl had to steer clear of the young white woman, the lady had given the girl a fine idea.

Chapter Thirteen

GRACE

It took me more than a week to find out that the girl slept in a dilapidated shed on the old voodoo man's property, right where I'd seen her the first time. The boy who told me as much would not even tell me her name, however, but would only point out the sorry place where she lay at night. He was reluctant to do even that.

One day, when I could hear the voodoo man snoring again, I let myself into his weedy overgrown yard and then ducked my head into the shed where the girl stayed, a dusty little windowless hovel with junk pushed against the walls. Inside were some old army blankets, a washtub she must have used for bathing, and a slop jar. I managed to stave off repulsion and crept in, and I was ever so happy I'd done so, because farther inside I made the most incredible discovery.

On the packed dirt floor of the shed were numerous scraps of paper, and in the handwriting I assumed was hers were snippets of poetry, and I recognized many of the lines. The verse of Emily Brontë. She wasn't an imbecile, nothing even close to it. Not only was the girl no idiot, she was literate. Elation flooded me, and then a sense of relief, and then something even larger.

Later that day, as we were distributing goods and food, I told Ira what I had seen.

"You entered her dwelling?" he asked with concern on his face. He stopped and turned to face me. "While she was gone?"

I deflated. "Y-yes."

At first, he said nothing.

"You think it was not a good thing to do."

His soft eyes held concern rather than incrimination. "I think we have to respect people's privacy."

"But she's still a child."

"She doesn't live like one, does she? She takes care of herself somehow."

His words were like soft nudges. Ira seemed to be giving me time to reconsider my ways. And then my regret was huge. I was as lost here as I sometimes felt alone at night. Down here a code of ethics still prevailed, and I had just broken it.

"I'm sorry, Ira."

He nodded, and we continued walking, doing our work.

He said, "I had a feeling she was not ignorant or afflicted."

"I'll be more careful. I promise."

During our stroll and food delivery, Ira sometimes prayed with people who requested it, but I never once heard him use sententious language or make moralizing comments, which one might have expected of a minister. He listened to everything, from stories and jokes to concerns and dire problems, with the same rapt attention, transfixed by one and all, but he didn't give advice unless it was asked of him.

Once he offered me his arm, and I heard a quick intake of breath when I touched him. Was he a tiny bit enamored of me? Often I was aware of him watching me, and once I glanced back to see his face, inquiring, contemplating, and maybe a little entranced. Perhaps he had never spent so much time working near a young lady.

I enjoyed all of my duties with Ira Price, particularly the work with the children. My favorite things were taking them to play in the ocean, leading them in games, and teaching them songs. This in turn gave me fresh memories of when my father was alive. Though memory before age five is a dim and fleeting thing, I recalled a day when he was stretched out flat on the grass beside me, and together we had studied a nearby colony of ants. We had watched them build a hill, and it was fascinating, all those tiny creatures carrying grains of sand, making something substantial together. Another memory returned to me, too, of my father and myself studying the back of a leaf, until my mother suddenly appeared and snatched our leaf away.

We worked daily among the adults, families, outcasts, and sick people. Ira and I had to ignore some gambling, cockfighting, and drinking, and most of the time we didn't try to "move mountains," as he put it. We did stop a phony druggist from selling morphine, but for the most part we took things "one act at a time," as Ira would say. We escorted a man who suffered from apoplexies to the hospital. We attended funerals and burials at Potter's Field. At the burial of one older man, an emptiness came over me. I longed to be able to visit my father's final resting place. My mother had never held a funeral service for my father, saying that he didn't believe in them. She told me he'd been buried in New Orleans, but we'd never visited the grave, as Mother had disliked that city from the moment of his death onward; in fact, she despised the entire state of Louisiana.

Ira wore his occupation as easily as he wore his simple clothing and gleaming glasses. His white shirt was neither perfectly white nor well pressed, but it was well matched with his comfortable demeanor and air of wisdom. Despite his rumpled hair and the frequent sunburn flaming raw on his cheeks, his presence was powerful but gentle. He wasn't a man of the streets, but he fit anyway—a small but essential piece of a complex puzzle.

In this hard part of the city, I helped load crates and even did some lifting, despite Ira's frequent objections. One time I ran for a doctor for a young woman giving birth. The labor was taking much too long. I waited outside during the labor and birth and became filled with the most profound sense of loneliness as I listened to the screaming and sounds of pain I would never forget, wrapped up in my own musings until I finally heard the words "Mother and baby are well," and in those moments of unfolding life, that old empty place was suddenly filled with all that was raw yet hopeful. A flash of memory—my father carrying me up the stairs, tripping a bit and then laughing, but I had felt no fear. He had held me, just as this community held its arms tightly around itself.

I would never forget the face of the baby his mother named Emmanuel, meaning *"God is with us."* I saw myself not as the center of my own life, but just one person in a teeming world of humanity. Around me were men who laughed with abandon, women who were not ashamed of their flesh, and children who created adventures, just as Jonathan and I once had.

I found myself searching for *my* place to fit in and also trying to solve the riddle that was Ira Price. He was a mystery to me, even though he was as open and bright as a spread of untouched sand on a sun-filled beach. I had begun to welcome his solid warmth beside me as we worked, the way he leaned forward ever so slightly when I spoke, the way he unconsciously nodded and smiled as he looked over donations.

The people of my social circle had no notion of the activities in the shacks and shanties and hovels and rookeries behind them. In the alleys, despite some miserable existences, what surprised me most was how much laughter and music I heard during my days. The alley behind Trinity Episcopal Church, attended by many people I knew in my social circle, was a most lively place. Alley dwellers changed residences a great deal, shared houses, washed clothes, peddled charcoal, played fiddles, made whiskey, picked figs, fried fish, gave birth, died. I would never have known all this had I not been sent here by my mother.

Several people became dear to me—the boy named Joseph, who was afraid of the water, and an old woman named Daisy, who had some malady of the neck that kept her face always turned to one side, but still she cooked for every single funeral, whether she knew the deceased well or not. Charles, with his sense of humor, and his grandson Isiah were favorites, too. Then there was a spry old man named Jules, who could play everything on the violin from concertos to jigs.

"He can also play spoons," Ira told me once.

"How does one play spoons?"

A smile crossed his face. He seemed to take genuine pleasure in my company, and I was ever so relieved that I hadn't become a burden to him.

He said, "Don't tell me you've never heard someone play the spoons before. Why, we'll just have to ask him to play a tune for you. Perhaps something special for a special young lady."

I had never expected anything close to a compliment from Ira, and at this I looked away.

Eventually the music man, as we began to call him, did play the spoons for me. He and I became friends and often talked of concertos and symphonies and art in general. I never asked how he came to know so much. It was a conundrum, but he could converse on the arts as well as anyone I'd ever known. I gave him some of my sketches, which pleased him.

But most of all my interest fell on the girl who possessed animal-like fear and hid from us, who knew poetry but didn't speak. Her isolation set her apart, and my attention was hooked.

I walked the beach almost every day before going home. And every day I stopped, faced the sea, and closed my eyes. What an opportunity I had been given. I could've so easily never known this, never recognized this. Had Etta not come, had I not betrayed her confidence, had my mother not "punished" me by sending me to work with Ira, I would have missed the experience of a lifetime. I might never have really *seen*.

Chapter Fourteen

ETTA

There were so many places to go, people to meet, and things to do. Etta attended a performance of the New York Metropolitan Opera Orchestra, hosted by the Galveston Quartette Society. She was invited to a Japanese bridge party, where the guests wore kimonos bought overseas (Etta donned her aunt's) and the prizes were a silver compote, a crystal puff box, and other intricate and expensive trinkets.

She viewed art collections and an antique Persian rug recently purchased by one of her aunt's friends. She attended a wedding held in the private home of her aunt's dear friend Olive Dougherty, whose niece married another island boy in the garden on a Sunday afternoon, and then afterward a private supper was served in the dining room over thick crimson carpets, with only a few select friends present, though Etta barely knew the newlyweds.

She had been accepted into an inner circle, a group of young people who owned Gramophones and Brownie cameras and read *Harper's Weekly* and had been to Atlantic City, New York, Paris, and London so many times they mentioned their last trips in passing.

She celebrated the graduation of a rather boorish young man who smoked a pipe and played with his hair while he stumbled among the guests at the party hosted by his parents, and she tried to look cheerful. Etta thought him to be uninterested in the party and its guests. Those who had so much as always failed to appreciate it.

Under high ceilings lit with chamber-sized chandeliers and to the music of a full orchestra, its musicians dressed in black tuxedos with white roses on their lapels, Etta danced with almost every young man at that graduation party. Her prospects were lining up. And now that she wore gowns with designs overseen by her aunt, now that she had allowed her aunt to take her under her wing, advising her on everything from jewelry to hair accessories and perfumes, even her suitors' parents approved.

She danced with a young man who was studying in the School of Medicine of the University of Texas. He was a gentleman but much too nervous in her close proximity, and when he started talking about a paper he was to give on hookworm disease, and then about the need for pasteurization of milk and cream in the Southern states as a public health matter, she allowed another young man to cut in.

The next dance partner was the son of the owner of Cohen's Clothing Store, among other established businesses. He was an excellent dancer, but he perspired too much. After she took her turn with him on the floor, Etta's hand was damp, even though she wore lacy gloves. Another man, an executive on the Short Line, talked too much, as if he was far more interested in his own version of everything than in learning more about her.

None of them affected her the way Philo had. She missed it, that feeling she'd exploded with for a brief period of time. She wanted to feel that overwhelming thrill again, that instantaneous attraction, a pull so magnetic it had almost made her ill.

She preferred the days spent with her aunt. They took shopping excursions, sat for coffees and teas, and visited the Galveston Athletic Club.

Dressmakers came by in the afternoon to offer fabric choices for Bernadette's new winter dresses, although her wardrobe was already filled with lovely suits and gowns and the most elegant and tasteful of accompaniments. Bernadette chose carefully but without regard to cost. She devised a menu for every dinner and wrote notes to the cooks suggesting means of preparation and presentation. Even in her everyday life she demanded only the best. Nothing less than pricey perfection would suit.

With her aunt, Etta was the curious one. Once she asked a question that could've come out of Grace's mouth. Or would it have been Jonathan's, or Wallace's? "Do you prefer beach side or bay side?"

Bernadette had been sitting, poised and reflective, in her private parlor. "Perhaps I'm odd in my fancy," she answered, "but I prefer the quiet of the bay. I find it more soothing."

Etta would continue, asking questions such as "Which is your favorite store?" "Your favorite place for dining?," always trying to find her way in.

Once she asked her aunt, "Who is your closest friend?"

"Why, my dear, I don't believe in ranking them," Bernadette answered. "That's not a courteous or a grateful thing to do."

Etta glanced down and tried to appear contrite. "But surely you have a preference."

"If I do," said her aunt a bit more harshly than Etta had expected, "then it's one I'll keep to myself."

Etta was sure her face reflected hurt. With her aunt she found herself less guarded.

Aunt Bernadette unstiffened. "My dear, it's simply the sort of thing one learns over the years. The trick, my sweet, is to make each and every one of your acquaintances a dear friend, and then you shall always be surrounded by favorites."

Etta looked up then and nodded, listening with all her might.

"Each person possesses his or her own unique gifts. Some adore music and the arts; others are experts on literature and museums. Simply make sure you call upon those whose gifts are best for certain occasions. Show no preferences, and in the end you shall always be preferred."

Of course. Etta was already doing just that, wasn't she? Hadn't she come to nearly the same conclusion on her own? Remaining friendly but reserved; choosing when and how to be around whom and under what circumstances. Discerning. Hearing it from her aunt was a powerful substantiation. It occurred to her that she and her aunt were more like mother and daughter. Etta was much more Bernadette's daughter than Grace could ever hope to be. And Etta was learning, picking up little tidbits of information, taking verbal and unspoken cues, becoming more of what she'd always longed to be but simply hadn't known before. She longed to become a woman like Bernadette, wealthy but generous, powerful and astute but also kind. Galvestonians not only respected Bernadette, they esteemed her.

Everything changed one morning when Etta learned that Bernadette would be unavailable, and for an entire day at that. Up to that point, Etta had been accompanying her aunt everywhere. Even though some of their jaunts had been less interesting than others, especially trips to view the construction of the new Rosenberg Library, Etta immediately sensed how much she would miss her aunt's company.

When she learned of this distressing news, she and her aunt were seated at the table on the back portico, taking their morning tea before her aunt was slated to leave. Grace had already departed for the day.

"What are your plans?" Etta asked her aunt quite innocently.

Bernadette didn't look up. "Business, I'm afraid."

Etta hadn't spent a full day alone since her arrival. "Perhaps I might come along and be of some assistance."

"No, thank you," said her aunt.

Etta blew into her tea to cool it and then stopped when she caught a disapproving glance from her aunt. "I wouldn't mind."

Bernadette sipped her tea and set down her cup with a little clink. "This is business I must do on my own, I'm afraid."

"Please don't think I'd find it boring."

In fact, Etta imagined that her aunt's business might be financial, and she would be ever so curious to know how much her aunt was actually worth. "Before coming here, I was preparing to take a post at a bank."

Her aunt finally glanced Etta's way again. "I didn't know that."

"So if you think I would find finances and figures of no interest, you'd be mistaken."

Bernadette closed her eyes, and for a long moment her face was different—older and more drained. "I'm sorry, but please don't press me on this, Etta. I must go alone today. We shall have the entire day tomorrow together, I promise."

Etta gulped. It was the first time her aunt had declined her. And doing so without any explanation made it all the more crushing. Perhaps the day didn't involve business or financial work at all. Perhaps it was something more important than that. Not being included was one thing, but not knowing was even worse.

Etta said, "Where will you be? I mean, I ask only so I won't worry and will know when to expect your return."

Bernadette hesitated as she normally never hesitated, and when she finally spoke there was a strange tinny quality to her voice. "I'll be on The Strand, and I know not when I'll return."

Etta sat in silence. She was convinced her aunt was lying. Very odd, very odd indeed.

After breakfast Bernadette went upstairs to gather a few things together, but before she disappeared she ordered Seamus to bring a carriage around to the front of the house.

An idea came to Etta. Out of her aunt's sight, she pulled aside the new manservant, hired only a week before, and told him with urgency, "I'll be needing the old carriage, but I want you to be unnoticed. Bring it to the side of the property at once and await me there."

"The horses ain't hitched, Miss Etta."

"Then do it as quickly as possible."

"Yes'm."

As soon as her aunt headed out of the main door toward the carriage in front, Etta slipped out back and met the other driver. Her aunt's carriage was long gone by the time the old carriage was ready. "Find my aunt's carriage. It should be on The Strand," she ordered.

The old man turned in his seat and studied her with disbelieving eyes. Etta was tugging on her gloves. She glanced up at him. "Please."

Etta's driver cracked the reins. The air was humid, and the neck of Etta's dress clung to her skin. There wasn't an ounce of a breeze, and as Etta fanned herself with her handkerchief, the carriage slowly lumbered onward. They made several turns, the sunlight dappled between over-hanging tree branches.

Etta's suspicions were confirmed. Exactly as she had suspected, her aunt did not go to The Strand; her carriage was not to be found anywhere in the close vicinity. So Etta instructed the driver to comb the major streets of the city. On the bay side, they finally spotted her aunt's carriage at Union Station, where they glimpsed Bernadette stepping out and then disappearing into a crowd of arriving train passengers. Perhaps her aunt had waited in the carriage until minutes before her train, the first one of the day, departed, perhaps savoring the shade inside before having to face the crush of other people.

Etta sat back into the upholstery and pondered her options. She had taken no money with her, and the train to Houston cost one dollar. She was unprepared to follow her aunt any farther, and she couldn't risk being seen on the train. Etta therefore returned to the house. Before she exited the carriage, however, she informed the driver that should he say anything about her little jaunt, she would deny it, and no one would believe him. She told the manservant the same thing.

She made a tactical decision then and began questioning her favorite servant, Dolly. Etta asked where her aunt went, how often she went there, and for what purpose, but to her dismay, she found out only that her aunt frequently took day trips by herself, but no further information.

Dolly even said, "She don't catch no train," which was very interesting. Either the servants didn't know, or they were protecting Bernadette, a possibility that Etta found even more fascinating, as well as baffling. Etta wondered what could command such silence.

"I'm mistaken then," said Etta. "Please don't mention my inquiry to my aunt."

"No, ma'am," Dolly said with wide eyes. "I'm fixing to stay outta your way."

That evening over dinner, both Bernadette and Grace seemed preoccupied. After they had eaten most of their meal in silence, Etta, who had spent the day unable to nap, unable to sort through her correspondence or write a single letter, who had wasted the day feeling unappreciated and abandoned, asked her aunt, "And how was your day?"

Bernadette silently set down her fork. "Productive."

Etta had been concocting these questions, to be so innocently asked, all day long. "Did you complete your business?"

"Yes."

"You were gone for so long, I became worried."

Bernadette lifted her napkin to first one and then the other corner of her mouth. "I had a meeting in the morning, then lunched with friends at the hotel, and concluded more business in the afternoon."

"You didn't return until nightfall."

"Yes. I got carried away, I suppose. I lost track of the time."

But Bernadette never lost track of the time.

Etta held this new information quietly inside her. Her aunt had lied. She hadn't been to The Strand at all, and no mention had been made about the train depot. In the five weeks that she'd been in Galveston, Etta had found her aunt to be the most honest person she'd ever known. So whatever had taken her away today must have been vastly important and personal for her to feel she must lie about it. And deception, when it was aimed her way, drilled into her like a nail.

Jonathan came over for a visit with Grace later that night, and he appeared as forlorn as Grace had been looking lately. Etta found him on the front portico, waiting for Grace, who had insisted that she change her dress yet again before receiving him.

Remembering her aunt's advice, Etta had decided she should remain friendly and on good terms with everyone, including Jonathan, maybe especially Jonathan. After exchanging the usual pleasantries, they remained standing, facing the front lawn and the balmy night.

"Grace is coming down soon," Etta said, "though Bernadette is otherwise engaged."

Jonathan smirked. "All is as it should be then."

Too bad Grace's fiancé was actually an agreeable young man. Although he wasn't interesting enough for her, and he was off-limits to her, he often made her smile. She said, "Jonathan, I owe you an apology. I was much too hard on you the other night."

134

A wretched smile spread across his face. "I won't defend myself. I have been curious about you, perhaps too much so. You've managed to beguile almost everyone. I suppose everyone wants to know you better."

"I'm entirely knowable. You may ask me anything you wish."

"I don't want to pry."

"I'm inviting it. Go ahead. Free yourself of what is bothering you."

Hesitantly he darted a few guarded glances her way and then finally said, "All right, you've convinced me. Tell me then: Do you ever reveal your true self?"

She stared at him harder. "Yes. You already know this. I opened myself up to the wrong person. I told Grace something that I hadn't wanted spread as common gossip."

He was facing her now. "Yes, she betrayed you. But I was talking about opening up your heart."

Etta shrugged. "Of course."

Jonathan seemed to be dancing around another question, looking over at her, moving his mouth as though about to speak, and then stopping himself.

"Go ahead. Ask me what you're thinking."

"Did you love the circus man?"

"Yes."

"Why are you here then? Even if your family sent you, you could still leave. You're not a prisoner."

"Hmm. I didn't love him enough, I guess. My mother panicked for no reason. He loved me—that I know—but he didn't ask me to go with him."

"What a fool." His face showed that he was serious.

"Maybe he was wise. Maybe he knew something better would come along for me. And here I am."

"What do you foresee for yourself here?"

"I'm not sure yet. I'm looking for someone who fascinates me, and so far the only person who does that is my aunt."

"You're joking, right?"

"Not at all. You've spoken as if I am a mystery. *She* is the mystery."

Jonathan scoffed. "You must have an overactive imagination. There's nothing mysterious about Bernadette. She's the most domineering woman I've ever known. That's her most overriding quality—the ability to direct others."

"But there must be a reason for that."

Jonathan looked away. "I don't care to know. I simply can't wait to take Grace out of this house."

Etta found it appalling that he was enamored of her and yet still planned on marrying Grace. But maybe his infatuation with Etta was already fading. That was a bit disconcerting, but it was also necessary. "Now, may I ask you a question?"

He blinked a few times. "Of course. Fire away."

"How much does it cost to go to Yale?"

He seemed surprised. "My classmates would say it costs one's sanity."

"Funny."

Most of the time Etta acted as if money were of no consequence to her anymore, but with Jonathan she was taking a different tack. She didn't care if he knew she was curious about wealth. "Seriously, what does it cost Daddy?" Then she bit her lip; maybe she was being too mean and letting him see too much. She was giving him little glimpses into hidden compartments of her mind that she didn't want others to know about. Oh well. She was beginning to long for a nourishing exchange of unbridled ideas.

Jonathan rocked back on his heels. "Ah, contempt."

"You're avoiding the question."

He waited a moment, then, "How much does it cost to attend Yale? About nine hundred dollars a year."

Etta let that sink in. "My sister and her husband bought a farm for a hundred and twenty-five dollars."

"Am I to be impressed?"

"They had to borrow the money."

"I'm sorry."

"I'm not," said Etta. "I'm just stating the facts."

He seemed to choose his next words carefully. "I doubt you're ever sorry about anything."

Etta smiled. "Sorrow is a waste of time. Look at Grace. It's eating her alive."

Jonathan's expression darkened as his arrow eyes perused her. "She has a heart."

"Maybe she's getting an introduction to the harsher realities of life."

"I hope to shield her from some of those."

"Like a father. Like the father she never knew."

Jonathan's face paled and then opened up with what looked like sudden comprehension. It was as if something was thrusting up from the slush of his brain, like a fish surfacing out of a murky swamp. One didn't see something that should've been obvious—Grace needed a fatherly type—until it was right *there*.

After that he made no more comments. They stood, each lost in the warmth of the night and the emergence of insects, in those heart-plucking hums and rumbles. Alone with private thoughts, and yet a bridge of sorts had been built. They were starting to understand each other, beginning to speak freely to each other. Perhaps even becoming friends.

All was going well except for her aunt's secret, eating at her like termites.

That night Etta considered questioning Clorinda, her aunt's favorite maid, a tall, muscular woman who quietly commanded the rest of the servants and carried out Bernadette's wishes as if they were royal decrees. Surely she would know where Bernadette went on these jaunts of hers, but Etta hesitated. There was a fierceness about that woman. She would probably tell her aunt about her inquiry. Clorinda was intelligent and, even more dangerous, she was loyal. So Etta decided it would be less risky to find out through her own means. She was planning a long stay in Galveston, the rest of her life, in fact, so there was plenty of time.

Chapter Fifteen

The Girl

Reena fed her fried chicken, butter beans, and baked tomatoes left over from the meal she'd cooked in the main house, a nice dormer cottage on a front street, and later, as the sun was just beginning to touch the mass of sprawling land behind them, the girl finally took her leave and wandered back to her shed in Madu's yard.

In the air was the scent of summer flowers—jasmine, honeysuckle, magnolia, and gardenia. If she turned her head toward the wharves, the smell of barnacle-encrusted dock timbers, salt-caked planking, cotton warehouses, and fish.

She ducked inside the shed. Someone had been inside! She caught a scent, a decidedly feminine scent: maybe lavender with a hint of vanilla. And the girl's notes, all of her scraps of paper on which she had practiced her handwriting, had been disturbed, too. The girl picked up a scrap, one written with words recalled from her days of reading poetry with her mother. Obviously whoever had invaded her shed had read it. Now she would know that the girl had at one time gone to school. That was dangerous.

The next day, a cloudy and drizzling afternoon ruining her fun, the girl was sitting in her shed in Madu's yard with her scraps of paper, using a candle for light. With a stubby pencil in her hand and her brow furrowed, she drew the outline of a fish. After staring at it for a few moments, she thought, *It looks flat.* She closed her eyes and imagined how the fish appeared when they swam in the shallows where she could see, and then she began to shade the underside and tail of the fish to be darker than the rest of its body. She drew curved gills and a large dark eye. Sitting back on her heels, she thought, *Could you teach yourself to be an artist?*

A knock sounded on the door. The girl blew out the candle and didn't move. Few people knew where she slept, and even those few never entered her space. Harry never came to see her here—she always found him—and Reena and Madu simply shouted for her to come out.

"Hello," called the voice, a woman's sweet, lilting voice, but that didn't make it any less frightening to the girl. In years past, it had been women who were the most determined to seek her out and put her someplace else.

The door creaked open, and a wedge of muted light streamed inside. The drizzle had stopped. The girl scooted back into the corner of the shed, her back pinned against rusting tools, old pots and pans, and spiderwebs.

"I'm sorry. I didn't intend to disturb you," said the woman as she crouched over and stepped inside. Her skirt and shoes were wet. "My name is Grace. I've come to hand over a dress I thought you might like. You appear close to my size."

The girl stayed huddled in the corner while the rich woman reached out her hand into the semidarkness.

The girl had no place to go. Her only exit was blocked. The hot oppression became overwhelming, as if melted candle wax had filled the room, and then her lungs filled with it, overwhelmed her, as if she were choking. She cowered.

So fast, so fleeting. Her freedom over.

The woman named Grace said, "May I see what you're writing? I saw that you can write when I came to visit before. You weren't home."

The girl had been right. This woman had been inside her place before. But the girl's tension eased a bit. If Grace had known for days where the girl lived and not done anything about it, maybe she was safe, like Reena and Madu. She let the fish drawing fall out of her hands.

Grace picked up her drawing and her face broke into a smile, showing perfect teeth. "Why, you're an artist."

The girl shook her head.

"This is good. The proportions are right, and you've shaded it well. Do you want to become an even better artist?"

Reluctantly the girl nodded.

"This is wonderful news!" the Grace woman said. "I'll bring you supplies. I'm an artist, too. I have an entire studio filled with paints and charcoal pencils, chalks, canvases, and tablets."

The girl said nothing, although she wished she could request a charcoal pencil and some paper. She had no idea what to do with paints.

"Would you like that?" asked Grace.

Reluctantly the girl nodded again. Was she making a mistake? Was she letting her guard down when she shouldn't?

But it seemed the young woman did in fact want only to hand over the dress and be friendly. The girl took the dress, stuffed it into a ball behind her back, and gestured for the young woman to leave, which she did.

After Grace backed up and vanished beyond the door, after her light footsteps could no longer be heard, the girl finally exhaled. She retrieved the bundle from behind her back and unfolded it. The dress was of yellow cotton, with white eyelet trim on the collar and cuffs.

Rolled inside the dress was also a petticoat, and even a pale-yellow bonnet to go with the dress.

She ran her fingers over the dress front, barely touching the lightweight fabric, which was tightly woven, fine, and smooth. She checked the bone-white buttons and the intricately sewn hemline, finished with the tiniest stitches she'd ever seen. She brought the dress up to her nose and inhaled. That scent again. Lavender and vanilla. She loved the dress. She also loved the idea that the nice young woman might teach her more about drawing. But doubt still plagued her.

This community of bartenders, junkmen, and house servants had hidden her well. At least that was what Reena, Harry, and old Madu said. No one had shown any great interest in her whereabouts for a while, but now the pretty young woman was interested enough to enter her shed and look through her things and then return without being invited.

A chill moved through her. The girl felt exposed, as if she were walking out on a plank with nothing, not even water underneath her. She didn't know what the young lady called Grace wanted. The girl remembered the woman's face, soft yet determined, and knew without a doubt that Grace would come back and want more. The girl couldn't stay here now that her home had been entered against her will, even though then she wouldn't get her drawing supplies.

She didn't waste any time. She gathered up her belongings—her washtub, candles, pieces of paper, her collection of salvaged scraps from her family's destroyed house that she kept in a cigar box, a pair of ripped stockings, all her old boys' clothes, along with the new dress—and she bundled them together and left the shed. She climbed up the three peeling steps to Madu's door. The paint on the tiny house, a two-room dwelling that faced the alley, was so long gone she couldn't tell what color it had once been. She rapped once, waited, and then rapped again.

When the screen door creaked open and Madu appeared in the doorway, she could see that he'd been sleeping. His eyes were foggy, and his skin drawn. The old man had his days and nights mixed up. Most nights he stayed up late talking to himself and making his magic, putting colored powders into little jars, and then he made up for lost sleep during the day.

Looking annoyed, he asked, "What you want?" as he shuffled his way out onto the porch.

She held her things up in front of her as explanation.

"What happened?"

She shook her head and pointed in the direction of the shed. She must have appeared miserable, because Madu's face fell. "I knows. I done heard her fiddling about. She helped herself to the inside of your shed."

The girl wanted to ask him why he hadn't stopped her, but she knew the reason. It was best—safer at least—for the Negroes to leave white folks be.

Madu moved his lips about in the odd way that was his alone. "Now where you gonna go?"

The girl lifted her shoulders and then let them fall.

Shaking his head, the old man tried to look angry with her. "You too much trouble, that's what. You been in my yard for too long anyhow. Go on now. Find yourself another place to hide."

She pointed in the direction of Reena's house. She'd stayed there before, in an old chicken shed with a tin roof that had only about four feet of room inside. But she'd been much smaller back then, and Madu's full-size shed had been a welcome relief when she'd figured out she could have it. In fact, Madu's shed had been her best home since the storm, and here sometimes her grief lifted, as if on wings.

On the other side of Twenty-Fifth Street were the best alley houses, their yards full of wild plum, pomegranate, and pecan trees, but the girl didn't know anyone who lived there. Class distinctions existed even in the alleys. Going back to Reena's was her only option.

"You gonna go with that Bible banger again, is you?"

Madu and Reena had never been friends. Reena considered Madu's black magic evil, and he considered her veneration of Jesus Christ as nothing but brainwashing by white folk. The alleys and the girl were about the only things they had in common. "Well, good luck to you, then."

Before turning to leave, the girl nodded and waved good-bye.

Old Madu was still standing in front of his doorway, twisting his hands together in front of him, no longer sleepy. She let herself out of the rusty gate that enclosed his small overgrown yard, and then she stopped and looked back. He was still there, watching. She walked on, stopped again, and turned back one last time, as if to ask, *What is it?*

"You go on now," he shouted in a cracking voice. "I don't care nothing about you anyhow."

The girl turned on her heel and walked away, smiling. A block and a half away, she found Reena outside scrubbing clothes on a washboard over a large tub of sudsy water. Reena looked up, noted all the things in the girl's arms, and quickly went back to her work.

"You pulling up roots again, I see." Reena stopped scrubbing, wiped a fleshy hand across her brow, and said, "Well, let me see. Lester thinks he's all grown up and is gone off to Houston to get a job. We has plenty of room for you in the house."

Reena had made the same offer in the past. When the girl had stayed close to Reena before, on rainy nights, or when winter storms had made it too cold to sleep in the old chicken house, the girl had slipped inside a time or two. She'd coiled up like a snail in the bed with Reena's youngest boys, enjoying their warmth and boyish smells. But after a while the girl had started having trouble sleeping.

She kept seeing all those twisted lumps of debris that had been houses before the storm, and she began to feel boxed in. She preferred a simple shelter, one that she could escape in a blink, even if the weather sometimes made it uncomfortable. At least there she could close her eyes and sleep. And on warm summer nights she'd take the open night sky, lying on a bed of wild sunflowers or beach morning glory, any time.

Reena said, "You ain't staying in that chicken coop again." She shook her head. "No, ma'am, you ain't gonna do it. The man of the house kept him some ducks in there a while back, and now it's no place for a person. No, this time you gonna have to come into my house and stay in there."

Narrowing her gaze on Reena, the girl slowly worked up to a little shrug.

"Well, go on, then," said Reena. "What you waiting for?"

The girl took her time walking up the steps to the backhouse and went inside the dark two-room structure, which smelled of cooking grease and some kind of meat—pork, she thought—the floorboards creaking under even her light weight. She put her bundle of things in the single bedroom, where the entire family slept in narrow beds pushed up against the walls, and told herself she could do it now, that she could sleep in such confinement.

Later when the sun came out, she helped Reena wring out and hang the clean clothes, sort through some potatoes, tossing out the rotten ones, and then start the cooking on the back porch of the main house, where it was cooler. After dusk, the girl crawled into one of the beds with Reena's ten-year-old son, Maurice. She felt his warmth and remembered at once how soft a real mattress was, how compliant, how it fit the body resting on it.

But later she dropped into the soft underbelly of that mattress too deeply, the same way her feet used to sink when she stood too long on the damp sand at water's edge. Hours later, she was still shifting and tossing in the bed, tangling herself in the covers and disturbing Maurice, all in an effort to free herself.

Finally she figured out what the problem was. The mattress wasn't firm enough to support her bones, which had become used to the ground. Everything inside her was collapsing into the other body parts, and her air was getting lost somewhere inside. She could not breathe in such a soft bed.

She had to get up and lie down on the floor, where she belonged.

Chapter Sixteen

Grace

After two weeks of working with Ira, I started asking Seamus to come for me later in the day. At first, I asked him to give me an additional hour, then two, then three. The days were long and my tardiness for dinner had become routine, but I always returned before nightfall so Mother would not worry.

Each day I walked the various alleys with Ira, where we distributed all the goods we had received, giving priority to any food items that could spoil in the heat, as we had no icehouse at our disposal. By then I wore only plain dark dresses and the simplest hats I could find to shield my face from the sun.

Later in his office, Ira asked me why I had changed my appearance so drastically.

I answered, "It's simpler this way."

"I see."

He moved around the small room and then stopped.

I smiled wryly and said, "Well, that's not altogether true. Again, I do things for selfish purposes. I grew uncomfortable wearing my finery down here."

"I see," he said again.

◆ ◆ ◆

Ira shared jokes with the men and helped them find jobs. We talked to the women, even some I suspected were prostitutes, and Ira tried to find them more suitable employment if they were so willing. We played with the children.

My feet were heavy as I walked alongside him. I still regretted that I had been initially forced into this duty. Although now I came on my own volition, I would never be as gifted as Ira was. I never saw him lift an eyebrow or raise his voice, although he was aware of everything that went on around him. His concentration and watchfulness were so powerful that whenever his eyes fell on me, his gaze was palpable, like a touch.

He could sit and talk for hours with anyone on any subject, from the best way to piece, flour, and fry a chicken to the most difficult of spiritual issues, such as the nature of discipleship. He had the gift of circuitous conversation, yet he could reduce the most complicated matter to a simple thought.

Once he was counseling a woman who had been spurned and left by her husband. She ranted about his betrayal and spoke of her desire for revenge. "I'm gonna stand up in church this Sunday and tell it all before God, I am."

"She shore is," said the woman's friend, who was sitting behind Ira, adding her encouragement every now and then.

"What purpose would that serve?" Ira asked in his quiet way.

The woman straightened her back, her face trembling with hurt. "It would pain him."

"And you want to hurt him," said Ira, more a statement than a question.

"I do. I'm cut down to the core, I am."

"She shore is," said the other woman.

The woman looked confused, lost in all she was feeling, but her voice was low and forceful and spoke of determination. "I'm a-hurting, and I'm aiming to hurt him back. What else should I do?"

Ira looked over her wavering face. He asked softly, "What do you think of forgiveness?"

"For him?" the woman scoffed. "I ain't never gonna forgive that sorry excuse for a man."

He waited for a long moment. "Give it time," said Ira.

Blissfully calm, he didn't tell her what or what not to do. But he had made her think about it. His kindness and restraint were amazing. Often I had to tell myself he was only a man.

I found out that the boy I'd first met on the beach, Joseph, was a strong reader, that in fact he was one of the best students in his school. I went into the library at home one night and pulled out some favorite childhood books that my mother was keeping for sentimental value. They had no practical use, so I crated them and brought them down to Ira's office, where I cleared a spot on a shelf for storage. I decided I would loan the books out to Joseph and any other children who were interested, and that if I could manage it nothing would give me more pleasure than eventually opening a library down here.

Later I learned that if I walked around with a book or two in my hands, before long a child would ask me to read or show him or her the pictures. Soon I would have a little group of children gathered around me in a circle. It became a favored time, this unplanned reading.

Sometimes people would walk by and say such things as "Good for you, miss. Keep 'em out of trouble."

As I read, time ceased to pass. The children and I journeyed over mountains and into the minds of animals. Sometimes I reminded myself to take a moment of pause, to watch as bliss poured from pages to faces.

Ira soon told me that he thought fostering a love of books was a fine thing to do as part of our mission, and therefore he decided to formalize my readings by posting storytelling times on a board outside the office, where he also posted his hours of work and means to get in touch with him in case of emergency. The people passed around news of our activities like precious collectibles. Only later did I realize that Ira was divining qualities in me I'd never known I had.

My personal life and experiences had never felt so small and trivial, as I now knew how diverse this tiny island was. Before, I'd awakened every day with myself as my primary concern. I'd never had to take care of another soul on this planet. I could paint, but otherwise I had been useless. Until now.

When we weren't out in the alleys, we were writing letters, working with children, collecting donations from churches and estates left to charity, and purchasing goods using the monetary contributions we had received. Ira kept meticulous records so there could be no doubt as to our integrity.

The days were long and hard, but I found that time passed effortlessly while I worked. Productivity was such an odd but rewarding feeling. I completed every task that Ira requested and started to take on other projects. I remained on alert for the girl, but I saw only occasional glimpses of her. She had moved out of the shed on the old voodoo man's property. Apparently she had always moved around often, but I was assured by those who would hesitantly speak of her that she was still around. I was not overly concerned about losing her. Eventually I would get the time with her I sought. I had a satchel full of art supplies to give her, so I handed them over to the voodoo man, as I was sure *he* would be seeing her again.

A few days later, when I asked him if he had managed to get the supplies to her, at first he didn't answer. He was one of those who had little use for Ira and me. Never rude, he kept his distance nonetheless, and after I asked the question, he gazed at me warily as he sat on his stoop and smoked an odd-looking pipe.

"I mean the girl no harm," I said softly. "She was drawing the last time I saw her . . . and I believe she'd love to have those supplies."

"They ain't here no more, is they?" the old man said.

"Does she have them?"

"I ain't no thief. Of course she done has them."

"Thank you," I said, turning to leave. Then I swirled around and faced him again. "I sincerely thank you."

He nodded once and stared at me as if with a poison arrow.

Ira was already scolding me about my long days. "You should go home earlier. I'm afraid you might be straining yourself. It's almost the dinner hour," he said one evening.

After organizing the donations we'd received that afternoon, I was trying to decide where best they should go, where they would be most beneficial. "You're still here," I said to him.

"I need to be."

"So do I."

"But you're not accustomed to this work."

I shoved a box into the corner, then shifted some others so that we might move about easier inside the small room. "I've wondered something about you."

"Yes. Go ahead."

"Why are you not a minister in a church? Why do this instead?"

"Ah, that is a question I am frequently asked."

"I would imagine."

"I'm associated with a group of missionary ministers who feel much the same as I do; I feel closer to our Savior when I'm here, or in a similar place. Someday I may find myself before a church congregation, and often I'm a guest minister for a Sunday service, but for now these people are my congregation, even if they don't realize it. I find that most people in churches are not in need of such essential help. They are already saved."

Puzzled, I said, "But if I may be so bold, you don't seem to be in the business of saving souls here, Ira."

"Some of these people are fine Christians already, and as for the rest, they must be fed, clothed, and cared for first. I find that given time, some of those without faith will ask me about mine. And then they are more receptive to the doctrine of the church. It isn't forced upon them then, you see."

It did seem that things worked better if we let people come to us. Maybe they gave up less of themselves that way. "Where did you study?"

"Boston."

"There's a good art museum there. I took a course in oils there once."

"So, you are an artist," said Ira, looking pleased. "I should have known."

"Oh, and how so?"

"I see it in the way you move, the way you walk. You're always studying things around you."

"Perhaps I'm too removed."

"No, I don't see you as removed."

There followed an awkward moment, during which neither of us knew what to say.

Finally Ira spoke. "I'm often asked why I went into the ministry at all." He cleared his throat and went on. "I always loved the church, even when I didn't know why. When I was about fourteen, my father and I were on a journey outside Boston. We stopped for water at a well in a small country town, a place surrounded by poverty. While my father pumped the water, I wandered into a tiny church that held only a few plain wooden pews and a simple altar covered with a tablecloth, a hardwood cross above it that was polished to a luster. I looked at that cross and something happened."

"Did you receive a vision?"

He shook his head. "Nothing as grand as that. I was simply filled with the knowledge of what I should do. I've had no personal message from God." He stopped and smiled, obviously remembering something amusing. The light shone on his cheeks. "But once I did become faint during a church service and had to sit down. My grandmother thought I had been stricken or 'called,' as she put it, but I was simply taken ill. All I had accomplished was to ruin the church service."

"You have no regrets, then, about your vocation?"

"My rewards grow larger every day."

"I admire your philosophy and your faith," I said, and then a moment later, "I admire you."

He didn't respond, but his face colored and he turned away. I had overstepped. Working this closely with him had changed me and had broken down some of my usual reserve. His frequent searching glances were piercing holes in my carefully crafted façade. With his back to me, Ira silently began to wipe his spectacle lenses in careful circles, his head down, and his hair soft against his collar.

Behind the joy, I sensed something raw and open about him, some unspoken pain that perhaps drove him to do the work that he did. Perhaps some people take on other people's woes instead of their own. Perhaps those people in fact need caring for more than others.

But instead Ira doted on me. He frequently took my hand to help me around a puddle of water or a pile of rubbish, even though by then I could handle myself without his assistance. In the rain, he removed his coat and held it over my head so I wouldn't ruin my dress. Sometimes, though, when we were alone in our office, he left me abruptly. And once I came upon him holding my hat, which I had removed earlier. He blushed, handed it over, and whispered, "Lovely." My cheeks grew warm.

He was surprised to find out that I'd never ridden the trolley. I hesitated to tell him that my mother had never allowed it, since we had carriages and drivers. So for no reason other than fun, we rode the trolley up and down Broadway, and I turned my back when we passed my house, without pointing it out to Ira. When the trolley filled and we were shoved far to the left, Ira hung on to the side and purposefully leaned out over the track.

"My friends and I used to hop on trains when we were teenagers," he said, smiling, over the clacking of the trolley. "We would ride for a while and then jump off."

I hung on with all my might. "It sounds dangerous. What compelled you to do such a thing?"

"It impressed the girls."

I spurted out a surprised laugh. "So, how did the girls show their appreciation?"

He laughed, throwing his head back in the wind, and I was afraid he might lose his balance. *Don't fall.* Crazy feelings surged through my brain. I cared too much what this man thought of me; I cared too much for this man.

He answered, "It's not a very interesting story."

Gathering myself, I said, "Let me be the judge of that."

He drew his body closer to the trolley car, closer to my face, where I could pick up his scent. Masculine but sweet. A flush rose from my neck into my face. What was happening to me? My mind wasn't right.

"They teased us into believing they might go on dates with us, but they didn't."

"That's not very nice."

Patting his stomach, he said, "I was the fat boy in school. And my friends—Temple, he had a crippled arm from polio, and Roger, he was the smallest boy in our class—we weren't very appealing."

He said this with a smile, which made it all the sadder to me. I had to blink away the beginnings of tears. "I'm sorry to hear that your childhood was . . . difficult."

"Not at all. I've given you the wrong impression. Those two—why, they were the best buddies anyone could ever want. We had something rare: true friendship. I'm close to them to this day. We write once a week."

"I-I . . . How wonderful for you . . ." Desperate to know more about his life, I opened my mouth and hoped for something appropriate to come out. But just then a baby on the trolley started howling, and the wind whipped up and swept my words away.

In the evenings I always returned home in time to share dinner with my mother and Etta, and sometimes with Jonathan as well. Still mulling over my day, I picked at my food after such demanding and emotional work, while Etta ate voraciously. I had been on my feet all day, whereas Etta had been sorting through her assorted invitations and going on excursions and shopping sprees. And yet my heart held no ache of envy.

After the dinner hour, I was usually too fatigued to go anywhere; therefore, I was declining most of the invitations sent my way. I was not becoming antisocial, but rather many of the parties and celebrations had begun to feel a bit silly. We gathered together all the time simply for enjoyment, ate lavish meals, and enjoyed expensive entertainment, and seldom did anything that could benefit others.

Mother usually studied me for a moment and then accepted my explanations without further questioning. But Etta watched everything. She studied me with Jonathan, she watched me as I ate or didn't eat, and she hung on every word uttered by my mother. Over dinner, which was the only time I saw Etta now, she would often say to me, "How was your day? Tell us what goes on down there to keep you so preoccupied."

Typically I gave some vague description of one small event and left out any specifics. The city belonged to me even more now that I knew its contrasts and needs, those unseen screw men and dancehall girls, barmaids and charcoal peddlers. But there was no way to describe my experiences to Etta. Not even Jonathan could understand. When we spent time together, he filled me in on the latest stories: who was courting whom, where people were escaping the heat, and what new game or activity was currently in vogue. I found my mind wandering while he spoke.

No longer angry with Mother, I was relieved, released from being a center of attention I no longer desired. My mother, if she noticed the change in me, didn't say. Of course she would think it a temporary lull. But at night I had dreams during which my legs were unloosed from twine while I was carried away by floodwaters of different whirling colors, my head always above the waterline, watching things go by.

Chapter Seventeen

ETTA

She was invited to go sailing for a day aboard a yacht owned by Viola Waverly's father, one of the founders of the United Fruit Company, which had holdings spread across the Caribbean. A servant delivered the invitations to both Grace and Etta after dinner one night.

The three women of the Hilliard household were spending some rare moments together in the parlor. Bernadette was embroidering, Grace was reading, and Etta had been daydreaming.

After opening the invitation, which was for Friday of the same week, Etta looked over at Grace, who had just put aside her book and opened her identical invitation. "Where are we to sail?"

"I guess wherever the winds are favorable," Grace answered. "I've gone out many times, and I've never asked where beforehand. It's exhilarating. Have you ever been out on open water?"

Etta said, "No."

"They most likely have planned a picnic on Red Fish Island. You'll get from the yacht to the island by rowboat," piped in Bernadette.

Grace said, "You'll enjoy it. There's no other feeling like sailing."

"Are you going?" Etta asked Grace.

"Friday is a workday for me."

A spark of tension ignited in the air, and Bernadette set down her embroidery hoop. "Grace, this is becoming ridiculous. You must take a day off and go. In fact, I insist."

"I have a prior commitment."

Pursing her lips, Bernadette said, "I never meant for this duty of yours to take over your life. Perhaps you've done enough. I'm certain you've made your apologies to Etta, so for now let bygones be bygones. You haven't painted in weeks. I scarcely see you."

"Are you saying my penance is over?"

"Yes."

"Very well. Now I'll be going on my own. I feel much better about it then."

"You wish to continue?" Bernadette swatted a hand in the air. "Nonsense. You must get back to your life. Reacquaint yourself with your friends and Jonathan."

"Jonathan is busy all day. There's no reason why I shouldn't be, too."

"You're getting too carried away about your work and letting your social life suffer. I'll have none of it."

Grace simply smiled and picked up her book. But not long after, she left the parlor in favor of her room.

"Oh, Etta dear," Bernadette said pleadingly. "I don't know what to do with her. I know I'm not the warmest person, but I do love my daughter. Why must she defy me like this? She has never been this bold before."

Etta moved quickly to her aunt's side. "May I offer you my opinion?" When Bernadette gave a tiny nod, Etta continued: "I think you should let her go as long as she pleases. This has clearly become some sort of rebellion, and if you try to stop her, it will only make it worse. Her determination will grow stronger. Let her go until she tires of it. What harm could there be? She's doing some good for the poor, probably learning a little humility, and she'll grow weary of it eventually."

Bernadette stared into Etta's eyes with a kind of appraising concentration, and Etta feared she may have overreached. But then Bernadette's shoulders lowered and she finally said, "Yes. I believe you may be right."

How perfect. This would give Etta more time with her aunt. Let Grace exert her independence for the rest of the summer, or forever.

Her aunt whispered, "Thank you," and the genuine emotion in her voice touched Etta.

"You're the one I should be thanking. For everything."

"Such a dear you are."

Etta gazed down at the rug, where her invitation for sailing had fallen. She picked it up and sat again across from her aunt. For the first time, Etta was dumbfounded by an invitation. Parties, dinners, luncheons, and outings on the island had been enjoyable, but on the ocean? Or even the bay? Normally adventurous, she had retained a fear of the water, although she rarely admitted it. Why go out on the water unless one had to get somewhere? Why take risks on the scary seas with no destiny in mind, for no purpose whatsoever?

Bernadette asked, "What is your hesitation?"

"I'm not fond of the water. I like to look at it, but I can't swim, and I don't think I'd enjoy the outing."

Picking up her embroidery hoop, Bernadette started stitching again. "You don't have to accept every invitation that comes your way, dear."

Etta pondered her dilemma. Viola had probably invited the rest of her cousin's inner circle, and that meant Wallace, as well as Jonathan and Larke. Etta's circle of friends had expanded beyond them, and sometimes she ran around with a flashier crowd, but she hated to miss seeing these friends, who were the first to take her in. And who knew what other young gentleman might be there?

"Maybe I'll decline the invitation to sail but . . . will they all go to dinner afterward?"

"Most likely they'll dine aboard the yacht after they come back to port." Bernadette stopped stitching and gazed away wistfully. "Oh, it's lovely to sit on the deck of a fine boat after a day of sailing. Most invigorating."

"Would it be proper to ask to join the group just for the dinner?"

"I don't see why not." Bernadette nodded. "In fact, I think that's a fine idea. I'll suggest it to Grace as well."

Therefore, on Friday evening Seamus drove her alone—Grace had still declined—to the dockside as the sun was going down, the sky turning the color of overripe peaches and the wind settling into a mere whisper of what it had been during the day. Probably the group had enjoyed a fine sail. When she disembarked from the carriage, Jonathan was standing there to greet her and escort her on board.

The boat was huge, and Etta had no idea what type of sailboat it was. Named *Joan of Arc*, it had two masts and was all rich teak, polished brass, lines held taut in fancy knots, furled sails, servants standing by, and an aft deck set up with a dining table and slatted chairs, adorned with pillows and cushions.

Disappointment was a cold wave washing over her, however, when she saw that it was the same old crowd, with no new additions, except for the captain, a weathered but well-appointed middle-aged man in uniform.

"You missed a wonderful day out there," Jonathan said as he walked her to the table, where everyone was sitting and sipping on champagne.

"I missed being frightened," Etta replied quietly as she took her seat and greeted everyone.

Jonathan spread his arms wide. "Look at this beauty. Best sailing yacht along the Gulf Coast. It would take an act of God to sink her."

"That's what they always say," uttered Etta under her breath as she smiled at the others.

"We saw dolphins," Larke exclaimed. "How do you like the ship?"

Etta put on her pretty face. "I'm charmed."

She settled in, ready for an evening of attention, but was surprised that the talk was all about sailing in the Caribbean. Viola's father would be taking the yacht to the West Indies over the winter months. They would be visiting Cuba, Puerto Rico, and several islands of the British West Indies, including Jamaica and Barbados. All of the dinner guests had already visited the region, and they talked of reefs, shipwrecks, and storms. Fishing trips and visiting friends who owned plantations. Weather and adventure.

For the first time since her arrival in Galveston, Etta found herself left out of the conversation. She'd never even heard of some of the islands they mentioned, and she had no desire to visit a single one. On this night, a clear difference between her and these people emerged: the rich were more fearless than regular people. They took off for foreign places and crossed oceans as if their lives were so valuable that God wouldn't dare let anything befall them. They were simply untouchable, invincible. They didn't hesitate to do hazardous things simply for fun and to be able to relive their experiences later with others. Possible dangers were mentioned only in passing, as if they were little bothersome things that sometimes got on their nerves but ultimately added to the adventure. They had never tasted trepidation on their tongues, had never felt doubt creep over their scrubbed, smooth skin.

Her eyes drifted over to Wallace. Poor Wallace. As the one who had let it slip about Etta's circus man, he had kept his distance from her ever since. Wallace had a clean-cut, baby-faced attractiveness that had not especially appealed to Etta before but on this night seemed more enticing—perhaps by keeping himself removed. And he was growing a beard, probably trying to offset his cherubic looks. Normally Etta didn't appreciate facial hair, but it was rather fetching on Wallace. And it did make him appear more mature.

Someone was speaking to her. Viola. She had said something about Grace.

"I beg your pardon. I didn't hear."

"Why didn't Grace come?"

Etta said, "She's busy."

"We've missed her," said Larke.

"I wonder what she does all day down in those . . . alleys," said Viola.

"She works," Jonathan said.

"I saw her the other day on the trolley with a man I assume was the Reverend Ira Price we've all been hearing so much about at church. They were laughing and hanging on like children. It didn't look like work to me," said Larke.

Foolish Larke's comment made everyone pause. Etta snapped a glance at Jonathan in time to see his face fall. Etta couldn't believe that she had once thought of Jonathan as a rogue. He could never get away with deception of any kind, because everything he felt showed on his skin and in his eyes—he couldn't mask a thing. However, he recovered quickly. "They work hard; this I know. Grace speaks highly of the Reverend."

The conversation moved on, and after dinner Wallace asked if he might give Etta a tour of the ship. After she agreed, he took her below to view the salon, cabins, galley, and wheelhouse. Etta found the interior constricting and asked if they might stroll above deck instead.

Soon he had taken her to the bow, which pointed out into the bay, and Etta could finally breathe again. "You've been avoiding me, Wallace, neglecting me, in fact."

Wallace frowned. "I had no idea you had been missing my company. I was sure that you would want little to do with the likes of me, the indiscriminate one."

"Such old business," Etta said. "It's already forgotten."

"I'm so pleased."

Etta saw opportunity there. So far she had met many people, but despite her social standing and bright prospects in the beginning, she had not yet been sought out for any serious courting. Men had lined up to dance with her, but few had come to call. Maybe she needed to initiate something more substantial. "Grace has left me to my own devices. Not that I'm helpless . . ."

"You? Of course not."

She waited.

"I'd be delighted to call on you."

"Please do," she said with a smile.

He looked elated.

At the evening's end, Jonathan offered to escort Etta home, and once they were in the carriage he said with a drawn face, "Grace never told me about the trolley ride."

Etta almost smiled but restrained herself. Jonathan had looked rattled ever since Larke had mentioned seeing Grace with the minister. And now he obviously considered Etta to be a friend, a confidante. "It's nothing. Perhaps they were simply running an errand."

"She has never mentioned taking the trolley. She told me they go about on foot."

Etta sat still. How interesting it was that Grace was apparently not telling her fiancé everything.

He gripped the door handle and gazed out into the twinkling lights of the streets. "She tells me almost nothing now. It's as if the girl I knew is gone."

"Come now. Grace is probably incapable of hiding anything from you. Don't you trust her?"

"I did," he said through a sigh. He seemed like an unwanted pet or discarded toy. Staring out the window, he sounded achingly vulnerable as he said softly, "But I'm not sure of anything anymore."

She chose her words most carefully. She had never desired discord between Grace and Jonathan, but now that it was here, there was something intriguing about it. Why were people drawn to watching house fires? To surveying the scenes of accidents? "You're having doubts."

"Not really . . ." He shook his head and continued to stare blankly outside. "Maybe."

Etta said nothing more; she listened to him breathing and sat waiting for him to speak again.

He raked a hand through his hair. "I have a terrible feeling of premonition. There's something lingering in the air, something unsettled. Several men have been seriously injured working on the wall. Soon every building and tree is to be raised off the ground and dirt brought in to raise the elevation of an island that nature intends to wash away someday. The heat is more oppressive than ever. Every day I watch men slaving in the heat. I rarely do anything else. And the people in my social circle are restless. They seem fevered. The gossip is worse than ever."

Such silly concerns, Etta thought, but she held herself in check. "Haven't they always gossiped? Why does it concern you now?"

"They can say all they want about me. But when it comes to Grace . . ."

This was getting more interesting. Etta perked up. "So her work in the alleys has become something of an oddity, and people can't resist discussing it. It'll pass."

"It's not about that. And it's not really about Grace. Well, not about her exactly."

Etta kept her voice light. "Then what?"

"I'll not repeat it."

Etta sat still and silent until they had arrived on Broadway. "You're troubled. Perhaps you would feel better if you talk about it. I won't breathe a word of anything you tell me. You have my promise."

He turned to her then. "I can't say more."

Chapter Eighteen
The Girl

The girl had taken the satchel from Madu without hesitation. Then she ran all the way back to Reena's without opening it, hoping that no one would see her. The satchel was made of fine, soft leather, and people might think she'd stolen it. Besides, she had a feeling she wouldn't want to share what was inside.

Safely inside the privacy of Reena's yard, the girl opened the satchel to find a book of blank papers and a box of thick colored sticks, almost like crayons but chalky instead of waxy. She touched them lovingly. So many colors, even several shades of blue.

The girl picked up the dark-blue one and placed the tip on the first blank sheet of paper in her book. The art sticks, as she began to think of them, left a bold color on the page. Across the page, she drew a straight blue line like the surface of the sea. Soon she figured out that the color could be smudged and blended with the other blues in the box to make a multicolored ocean. She worked for hours on the sea and the sky above it, even adding the dark silhouette of a boat against her imagined horizon.

Her drawing was not good. She had not even begun to capture the beauty of her favorite place—where the sea met the sky. It always sparkled and shimmered out there. What color would an artist use for that? White? Yellow? She didn't know, but despite all her questions and self-doubt, this felt like a beginning. Maybe the woman named Grace would teach her to become a real artist.

When the girl stopped for the day, her hands were covered in pigment. She put the supplies back in the satchel, hid it in a special spot under the house, and then washed her hands free of any evidence.

The next day, she had to make herself more useful. It was a hot morning. At Reena's feet, the girl dropped a pail of crabs she'd been sent for. Reena smiled approvingly into the bucket of crabs, which would go fine with the Spanish mackerel she was cooking for supper that night. As always, Reena smelled of some sort of food and cleaning supplies; today it was sweet potatoes and laundry soap. Laundry was just one of her many duties, which included all the cooking and cleaning, polishing silver and dusting crystal, marketing and gardening, as well as washing and pressing everything from doilies to woolens. Yet seldom did she complain, because as she told the girl once, her employers "was better than most."

That day Reena looked back in the direction of the gulf, where the house on Avenue Q had stood, and she slowly shook her head, the whites of her eyes beamy and liquid. The girl had noticed that her presence often made Reena remember . . . "Lord knows that storm was the devil's making."

Then she shook her head, let out a long sigh, and adopted a wistful expression. "At first, I was hoping it might have done washed away everything all clean and new so that everything could just start all over again. All different."

With the girl simply sitting and listening, Reena sighed again and finally moved on to another thought.

Reena hadn't completely given up on getting the girl to talk; she was the only one who hadn't, and today she sat her on the steps and plunked down across from her in a hand-me-down chair and said, "Now, when is you gonna stop all this foolishness and start talking again?"

The girl didn't move.

"Now, come on. I know you can do it. It's in there somewheres, I know it is."

The girl looked away, and Reena went on. "Just try, will you? Just do it for me? Come on now. Just open up that mouth of yours and try. Don't matter what it sounds like. Lord knows you're out of practice, but just go on now and try. Come on."

After Reena's demands went unheeded, she sighed again in that mournful but accepting way of hers and said, "Well. Maybe that storm really did steal it out of you, or maybe a thousand other storms are up and trapped there inside you."

The girl waited and listened, because if you spent time in the company of someone who could put together words like that, why did you need to talk anyway?

As though she might pluck answers from her fruit trees, Reena gazed around. Then she stared back at the girl. "But whatever it is, it's all done closed up behind a big ole door in there, ain't it?"

The girl nodded.

"And locked behind a big ole padlock, too, ain't it?"

The girl nodded again.

Reena stood and lifted the girl for a hugging spell and then pulled away and held her at arm's length. "Honest to Pete, I don't know what to do with you most of the time. But I do know one thing. You listen to me now, child. You been going around in that fine yellow dress, and there's people who done stopped searching for you that's gonna start up again. It was best when you looked like a boy. You hear me? Don't you go running around in it no more."

The girl backed up; she hated to argue with Reena. She wrapped her arms around the porch post and gave Reena an expression of feigned obedience that promised, *I won't.*

"Lord, I pray you be telling the truth." Reena wiped her brow, and then seeming hesitant, she went back to work, the girl assisting her.

Even though it was still early morning, the day was hot enough and the scrubbing hard enough to bring a sheen to Reena's ripe-plum-colored skin. "I know some fine lady done gave that dress to you. I just hope she's a good one."

The girl shrugged.

Reena gazed off into the distance. "Maybe . . ."

Something in Reena's voice made the girl dart a look.

"Maybe this time . . ." Reena stopped and shook her head.

The girl made her face into a question mark, asking, *What are you saying?*

"It's nothing. I was just hoping that maybe this one could do something, maybe just a little something, good for you, child."

The girl shrugged, looked down, and started drawing patterns in the sandy ground with her big toe. They didn't speak again for a long moment. Then Reena finally said, "Well, anyway . . . I has news for you."

The girl glanced up.

"Harry's got himself something to show you. Down on the docks. It's an important thing, and that's why I'm scooting you off to see it. But I want you to change out of that dress first."

Why had Reena waited so long to tell her there was some news? She sprung up and grabbed Reena by both of her upper arms. Then she squeezed in a way that said, *You must tell me.*

"I most certainly is not saying nothing more. You go on down to the docks and see for yourself."

After planting a kiss on Reena's cheek, she tore out of the yard and down the alley. Faintly she heard Reena call after her, "You ain't changed outta that dress!"

Friends of Reena's were outside in their backyards or on their shaded porches, starting their washing or shucking corn or swapping stories about their white families, and the girl waved as she passed them by.

The alleys were sandy and unpaved or covered with oyster shells, which crackled as she ran over them. She hurried silently past Madu's house, where all was quiet. She didn't want to rouse him from his nap. She reached Market Street and entered a different world of shops, selling everything from French perfume to Cuban cigars. Wooden block paving on the elevated sidewalks was as solid as bedrock beneath her feet, although during high tides the blocks tended to pop up and float around. The sun was coming up big and lemon bright, and around a corner she caught a first glimpse of tall masts and furled sails on Water Street at the port.

The girl headed to Pier 19, where the handcrafted, family-owned boats, called the Mosquito Fleet, rocked in the water. Soon she was hidden among their skinny masts, crusted nets, and sails the color of bleached bone.

Galveston was once home to pirates, then it was the largest slave market west of New Orleans, and now it was one of the biggest cotton ports, but down here on Pier 19 the businesses were still run by families who lived on their boats. She walked past piles of fresh gulf shrimp, crabs, and scallops spread out for sale on straw mats, along with stacks of firewood, fresh oranges, green bananas, and pots of honey brought back from sails up the bayou.

The girl spotted Harry by the hair that always stuck up out of his head, thick tufts of mixed blond and brown perpetually windblown in every direction. He was knocking about in the stern of a small shrimp boat, and as soon as he saw her he stopped what he was doing and squinted up in a grin.

"Well, here you are," he said.

Harry tossed some lines aside and reached up to help the girl on board. He acknowledged the question on her face, *Is it yours?*, and answered, "Would I be working alone on another man's boat?"

She looked about hard. The boat was an old, hand-constructed skipjack with a racked mast, a jib, and a leg-of-mutton mainsail, newly painted and outfitted with nets and equipment so that Harry could make a living on the sea, just as his father had. After the storm, he had traveled back up Buffalo Bayou in search of his father's boat one last time. It had been a skipjack like this one, but he hadn't found even one plank. Ever since, he'd been living with relatives, on other men's boats, or in spare rooms not far from the docks, working at the wharves and warehouses and on other people's boats, trying to earn enough money to buy his own. Now Harry was a full-grown man, a fisherman, who could stand on his own.

Harry struck a match, lit the rolled stub of tobacco on his lip, and sucked in the smoke, then immediately coughed it back out. "She'll do."

In the bay, the first river steamer of the day was chugging across the high line on the horizon. The girl pointed out to open water.

Harry directed his gaze that way, too. "Don't you remember what happened the last time you and me went out together?" He shook his head. "We don't have us a good record."

She held still.

Harry started working again. He checked the rigging and mended a hole in one of the sails. He spent about an hour making her suffer, acting as if he weren't taking her out. But the girl waited for the breeze to pick up, knowing there was no chance she'd let him go out on the water today without her.

When a good breeze started blowing in, Harry didn't say a word, just got everything ready and then pushed off from the pier, raised the sail, and they drifted quietly until the onshore breeze flew over the island and popped the sail. Soon they were skimming over smooth seas like silk on marble. They blew for the oyster shell reef in the bay known as Red Fish Bar, where Harry turned the boat into the wind, furled the sail, and dropped anchor.

For a while they simply sat and watched the water on both sides dip and drop, small waves cupping against the hull, like a parent whispering to a sleeping child, broken only by occasional clinks and pops.

There was no need to speak. The storms inside the girl settled on this calm water.

It had been almost three years since she'd been out on a boat, but even so she remembered. Harry had taught her and her brother the rudiments of sailing back when she was eleven, and she'd made a decent ship's mate. He'd also taught them about the sea and the life on it. She knew that plovers were the seabirds with short beaks, that sandpipers had long slender ones, and dozens of different species of gulls cluttered the air over the gulf. And oddly, oyster, clam, and snail shells could be found every day on the gulf side instead of the bay side, where they belonged. Harry grumbled that farmers and others on the mainland had cut up too much grass and chopped down too many forests, making for muddy rivers and an increasingly murky bay. When the sun rose high, the girl rolled up her sleeves and tore off her bonnet so she could face the sunlight directly.

"You're fixing to get burnt," grumbled Harry.

She gave him a look, and he scratched his chin while terns dove into small whitecaps over a sandbar. Finally Harry asked, "How do you like her?"

The girl studied the weathered wood beneath the paint along her railings and frowned, then fluttered her fingers like flames.

"I know. She's a tinderbox. If we don't catch her on fire, though, she'll do me right fine." Harry raised an eyebrow. "You want to start working with me?"

The girl nodded.

"That new yellow dress of yours is bound to get ruint," said Harry. "Where'd you get it?"

She shrugged again, as if saying, *It's of no importance.* But even though she tried to hoist up her skirt, it bothered her that the hem was getting wet as it dragged along the deck. She decided not to wear the dress for working again, to save it for special days.

"I don't expect you to be helping me for nothing." Harry paused from his work. "We can make us a deal, you and me. You help me on this here boat, and I'll give you a share of the haul." He tossed his head toward land. "Is Reena still cooking?"

Before the storm, Harry had been a frequent guest at her family's house for dinners, cooked primarily by her mother, but with Reena's help. The girl nodded.

"Reena's shrimp batter is the best on this island. Bring me some of her shrimp all fried up sometime?"

The girl nodded.

Harry was still studying her new dress. "Who gave you that? Some lady do-gooder?" Anyone could see that it could only have come from someone with money.

"I met me one of them society types once." Harry smiled. "Your pa, Anson, and me was sitting in one of the bars off The Strand when you was about six years old, and here this do-gooder comes waltzing by one day. Stops dead in her tracks outside the window when she sees your pa enjoying a bit of the spirits with a little girl on his lap." He stopped and winked her way. "You know, he never went nowhere without you. But your pa, he wasn't bothered by her hoity look. He just grabs you on up and walks out the door, right up to that lady, and introduces himself."

The girl smiled.

"You sure got his gumption," said Harry with a smile.

And that was a real compliment.

Later, as they sailed back to the docks, the girl watched the sun just beginning to touch land. Clouds drifted overland. Set on either side of the sun, they looked like long flowing golden arms, and the wind in the sails was prettier than a hymn sung by any church choir. Harry's boat was light on the water. The girl took a deep breath and enjoyed the ease of the day. With her hair of red ribbons streaming behind her, her face warm with the light of the sunset, she hadn't felt this weightless in three years, even when she glanced down and saw that her dress was soiled, the hemline drenched with seawater. Her face was burned again, and her arms were screaming new freckles, too, but it was no matter.

Madu thought she should hate the sea, because it took her family. But instead, out on these waters she felt closest to the family she had lost. She remembered her mother's hands, which had done everything from baking bread, to cross-stitching, to washing the grit off collected shells, to combing and curling her daughter's hair. She remembered her father, who despite a limited education (he couldn't read and could only sign his name) had managed to build both his shop on the beach and then a home on Avenue Q. He had babied her constantly despite her mother's protest to "let the girl be." And then there was her brother, who had been tall and big boned, had excelled at everything, and was destined to become the first in their family to go to college. But the girl blamed neither the sea nor the people on the island, who were warned about the 1900 Storm and did nothing, not even those people who stood by and watched, who believed the sea couldn't hurt them. She blamed no one really, not even those still foolish enough to believe that human beings could tame such a force.

Since the storm, everyone on the island was trying to re-create the Galveston that was, to rebuild everything in a way that would prevent another scourge of the island by hurricane. But fishermen like Harry had different ideas. Harry shook his head when he heard about all the plans to put Galveston back the way it was, only better and stronger. Harry wanted only to work off the island's waters, make enough money to feed himself, and find a safe place to put in for the night. Much of the city had already been rebuilt, but it was of little matter to people like Harry and the girl.

For them, Galveston had always been the sea, and the sea remained.

Chapter Nineteen

GRACE

"You're not yourself," Jonathan told me one evening after supper. We had slipped away from the house and were strolling the back lawn, lost among the rosebushes and spindly oleanders that he pointed out were in need of trimming.

"My day was long."

"I understand. But your days are the exact same length as everyone else's."

Exhaustion seemed to come out of my very feet, loosen my ankles, and then unpin my knees. I faltered in my steps. I could still feel the rhythms and music of the alleys in my head, and still see Ira's face beside me. Lately when Ira and I were alone, we both became overly aware of each other, and the atmosphere had transformed, as if a mysterious illness had overcome us. When we walked about, I found myself pulling closer into his shadow. "Have I been neglecting you?"

"I wouldn't say that, but I would like to do something amusing with you for a change. Perhaps we should go to a dance or a dinner with our friends."

I looked his way and smiled as a way of agreement.

"You aren't painting, either."

My days were so full of color and texture and movement that I hadn't felt the need to put more of it down on canvas. "I haven't been able to focus on art lately."

"Have you taken to this charity work?"

"Yes," I told him as we walked onward. "I have a hard time admitting that I'd never thought of helping others until recently."

A tremendous full moon rose over the salt cedars rimming the back of the property. "Perhaps we should look at things in a new way. Some of my college buddies are becoming Socialists."

Jonathan had been reading about Jack London. He looked to me for a response, but I could barely smile.

He said, "Like London, I admire some of the doctrine, but I don't see how it could work."

Socialism sounded much like anarchy to me, but politics in general had never interested me very much.

Jonathan said, "Americans will never give up their lust for money."

"I hope you're wrong."

He recoiled in an exaggerated way. "Please don't tell me you dislike being wealthy now."

"No," I said and laughed. Jonathan could always put the levity back into any situation. "No. I'm not planning on giving everything away, but the wealth of this world is so poorly distributed. If you could only see the disparity close up, you'd also realize that the wealth of the world could be spread so much more evenly."

"Things will never be even. Don't even hope for it, or you'll doom yourself to certain disappointment."

"Walt Whitman says that if we don't address the problems of the underclasses, our experiment in democracy will fail."

"So you see," he said with a smile, "you may be the Socialist in the family after all."

I gazed off. "I'm seeing the differences so closely now."

"I was teasing you, Grace."

"Oh. Well, I'm serious."

He stopped and faced me. "So, your mother's sentence isn't punishment after all. You're enjoying yourself. You have triumphed. You're the victor, Grace."

He meant well, so I smiled. "I don't feel victorious, simply overwhelmed at the moment."

"However, you choose not to talk about it."

He was irritated with me and obviously feeling ignored. But I didn't want to share; that much was true. "If I were to relive it all with words, I'd be exhausted."

"I suppose I should say I understand."

"I do hope so."

"Anyway, it will be over with soon."

But I wasn't certain anymore if I wanted that. I didn't presume to think my presence was so important that I would be missed down in the alleys. Life there would continue with or without people such as Ira and me. But there was something about the places and people I saw that I wanted to understand, a glimpse of something that if found would allow me to see what perhaps I needed to see.

The next day, when Ira and I were sorting through some crates, a very anxious-looking young man summoned Ira at the door. "You best come on," the young man said with a sense of urgency that tightened my throat.

Ira followed the young man down the street, with me on their heels, but when Ira asked what was happening, he received no answer. The young man only shook his head and simply said, "Just come on." I was struggling to keep up with them, and by the time we arrived on the scene, a small crowd was following us. I overheard the others saying that a young boy of about ten had just died of a fever in the wards of John

Sealy Hospital, the skills of modern medical practitioners apparently unable to save him. His grandfather was now in grave need, I was told.

At that point, I almost turned away, not wanting to be a voyeur of someone else's pain. But something told me to push on. The urgency in the young man's voice made me worry about Ira.

When we arrived, I saw that the grandfather was Charles, the same man for whom Ira had read a letter on my first day in the alleys; the same one I'd thought of as crass when I first met him. Then I remembered Isiah, the polite and charming boy I'd met that same day. Gone in the blink of an eye.

We found Charles standing wide-stanced among the tall, muddied weeds of his small yard. I'd never noted how tall and rail thin he was, and today his clothes hung off his body, his eyes deep pools of yellowish water. He looked out at the crowd, his face as blank as that of a corpse. He asked a mumbling question that no one seemed to understand.

Only then did I see the knife in his hand. The blade caught a glint of sunlight and beamed it back into the cloudy, lightning-split sky. I held my breath, having no idea if the man intended to use the knife on himself or to inflict harm on others.

Charles stumbled about the small yard as if he were drunk, but he'd had no liquor, I was told. Instead, some dark spirit, a soulless grief, had overtaken him. I looked to Ira for direction. I heard murmurings about summoning the police, but Ira held up a hand to halt this.

Another man, a very large one with sensitive eyes, entered the yard and approached the grieving grandfather. He tried to cajole the knife from the older man, but Charles pushed him away so hard that the other man backed off immediately, his hands up in the air, as if to say, *All right, I'll leave you be.*

Then I knew why I had come, despite the weakness in my knees. Ira might need to be stopped from putting himself in harm's way. If so, would he heed my call?

Charles gazed around for a few long minutes, everyone holding his or her breath, but he did nothing, and it looked as though his grip on the knife was easing. I thought for a long relieved moment that he would drop the knife and the crisis would be over.

Then, as we watched in shocked horror, Charles lifted the knife and placed the blade against his inner forearm just above the wrist. He began to press down.

Now the women around me were whimpering and whispering prayers to the Lord. A sourness churned in my stomach, and my breath was hot and urgent, my neck strung with tight ropes. Everyone appeared to be paralyzed. Ira was standing near me and still not moving. If a number of the men moved forward, they could stop Charles. Why didn't they try to stop him? I was too shocked to say it myself, and I supposed they were, too.

An old gentleman who wore a patchy straw hat said to the enraged man in a low rasping voice, "Don't do it, Charles. Don't do it."

Another man said, "You go on and give it up now. Give it up."

But it was as if the older man couldn't hear, his face blank and inhuman. He slowly and methodically pushed the tip of the knife into his flesh until a bloom of blood appeared. "Don't want . . ." he mumbled, "to go on now."

Ira and a few of the men started toward him, but Charles held up his free hand in warning. Then silence and sunlight shot through a crack in the clouds. In one blinding moment, Charles seemed to become aware of what he'd been about to do. He pulled back from the brink, dropped the knife, looked around at the crowd and squinted, as if a bright realization had suddenly been shined into his eyes. His wet, yellow gaze passed over the rest of us and finally settled on Ira. "Good thing you is here, Rev'rend. I just scared all these good folks half to death."

Ira let himself into the yard and took the man in his arms. I saw silent retching sobs but heard no sounds.

◆ ◆ ◆

Ira returned to the office hours later, visibly shaken. People rarely saw such absolute grief before their eyes. And I had thought Charles such a happy soul. How humbling was the realization that before I was at the center of nothing except my own small life, and that events went on in the world that were powerful and desperate and had absolutely nothing to do with justice or fairness. My hands were still trembling as I tried to pack crates for distribution. Ira and I had food that needed to go out that afternoon.

Finally Ira stood inside the doorway, his hands at his sides, quiet and still. He was watching me sweep around the room, yet his eyes held an urgency I'd not seen before.

Several strands of my hair fell into my face. I tried to rake them away, but they wouldn't budge. My forehead was too damp and my hands too shaky. I said, "I've almost finished. The food must go out soon."

Ira's eyes were glazed with something I couldn't describe. He had always seemed so strong to me, both in spirit and physique, but today he didn't look so hardy. Our eyes met, and his were full of light and vulnerability. In a whisper he said, "Don't leave me here alone."

His words came like a soft blow to the chest, followed by an emptiness, a longing so deep it felt like starvation, as if I'd been hollowed.

I ran into his open arms and let him hold me, his body as steady as ballast, and I whispered into his ear, "I won't."

Chapter Twenty

ETTA

Wallace came to call on a Wednesday afternoon when it was so hot and humid the interiors of carriages were almost unbearable. So instead of taking an excursion they remained on the portico, sipping lemonade. Despite the heat, Wallace had come dressed in a suit and tie, and Etta had worn another of the new frocks her aunt had funded. Her aunt had also given her spending money, but Etta had yet to figure out where she would spend it.

After he and Etta exchanged niceties, Wallace kept rocking on his heels and standing, refusing to sit. They made several inane comments about the heat, and Etta, fanning herself with one of her aunt's souvenirs from the Orient, said, "Something seems to be bothering you."

At first, he denied it, but he finally stood still, stared at her hard, and said, "I wonder why you've forgiven me and yet you won't forgive your cousin."

She smiled and wished she found Wallace more attractive. "For talking of my past?" He had shaved off the beard, which she had liked, and now he looked positively childish and angelic, not alluring or enticing at all. "How do you know I haven't forgiven Grace?"

"It's obvious. On the rare occasions when we see you together, there's an air of hostility. Everyone can feel it."

An arrow of annoyance shot through her, and Etta's forehead was beginning to dampen. "Why is everyone so concerned about Grace? Overprotective even, as if she's a child?"

Wallace said slowly, "She hasn't had an easy life."

Etta couldn't help it; she laughed. "Please don't say that, Wallace. I was starting to like you, but if you continue to make ridiculous statements such as that, you will make it near to impossible."

He licked his lips. "I mean that it's her father . . . or rather I should say the absence of her father."

"But people lose parents all the time. Some even lose both parents." Her annoyance was growing; this was not the way she had planned for the afternoon to transpire. She sweetened her voice and stopped fanning herself so that Wallace could see the sincerity in her eyes. "But never mind. I've been properly chastised, and I have forgiven my cousin. If that hasn't been apparent, I regret it. I promise to be on my best behavior from now on. And . . . besides . . . I'd rather talk about you."

He smiled hesitantly. "What do you wish to know?"

Etta positioned herself on a chair and looked up at Wallace invitingly. "Let's make this a little interesting. Oh, do sit down, Wallace, please."

He took a chair next to her a respectable distance away but close enough for quiet conversation.

Etta smiled mischievously and said, "Tell me something interesting. Something I've never heard before. Tell me . . . your secret."

He laughed a little uneasily. "Why do you assume I have a secret?"

"Because everyone does."

Clasping his hands together on his lap, he was clearly trying to appear nonplussed. "I disagree."

Etta leaned closer. "But in your case it happens to be true, doesn't it?"

He looked away and then gazed back at her. "Maybe."

"Do tell," said Etta and fanned herself again.

Studying her, he lifted one eyebrow. "Gambling."

Finally he hadn't held back; she liked that. And gambling did make dear Wallace seem more intriguing. At least he wasn't perfect, as some people claimed he was. She settled lower in the chair. "Hmm. That is interesting."

"I don't do it often, but when I do . . . Well, it's an adventure. Of course my parents have no idea . . ." He leaned a bit closer. "So there it is. I've been honest with you. Now it's your turn. What is your secret?"

Etta shrugged. She would keep it simple and superficial. "I suppose it's not a secret any longer. Many people, including you, know that I love to go barefoot, even to run barefoot."

Though his eyes showed disappointment, he smiled. "Not such a bad vice."

"I removed my shoes for tennis lessons the other day, and I was told it wasn't ladylike."

"So?"

"I kept them off anyway, of course."

Wallace laughed and then said pensively, "It must be tough on the feet, however."

Etta batted her eyelashes and then caught his gaze. "I promise that I have no calluses. Nothing but soft skin everywhere . . ."

Wallace colored but unfortunately had no clever response. She had given him the perfect opportunity to say something seductive. Oh hell, she would've settled for flirtatious. Viola had been right. She called Wallace a "choirboy" for good reason. Despite the admitted gambling, he was no match for her.

This had not been a good idea after all. She ended up sending him away earlier than planned, using the heat as an excuse. He acquiesced easily, but there was a change in him anyway: unintentionally, she had hurt him.

The next time her aunt told her that she must conduct another day of business, Etta was prepared. She dressed as if planning to stay in, and then at the last minute she grabbed a shawl for travel and took enough coins for train fare, following her aunt again in the carriage that she had ordered prepared in advance. She stayed out of view at the depot until Bernadette had disappeared, and then she gauged how long it would take her aunt to purchase her ticket and board. Then Etta entered the station and bought a ticket on the train sitting in the station, bound for Houston. She bought passage in a second-class compartment, where she was sure not to run into her aunt.

The train clacked across the bay. Today the ocean was quiet and still, in contrast to Etta's churning stomach and spinning thoughts. Perhaps she should feel guilty for following her aunt, who had shown her so much kindness, but Etta couldn't stop herself. There was a secret begging to be uncovered here.

In Houston she disembarked and looked about for her aunt while hiding within the throng and being careful not to be seen. She was in luck. Out in front of the depot was a line of carriages for hire, and she recognized her aunt's distinctive form as she stepped into a carriage that she had apparently just hired.

Etta quickly hired a carriage herself and told the driver to follow the one her aunt had taken, keeping a reasonable distance between them, and soon they had traveled through the hot dusty city—not nearly as attractive as Galveston—to its outskirts on roads that were as straight as drawn lines. They lumbered first on pavement and then on a dirt road that led through an area of vast cotton and cornfields, all as cool and green and orderly as markings on a map. The greenery made Etta momentarily daydream of home, but she quickly put her mind back to the task at hand.

Her aunt's carriage turned into the drive of what looked like a large, old plantation home, isolated from everything. Etta asked the driver to pull over under the shade of a moss-dangling old oak, where they were less likely to be seen. The house was unmarked and unnamed, quiet, with only a few trees and simple gardens in front, an automobile and several carriages parked before it. A man in a business suit was descending the front stairs.

Etta couldn't instruct her driver to go down the drive or she would risk being seen. Instead, she asked him to drive slowly by. So from a distance she watched as her aunt exited her carriage, then turned to face her driver. She appeared to be telling him to wait for her. Then Bernadette climbed the front steps, passed between massive white columns, and disappeared through an unseen door.

Etta then asked the driver to stop. With her aunt nowhere in sight, she studied the place. If she had simply passed by, she might have thought it a private home. It had a lazy feel, but on the other hand there was something uninviting about it, too, something silent and closed. Etta decided the house had the rather sterile air of a business establishment, maybe a place where people made secretive deals. But what kind of business, Etta had no idea. The trees stood perfectly still, framing the house like bars, and through the leaves the closed windows glinted in the sunlight as though teasing her. Etta couldn't understand it. Closed windows in such heat?

Her aunt hadn't reappeared, and Etta didn't know what she would do if she did. If Etta stayed there too long, she might be discovered. When finally the heat sank into her skin to the point of nausea, and after gaining no more information, she had no choice but to instruct her driver to turn around and disappear into the dust stirred up by the carriage's wheels.

Her aunt had included Etta in everything, but not this. And why the lies? What could her aunt be doing in there? What business could she be conducting, if it were business at all? And why didn't she want Etta to know about it? She had no choice but to leave the scene without answers. She had thought of her and her aunt as closer than mother and daughter. She had thought of them as alike and inseparable. And now she felt no more significant than a single particle in the midst of all that dust.

Chapter Twenty-One

THE GIRL

It was a rust-colored early morning, with dusty lines of pale-orange light leaking through the slats of the house walls. The girl awakened and imagined her favorite place on that ocean that never stirred. She had been trying to create that special shine and shimmer on her sea drawing but hadn't been able to do it. She needed to take a fresh look at it, make more of a study of it, with an artist's eye.

Not heeding Reena's advice, she slipped into her yellow dress, wishing she could wear it every day, but she didn't want to ruin it on Harry's boat, and of course there were the times when she couldn't wear it because Reena had washed it for her and hung it on the line. But even when she watched it dry in the wind, there was a feeling of pride. When she wore it with the matching bonnet, she recalled those days before the storm when she and her mother had dressed up and gone to church together. She had almost forgotten what it felt like to wear something girlish.

The girl donned the bonnet and walked down through the alleys. Too bad she didn't have any shoes to complete the outfit, but it was no matter. The bottoms of her feet were as tough as hooves.

It was early, and few people were up and about yet. She could chance it. The girl made speed until the gravelly soil underneath her feet had changed to sand. The city gave way, and she slipped across the road, unseen like a coyote, and then it opened out before her: the ocean waters, sunlight on dips and swells, a surf hushing against the shore, and out in the depths the silent and massive ocean, moving heavily like liquid metal.

She found her way to the water's edge, where slippery waves lapped at her toes and made a fine-textured foam with a regular cadence, a mere whisper today, and then she gazed back toward the city and began to stroll. There was only a light breeze, and the streets were still quiet. But with the seawall in the midst of construction, laborers and engineers were already at work on the project when she reached it.

Farther down the beach, on the completed part of the wall, people had already been taking to the top to enjoy the view. A promenade on the seawall was the newest and far and away the most exciting thing to do on Galveston Island, and several couples were already strolling there to watch the sun climb the sky. Even the women were willing to step up a ladder to see the view. Ever since she'd been watching the wall go up, the girl had wondered what could be seen and studied from up so high. It hit her then. Up there she'd be able to look out at that special spot she was trying to paint and see it better.

She found an old ladder and dragged it to the wall. After scrambling her way up the ladder, which didn't quite reach the top, she hoisted herself up the final three feet. She gazed out to the open ocean, out past the lazy waters, where seaweed floated. Galveston Island was nearly flat. Not since looking out with her father, up high on his shoulders, had she been able to see so far, to lose herself in those distant, planed waters that were her favorite, out to that shelf that held up the sky and made all the cries inside her die down. The sparkles and shimmers in her favorite place were silver, not white or yellow. She could create silver by blending her black and white art sticks.

After the quiet calm of that distant water settled into her bones, she felt like walking. She followed the length of the seawall, passing by ladies wearing high collars and long silky skirts who lifted parasols high over their heads, past men in waistcoats and tall hats. Her hair was flowing free under the bonnet, wild and tangled, and only then did she realize how noticeable it was that she had worn no shoes, heeding looks of disapproval from other strollers.

Slowing her pace, she tucked up her long red tangles under the yellow bonnet and tried to walk in a way that was sedate and lady-like. She alternately walked and stood and studied until the morning sun came up fully and the day was no longer quiet. People rushed along the walks on their way to conduct business. The streetcars were running, clanging on the tracks, and wealthy women were out and about, wearing hats and gloves, carrying baskets and going to market.

A group of knicker-clad and hatless boys moved along below the wall. They were looking up, squinting into the sun, walking along with her at the same pace as she was, following her progress. She remembered hearing about such boys. Along with the seawall promenade had come enterprising young men—boys, really—who made a penny offering their help to the ladies with a ladder.

A mistake! The girl had lingered too long, and by now the boys had homed in on her. A small pack of them were scurrying along the city side of the seawall, weaving through pedestrians, calling and hooting at her, offering her a way down.

"We'll get you down, girl," shouted one of the boys.

"Leave it to us," said another.

Heat gathered in her brow, and she thought of Reena's warnings, and also Madu's warnings, which she had so often ignored. She walked along for a while more in hopes that the boys would lose interest. But they stayed below.

The girl picked up her pace, glanced their way, and tried to give them a discouraging glare. She shook her head at them and frowned determinedly in an effort to dampen their spirits. But it did little good. She returned to the spot where she had first gained the wall. The ladder was gone. Someone had removed it, and she hadn't any way down.

Of course she didn't have a penny on her. She took a few deep breaths, then focused ahead and would not even gaze down at the boys again, feigning disinterest. But they continued to follow her. She'd have to outrun them, but her long skirt hindered her progress, tangled about her legs, and besides, the rowdy boys just started running below as fast as she did. She ran anyway, until she lost her breath, and still the boys jogged, matching her pace. She stopped running and tried to catch her breath, but there was only more heat, more unbearable, scorching, heavy heat.

"Come now, let us get a better look at you," said one boy with a face full of peppery freckles.

"Be a sport," said another. "Let us get you down now, girl."

She shook her head vigorously.

Another boy said with mock seriousness, "I don't believe we've met."

At that the others hooted and clapped their approval.

Finally one yelled, "All right, then. You win. We'll fetch our ladder for you and not charge a cent. Come now. Who are you?"

Reena had told her that the boys' real purpose was to sneak a glimpse of a woman's leg. But showing a bit of her leg was the girl's least worry. If they caught her, they would ask questions. They would expect her to talk. And when she couldn't talk, that might lead to someone figuring out that she was the one the authorities had been seeking off and on for the past three years.

Two of the boys were now dragging a ladder toward the wall. Soon they would climb it and gain the top.

The heat of the day somehow became even hotter. She wiped beads from her upper lip as fat lines of sweat traveled down the sides of her face. Even though the bonnet shaded her, the skin on her cheeks and brow and around her mouth was searing.

Along and below the seawall now, groups of people were watching the spectacle. The girl, scared but trying to act haughty, trying to escape. Some of the boys were on top now, running closer, determined to catch her. More people gathered, and a man was setting up a big black camera on a stand.

Running again and faster was her only option. This time the girl hiked up the yellow skirt and the petticoat beneath it, but she cared little who saw her legs. Now she could run much faster and make good speed on the hard surface of the seawall, faster than the boys below could run among the crowd, and thus she pulled out ahead, all to the enthusiastic shouts of watchers and passersby. She reached the end of the wall before the boys did and stopped.

Below was a pile of sand, but it had to be a ten-foot drop to get there. She would have to take the leap and pray she wouldn't be injured. The boys on the wall would probably not take the same plunge; they had mothers and fathers who would punish them for taking such a risk. If the fall killed her, so be it. With a glance at the boys closing in on her and with a relieved smile, she kissed her hand, lifted it into the air, turned, and jumped.

The fall knocked the wind out of her, and her legs trembled with the shock of the landing. But in only a split second she had conquered a distance even those daredevil boys wouldn't dare try. Instead, they only groaned in disappointment and shouted out their protests. She scrambled to her feet, while the crowd that had been following her plight below the wall began to close in.

She ran, gained the alleys, crossed streets, and still running, she took Fat Alley and Tin Can Alley, where no white person would ever go, elated that she'd outfoxed them and, more importantly, that she had not given herself away. Soon she was lost in the rears, darting among kids playing stickball, rolling tires, and throwing marbles.

She finally slowed her pace and made her way to Reena's backhouse, where she found a plate of cold breakfast Reena must have left for her sitting on the stoop. She ate the drying eggs, bacon, and biscuits and then stretched out on Reena's porch in the shade. She hadn't realized how exhausted she was, and before she knew it she'd finished reliving the episode on the seawall and had drifted off to sleep.

The next day, when she awakened the sun was high in the sky. Today she was to go out with Harry, so she slipped out of the dress and into some old clothes that had once belonged to Reena's boys. Then she walked through the alleys to the other side of the island and followed The Strand until she had made her way to the docks and Harry's boat.

He was working as usual. When he heard her, he looked up and fixed his mouth into a stern line. "You're late," he grumbled. She eased into the boat and helped him ready it for sail. Before they could cast off, the wind stopped blowing. Harry gazed about as though reconsidering his decision to set sail. And then came an odd pulling sensation in the air. Nearby a waterspout, a small tornado filled with water, was coming toward land. All the fishermen on dock that day stopped what they were doing to watch the unusual phenomenon play out.

The waterspout spun across the docks, leaving behind slippery trails of flipping, silvery minnows.

"You cain't save them all," said Harry, already knowing what she would do.

But the girl scrambled out of the stern and dashed down the planks, where she scooped up handfuls of minnows and tossed them back into the bay waters, all to the raucous laughter of the fishermen, who couldn't understand the fuss she was making.

When the wind picked up, they headed out on the gently swelling water. Harry put out the seine. Over the water, the sun was hot, but the breeze was sweet and the water calm. A perfect island day.

"There's gossip in town," Harry said without looking up. He coughed into his hand, wheezed, and then went on working.

The girl glanced his way. Harry was thin, and he had been coughing a lot lately, more so than usual.

"Something about a girl in a yellow dress outrunning some boys on the seawall."

She bit her lip.

"That new dress you got that you wore the other day. I was just wondering if it's the same one." He coughed again, then followed it with a gasp.

Meeting his eyes, she wouldn't deny it.

Harry shook his head.

"Anyone asks, don't let on."

She nodded.

"You hear?"

She nodded again.

Back in the alleys later that day, nearing sunset, Reena looked the girl over, too. She pursed her lips. "I been worried about you."

Reena lifted a water bucket and carried it away from the cistern with one fleshy, strong arm, all the while pointing her finger. "I knows what you done. It's been all over. In the newspaper, too, I hear. Some girl in a yellow dress on the seawall." Reena let out a long exasperated sigh. "It'd be a good thing that most people don't know you in that frock. And now here you is, smiling 'bout it."

It had ended up being a thrill. Sure, she'd been trapped there for a few minutes, but outrunning the boys had ended up exciting.

Chapter Twenty-Two

GRACE

I stood on the beach with a group of children. After the children had been in the surf, wading and playing for more than an hour, they were finally tiring out. I had them sit on the dry sand just above the high-water mark, where Joseph stood on his own, still afraid to venture any closer to the waves. Already I'd found a sand dollar to show him that day, and we'd watched the sand crabs scurry sideways across the small dunes at our back.

We were down below the wall, near the segment under construction, and I had just taught the children to play London Bridge and some circle games. I thought I might see Jonathan on the wall, but unfortunately he must have found a way to slip away, or else he was doing his required observation in another spot.

Over three miles long, the seawall was being built of solid concrete. The top rose to over a foot higher than the top water level reached during the 1900 Storm. Crews had brought in the finest granite from west of Austin and the largest pines for pilings from East Texas. It was indeed a huge and impressive thing, sixteen feet wide across at the bottom and five feet on top. After the wall was completed, the entire city would be raised behind it.

In opposition to the seawall, some people had had the audacity to recommend that we relocate the city, or have a daytime Galveston for business and a nighttime Galveston for sleeping. But we would show those who had made such suggestions. No storm would be able to penetrate that wall, and Galveston would regain her former glory.

Before long, Joseph and the rest of the children were building castles and digging moats in the putty-colored sand, having a grand time. The water shimmered as if strings of jewels rode the swells. The wind sprinkled me with tiny grains of sand while I stood and watched the children at play.

As I led the children back toward the school, I heard shouting coming from the seawall. Men were working there, and my first thought was that someone had been injured, but then I heard laughter, and I looked up to see the girl, my girl, on top. She was wearing my old yellow dress. Barefoot, she had her hair tucked up under the bonnet I had also given her.

It was ironic that I'd been searching for her and picturing her somewhere hidden and secreted away, but now I'd found her again, and she was in plain view in a very public place. Not only that, she was causing something of a spectacle.

Many people were watching. A group of boisterous boys below her were following her progress. She was refusing them with a very definite shake of her head. Soon she began to run.

Oh, to run like that! To be so free!

She left my sight, and I was unable to follow, as I had the children in my charge.

I didn't know what had happened until I read about the occurrence in the newspaper the next day. An article described a so-called Miss

Girl, who had run upon the seawall, had successfully evaded the boys, and then escaped without anyone knowing who she was. The account was dramatized and interjected with humor, and it was liberating for a young woman to outrun boys of her own age.

It was also the talk of the town for the next few days. People speculated as to who the so-called Miss Girl could be, when she would return, and why she preferred to keep her identity unknown. Why not come forth and tell her story and bask in the attention for a while? A few young men even wrote love letters professing their undying devotion to her, which were printed in the paper. She inspired awe in men and pride in women.

The next day Ira was wearing a new suit of lightweight gray wool. "Ira," I said, "you've visited the tailor." Neither of us had mentioned our embrace on that prior day of such terrible grief, when we'd both forgotten who we were and why we were there.

He touched his right lapel. "I do receive a salary from the charity." He seemed embarrassed, ashamed of even this tiny streak of vanity. His old shoes were polished to a shine, and his beard looked freshly clipped, too.

"I decided it was time to purchase something nice to wear. I have meetings with some influential city leaders coming up soon."

I told him about seeing the girl on the seawall. At this new bit of information, he looked bemused. He raised his eyebrows, set aside his work for the moment, and said, "She is quite a puzzle, isn't she?"

"I'm thinking of trying to communicate with her. If she can remember a poet's exact words and write them well enough that I recognized them, then she has had schooling. I've also seen her draw. Her memory must be excellent." I turned to him. "Aren't you curious about why she doesn't speak? And about how she ended up living as she does?"

"Of course."

"Wouldn't you like to know her background? Where her family is?"

"Of course. I have a natural curiosity about people. As do you, I see."

"I've an idea I'd like to propose. I could borrow a slate board and chalk from the girls' academy and then see if she would write to me, if perhaps she would answer questions. Perhaps then we could learn why she doesn't speak and why she lives here in apparent hiding."

Ira was gazing at me in an unusual way. These days, whenever his eyes fell on me, I found myself in a dreamlike state, floating on water. If he touched me, most often inadvertently, I was paralyzed by both apprehension and a pleasing sense of heat. In my bed at night, I reexperienced those moments, perspiring under my sheets, stunned by the immensity of what I was feeling. Now I turned away and focused on work, my hands trembling.

Outside, storm clouds were gathering, and beneath them the sky had turned an ominous shade of green. I had no idea how I was going to get through the day holding in these feelings I had for Ira. "If she is receptive to me, however, I want to give her a few things. I've already passed on some art supplies. But perhaps another dress and some shoes. She goes about without shoes, and it's a wonder she hasn't cut her feet and come down with lockjaw. The yellow dress I gave her is the only one she owns, as far as I can tell, and already it's soiled. I found a book of poems by Emily Brontë in our private library at home. Don't you think she might like another dress and a book to read?"

Ira smiled and nodded. "You're excited about this. But let me warn you. For the most part, this work has its rewards, but other times we are disappointed when someone doesn't do the things we would choose for them."

"I won't try to choose for her."

"Very well," he said. "But don't think of the alleys as a laboratory, Grace. People's lives are fragile, especially down here." He looked away and then back at me. "Sometimes people live as they do, I've found, because they want to."

"But, Ira, you of all people know that sometimes they live as they do because they have no other choices, because they are trapped. This girl has captured my imagination, and I want to help her. I have so much, you see."

Hesitantly, he said, "For the most part, I prefer that we focus on those who desire our help. You mustn't force . . ."

"Is that what I'm doing? Forcing myself? Being pushy?"

"I'm sorry. I'm only trying to explain."

My eyelids stung and I had to look away. "Pushy."

"I don't want to discourage you, Grace, but you must exercise caution. It's a difficult balance to maintain."

I needed this now. And there was no way to hide it. Ira knew me, as if I'd removed my heart and handed it to him. "I have much to learn."

"If it's your wish to pursue the matter further, I won't stop you." He waited. "Just be careful."

I couldn't answer. Ira stood quietly, waiting, and his concern, his sincerity, were almost overwhelming. But the concern I saw went beyond issues of our work down here. There was something longing, something yearning in those soft pond-water eyes of his, and it settled on me like silt. He opened his mouth to speak, and I had the feeling that he was about to say something important, perhaps something that would change everything between us, but a rap on the door stopped him.

Joseph stood on the doorstep. He wanted to tell me about the high marks he'd just received in school. By the time I finished congratulating him and praising him for his work, Ira was standing behind his desk with a letter in his hand, and the moment had passed.

After Joseph left us alone again, we went back to talking about the girl. "If she resists me," I said, "I promise you I'll stop."

"Very well."

I began to move about the room, gathering up donations and sorting them into crates to pass out later. But as I worked, I felt Ira's eyes following me.

The room in which we worked was small, and Ira and I often brushed up against each other. My skirt sometimes fell across his shoes, or my elbow grazed his. Often I didn't take notice of the touches until I realized how much Ira had. He seemed shaken by them, but today I was the one so hindered. I moved my skirt out of his way and could hear his breathing, which was matching mine. I could scarcely wait to escape the close proximity that brought forth in me odd involuntary thoughts, such as *How would it be to kiss him?*

Did he feel the same way I did? Was he falling in love with me? Yet if that were true, he would probably never say so, since my mother had sent me to him, and this was supposed to be sacred work.

That evening, I sorted through my wardrobe and pulled out two dresses: a pink day dress with a matching jacket, and a pale-blue party dress I hadn't worn in years. I had intended to give her both, but I paused. Ira was concerned that I might be overstepping, and so I selected only one dress to give her now, thinking I would save the other for later. I wondered what she had done with the pastels and the sketch pad I'd sent to her.

The pink day dress would have been more practical, but I imagined her thrilled reaction to the blue party dress. Its color was very much like her eyes, and so I settled on it. Of course she would have no use for a party gown, except for dress-up, but still, it was the choice I made.

I filled an old traveling satchel with the slate board and chalk I'd managed to borrow, and then I folded the dress, slipped in the book of poetry, along with a handkerchief and some undergarments I was certain she could use.

As I undressed for bed that night, I wondered about my body as I'd never done before. I had no idea how I looked from another's eyes, a man's eyes. It would be completely inappropriate to study myself in a mirror, but I wished I could. Thoughts of Ira drifted down my body like my silky nightgown. I lay awake for hours, feeling as if I'd been kidnapped by him in the middle of a life journey that had previously been so carefully arranged.

When I arrived the next morning, the sun was bright and hot, and streams of dusty light slanted into the office through the only window. Ira, as usual, was there before me, and he glanced at the bag I'd brought along from home, then went on as if it didn't exist.

I tried to make light of his reaction. "I contained myself, I assure you. I could've given away so much more. In fact, I will go ahead and donate many other articles. Now that I see such need around me, it seems ever so silly and wasteful to keep the amount of clothing I have in my wardrobe."

Ira smiled my way and then lifted a stack of letters and began to sort through them.

"If you're concerned, Ira, I won't push ahead. Truly, I would do nothing willingly to cause you any trouble. I don't have to find her again if you don't want me to."

He looked up from the letters. "Have you learned of her whereabouts?"

"Just yesterday I was finally told by one of the children. She's living in a backyard near here, in the servants' quarters. It's close by. I can easily walk there and find her."

"Would you like me to accompany you?"

"No, thank you. I think I'd be less threatening on my own."

His voice lowered and softened. "I happened across someone like her once, a young boy. He had a lame foot—a clubfoot, I think it was—and all the other boys teased him. I paid him special attention and gave him extra things. I even slipped him money. But as a result all I did was make it harder on him. People teased him even more. They called him my cabin boy."

"Oh . . . Ira."

He tried to smile, but the pain of that memory was still shining in his eyes.

"What happened to him?"

"He turned away from me and from the faith. He fell in with the first group of people who accepted him as an equal. Gangsters, I'm afraid."

I managed a weak "You tried."

"Yes, but I tried too hard." He gazed down. "Often we make mistakes. Often we push too hard." He looked back at me then and held my gaze with a quivering in his eyes, and I already knew that he was also trying perhaps too hard with me, and he knew it. As I stood there, recognizing it for what it was, something silent and powerful plunged inside me, a sand fall of feelings.

But I was engaged to another man.

I dropped my arms to my sides and tried to act normal, but inside me the sand fall continued to pour off the rim.

As the day wore on, I grew more troubled. I kept myself busy with numerous projects, including reading to the children, attending a wake, and distributing some old hats and boots we'd received. In the heat of afternoon, I took the loudest, largest group of children I'd ever handled down to the beach for wading. The ocean was testing us that day, rolling and heaving loudly and boisterously, then retreating with a sucking pull.

I thought of the girl and not of Ira, but I ended up delaying my pursuit of her until the next day. The sea stirred up the disquiet within me, making me doubt myself as never before. Ira was here because of a faith larger than mine. He maintained an abiding belief in the goodness of humanity, especially goodness aimed at others, and yet he was skeptical we could benefit the girl. His words kept returning to me. *Don't think of the alleys as a laboratory, Grace. People's lives are fragile.*

Over a meal of roast duckling with sweet potatoes that night, Mother informed me that one of her china collections was cracking. Clorinda had discovered the problem.

I wondered about Clorinda as I never had before. She had been with us for all of my life, and yet I barely knew anything about her. Of course I knew the servants had lives beyond our house, and that Clorinda's revolved mainly around her church. My mother took pride in paying the servants well, perhaps as some type of penance for how the family money had originally been made. We had a house bigger than most just for the servants; they didn't live in shacks and sheds—in fact, nothing close to it.

"Such a shame. I don't think the pattern is made anymore. I won't be able to replace the pieces." She was still talking about the china.

"Buy a new set."

Mother stiffened. "Of course I can order a new set. But the pieces have sentimental value to me. It was our wedding china, you see, your father's and mine, and I'd planned to always hold on to it. Someday it was to be yours, Grace."

"If you wish to donate the china, I'll make good use of it."

But Mother looked pained, and I regretted my impulsive suggestion. "I thought you would still want it, despite the imperfections."

Mother would never use cracked china, and when I married Jonathan, I wanted to start anew. "I'm not marrying for another year. Why not give the set away and let someone else make use of it now?"

Etta, who had been listening intently, sat back in her chair and appeared aghast. "You would take your mother's china down into the alleys? At the very least find some nice family home, where it could be given proper use."

"Proper use?" I looked into her dark eyes that even in the gentle wavering candlelight were animated. "I used to believe as you do. That the poor have no use or no appreciation for fine things. But it isn't true."

Etta shook her head.

"They have likes and dislikes and tastes that run the gamut."

Etta appeared as if she wanted to say something, but she stopped herself and deferred to Mother, who said, "I see you're learning about the lower classes, and I'm pleased. I sent you there to learn. But didn't a wise man once say that a little knowledge is a dangerous thing?"

Not responding, I steeled myself against more criticism I was sure would come.

Etta said, "Are we to feel guilty because we have more than others?"

"No."

And then Mother added, "Be careful that you don't begrudge us what we have, Grace, simply because others have less."

"I wouldn't dare," I said.

Later Jonathan arrived, and I found him outside on the front portico with Etta. It was a gentle, warm evening, the smell of oleanders and beach fires in the air. Etta and Jonathan had been sharing a quiet conversation. I couldn't say that Jonathan seemed particularly pleased to see me as I walked up and gave him a smile, but I also couldn't say that I blamed him. For the past six weeks, it was as though I'd been sleepwalking through my evenings, my thoughts focused on the day I'd just completed or on the day of work ahead of me.

Something else: Jonathan had stopped whistling again, particularly around Etta, something he ceased only when troubled. And so I stopped seeing Etta's beauty as a flower, not even a wild Indian paintbrush, but instead a twisting vine.

Perhaps Jonathan had come over in hopes of talking to Etta instead of me. I was capable of jealousy, but now, if a threat did exist to my relationship with Jonathan, then it was fated to be that way, and I would do nothing to intervene. And I was hardly blameless.

Ira . . .

I ended up leaving them to their conversation, and as I passed my mother, sitting at the cherry table in the family dining room, she was looking over the pieces of china, sighing and lamenting the fact that so many were ruined. She held a teacup up to the light. "There they are. See them, Grace. Cracks everywhere."

Webs of fine cracks ran through the cup, almost indiscernible to the eye. The cracks were fine enough that the cup could still hold liquid, but bothersome to Bernadette. To me, the imperfections demonstrated character, like the wrinkles in a good pair of leather gloves, or in a learned face.

"I can't part with the good ones," said Mother. "Some of them are still intact. But I will turn over these more damaged ones to you, my dear. You may take them to your mission if you please."

"Thank you, Mother."

She couldn't let go of much, but she could part with those things she deemed less than perfect, that failed her touchstone, that were, in her mind, damaged goods.

Chapter Twenty-Three

ETTA

Curiosity and that clenching ache of being left out were driving her to distraction, so Etta considered her options. Her aunt had a cherrywood secretary in the library, where she kept papers and such. Etta could nose about at night, but she was fearful of being caught. There were simply too many other people in the house. Besides, she didn't know what she would be looking for, and she assumed any papers of real importance were probably kept in a locked box at the bank.

Her next idea was to write a letter. She knew the address of the large plantation home outside Houston, but she did not know the name, if it indeed had a name, nor did she know the name of anyone who lived or worked there. But she quickly decided to simply write a letter addressed "To Whom It May Concern," acting as a domestic inquiring about work, and ask about the type of business that was run there in an effort to explore their needs. To be convincing as a servant, she would have to write the letter carefully, without her usual flair, but she could do it.

But then came the manner of how to obtain a reply. All mail that came to the house was passed first to her aunt Bernadette, and should she see a letter to Etta from that place, she would know that Etta had followed her. Etta considered renting her own postal box in town, where she could receive anything she wanted in secret, but she then decided she didn't want to wait that long. Instead, she would observe her aunt longer and follow her again on her next mysterious "business" trip.

She took several excursions with Wallace, who had not let their last meeting discourage him. She went as his date, sometimes alone but more often with others. Each time she saw him, she hoped for something to flame alive: a sense of excitement, an increasing attraction, even more humor and conviviality.

One day on a beach picnic with a small group, she grew tired of the discussion about art and music that was consuming the others, and she excused herself to take a walk alone at sunset. At the water's edge, the sky was burnished copper and deepest blue, striped with clouds that looked lit from within.

She unlaced her shoes, rolled down her stockings, then left it all in a pile. She picked up her skirt and walked briskly, while memories of her moments with Philo filled the chambers of her mind. He had been surfacing more and more, against her will. She walked so far she could scarcely see where she'd left the others, who were sitting around in a circle on porch chairs brought to the sands by servants.

Eventually she stopped, breathing deeply. It was exhausting working so hard to become one of them, to be one of the pampered, clear-eyed girls of the elite, with all their inborn confidence and sense of entitlement. Sometimes she couldn't follow what they were saying; it was if they were speaking in a foreign language. During those times she had to plaster on a look of interest and understanding and simply nod like an idiot. And yet she wanted to be here, needed to be here, if she was going to have a winning future. What, pray tell, was waiting for her in Nacogdoches? She had to proceed cautiously. Being different and fresh was one thing, but she couldn't distinguish herself to such an extent that no young man would find her worthy. She was walking a tightwire.

Damn. Not thoughts of the circus again!

Removed and utterly alone, she stared out at a blackening sea shimmering with quicksilver until she felt a presence. A figure was approaching from the direction of the others. Wallace. He was carrying her shoes and stockings. Standing before her now, he explained, "The sun is almost down. There'll be no moon tonight, and you won't be able to see your way back."

"Dear Wallace," she breathed and looked up at the sky. The stars were already beginning their eternal wheeling around the Earth. "How kind of you."

He held the shoes out to her, and it was tough to face his eager, luminous eyes.

She smiled a tired smile. "Where am I to sit? I can't very well don them while standing."

"I'll hold you up," he said.

"Very well."

He held her about the waist while she slipped the stockings and shoes on first one foot and then the other. All she had to do was turn around and she'd be in his arms. She battled with herself all the while she was tying her shoes. It would be easy to start something. They were alone. No one would see. One kiss from her and he would be enraptured.

But in the end she couldn't do it. She finished tying her shoes and walked back to the others at his side, not touching or talking at all.

Etta lay in wait for another man who would affect her the way Philo had, while also lying in wait for her aunt. When Bernadette interviewed chefs for Grace's engagement party, to be held at the end of August, Etta watched. The house chefs couldn't come up with something special enough for the engagement gala, and so her aunt was interviewing chefs from all over the city, and even a few from the mainland, too.

After she had released today's chef interviewee, Bernadette sat quietly and thumbed through the newest issue of *Harper's Weekly*. The library smelled of knowledge and worldliness, and the sound of her aunt turning the pages was the only thing breaking the silence. Etta studied her aunt's face, where she could now see flashes of her mother—or rather, how her mother might have looked at this age if all the cooking and ironing and washing had not destroyed her appearance.

"Are you happy here?" Bernadette asked so quietly that Etta almost didn't hear her.

"I'm sorry, I don't understand."

He aunt gazed up from the pages and met Etta's eyes. "Are you adjusting? Are you doing well?"

Her aunt's scrutiny was so different from others'. It penetrated her skin and made her squirm. A touch of fear jumped into Etta's throat. Had she done something wrong? Or even worse, did her aunt know that Etta had followed her to Houston? "Yes," said Etta. "Splendid."

"Very well then. As it should be."

Etta let out her breath.

"But perhaps you should spend more time around people your own age."

Her words hit Etta like a spear to the heart. Bernadette was already tiring of her company. She stammered, "G-Grace is gone all day. She's down at the . . ."

"That's true, but you've met so many others. Aren't there any young men to your liking?"

Apparently all her aunt wanted was to see her mingling with the opposite sex. "There are many that I like. But I haven't felt anything"— she paused—"overwhelming."

The flash of a smile. "You want to be overwhelmed, do you?"

"Well," said Etta, "I prefer it over boredom."

Bernadette laughed. "Etta, you are so precocious."

"Thank you."

Etta watched as her aunt slowly stopped turning the pages, as her face took on a dreamy, distant quality. "That's how it was for me and Grace's father. I was mad about him. He read poetry to me." She stopped and smiled, her eyes wistful. "He filled entire rooms with flowers. And he could dance . . ." She blinked her eyes, then made soft, fluttering movements with her hands. "He was quite the waltzer. I'd feel as if I were being carried away." Then a smile and she looked askance, and Etta had the feeling the memory was almost too much for her aunt to bear.

Etta would've loved to learn more, but she didn't like speaking of the dead. And besides, she had no words of consolation or agreement. But she liked hearing her aunt talk on any subject, and for her to share such intimate details—why, Etta felt honored.

And then came a wave of guilt. Perhaps she should drop this preoccupation with her aunt's secret train trips. But she considered it for only a moment.

Bernadette said in a soft voice, "He hummed while he read books. Not when he read the newspaper. Only books." Her face held an expression of concentration, of complete immersion in the memory.

A moment later, she seemed to shake herself out of a daze. She touched both sides of her face with her palms. "It's funny what one remembers."

Etta was speechless. She wanted to love someone in that way, in that exact same way, with every bone and breath. The way she had once felt with Philo.

One morning over breakfast a few days later, her aunt complained about another day she would need to conduct "business," and Etta tried not to let her excitement show.

She raised the napkin to her lips and kept her eyes averted. "More business?"

"I'm afraid so."

"So soon?"

"Yes," said Bernadette, a tone of resignation in her voice. "I shall miss your company again today."

"Not as much as I'll miss yours, Aunt," said Etta, and she began picking at her food again. "How long will this business go on?"

A feigned smile. "As long as it's necessary."

Her aunt made the comment glibly, but a look of sadness clouded her usually piercing eyes, as if she needed to be saved. How Etta wished her aunt would confide in her. Tell her everything.

But Bernadette changed the subject, and Etta determined she would have no choice but to follow her again. The servant who had driven her to the station before must have kept his mouth shut.

Etta arranged to have a carriage meet her at the side of the house, and again she followed her aunt to the station, and then on the train to Houston, and then back to that same large plantation home dropped down away from all else. Again Etta told her driver to pass slowly by. She peered down the driveway and watched her aunt disappear inside the grand house. And again she asked the driver to stop.

What she saw next surprised her. Wiping her neck with a handkerchief, and frowning at the dirt that had collected there, she watched a woman dressed in nurse's clothing emerge from behind a hedge of bushes along the side of the house. The nurse was pushing a small hunched-over woman about the grounds in a wheeled chair.

So this place was some sort of infirmary, most likely a tuberculosis sanitarium, or was her imagination getting away from her? It was possible that the old woman simply lived in the house, a member of the family who had taken ill, requiring a private nurse. But later there were others in wheelchairs. They appeared to be patients in this place, and it looked as though they were being brought outdoors for a breath of fresh air. How confusing. What business would her aunt have here? As far as Etta knew, everyone in the family was healthy, and if they weren't, why would her aunt maintain such secrecy about it?

Etta sat in her carriage and tried to imagine a sensible scenario. The horses were awaiting the driver's directions and whinnying a bit as a little breeze picked up. Finally there was some wind out here in the still, flat, featureless plain, though it didn't stir up any ideas in Etta, only some clacking of branches in the trees, like the ticking of a clock. Time was running out.

Crows were calling out from the nearby fields in their ugly tones. The sky threatened rain as silent bolts of lightning touched stiffly on the ground with long, white-hot legs. Etta watched a moment longer and then experienced a small prickling in the small of her back, a tiny sense of disquiet that told her perhaps she should leave well enough alone. Perhaps she should drop this desire to know everything about her aunt's life. It was rather odd that she had wasted two perfectly good days to pursue Bernadette in this clandestine way.

But Etta didn't drop it. She simply couldn't stand being shut out. It hurt too much. So she sat in the carriage until she watched the patients being returned to the house, and then, before risking discovery by her aunt, she returned to Houston under that huge gaping sky, filled with all her questions.

Three nights later, she was attending another gala, this one on board a visiting British naval ship in port, hosted by her aunt's friends from the Daughters of the Republic of Texas. Her aunt was in attendance, as were Larke and Wallace McKay, but Grace and Jonathan had declined. Grace, apparently, was too tired after her day of doling out charity.

For such a special event, her aunt had ordered Seamus to drive the carriage with the horses checkered, with steeds of matching color arrayed diagonally, as she had seen done in New York City for going to operas and plays. After touring the ship, the guests watched the sunset over the harbor. They shared their opera glasses to view Galveston from the deck, and when that activity grew old, the guests were seated for dinner and served both tender veal steaks and slices from an enormous stuffed turkey.

Etta had grown accustomed to watchful eyes upon her at every moment. She'd borne the scrutiny well, in her opinion. Her manners were genteel; now she knew the difference between an oyster fork, a fish fork, a luncheon fork, a dinner fork, a serving fork, and forks to skewer pickles, and if she didn't know what to do with a certain piece of silverware, she simply waited until someone else began to use it and followed suit. But perhaps Etta had begun to blend in too much, becoming too much like them, making her less interesting. Lately she was not being sought out as often; maybe her allure was waning. Her newness and individuality could be wearing off.

Everyone was talking of ballet and opera and art, along with glorifying the seawall as usual, then bemoaning the grade-raising project to come. Nothing new, nothing of interest except the money and lifestyle it took to care about such things as ballet and opera and art. Then, as the vegetables were being served, Etta overheard talk of Miss Girl, the one so much had been written about in the newspaper.

"That's something I believe Miss Etta Rahn would do," said Wallace proudly. She only then cared that he was sitting at her side. "We all know she loves to run around without shoes."

At first, there was silence. Then Etta heard, "I'll wager it is her. Miss Girl wears no shoes."

"She's new here, and it makes sense, now, doesn't it? This other young lady simply appeared out of nowhere."

"She fits the description, does she not?" said another man.

"But she keeps her face hidden under a bonnet," said another woman.

One of the men said, "Miss Etta has the fortitude for it. She would love to create such a mystery."

"But will she confess?" said another woman, who sat to Etta's right two seats down.

Etta caught their stares, a pleasant sensation. This could change everything back. The anonymous Miss Girl had fascinated Galveston, so why not let these people think it was her? There was no need to react to an incorrect assumption. Let them think as they may.

The young man sitting opposite Etta said, "So do tell us, Miss Etta Rahn. Is it you who ran the seawall incognito?"

Etta cocked her head to one side, playing coy. "How did you guess?"

Larke McKay, who sat almost at the end of the table, asked her aunt, "Is it your niece?"

Bernadette laughed. "I wouldn't know. I don't know of her where-abouts at all times. Besides, Etta can speak for herself."

All eyes landed on her again.

"Seriously," the man across from her said, "we want to know. Is it you?"

"Do tell us, Etta," said another.

"Let your secret be known. Don't keep us guessing."

Let them think it; let them think anything they wanted. "Now, Henry, don't you see? Don't you know me by now?" She paused for the perfect amount of time. "I always keep people guessing."

Chapter Twenty-Four

The Girl

The woman named Grace found her again in only two weeks' time. It was late July by then and the hottest day of the year so far.

After having slept on the back porch, the girl awakened one morning, dew on her face and sunlight slanting into her eyes, and soon felt someone's presence. She rubbed her eyes and looked up. The young woman was standing just outside Reena's gate, peering over the fence into the yard.

The girl quickly stood, folded up her quilt, then set it down on the planks, as if to say, *I live here now. I'm no longer in the shed. You can leave me be. I'm doing just fine.*

No one was stirring inside Reena's house yet. It was a Sunday, and the house servants were allowed to sleep in a bit later than usual. Reena didn't have to serve breakfast until nine o'clock.

The girl looked at Grace, standing there in the alleys on a Sunday morning, and thought she had never appeared so out of place. Why wasn't she singing in the ornately carved pews of a wealthy church, gazing through tall stained-glass windows, and listening to an organ? Grace was wearing what could have passed for church clothing, but the long gathered skirt with matching tailored jacket and plain white blouse underneath were probably just her everyday wear.

The girl tried to flatten down the sides of her hair. She straightened the shirt and knickers that had twisted around her body in sleep, and as she sat on the bottom porch step, she folded her legs underneath her to hide her dirty feet.

"May I join you?" asked Grace and then pointed at the gate.

The girl hesitated, but Reena, her husband, and sons were just beyond the door, assuring her of safety, so the girl reluctantly nodded at Grace, who opened the gate silently and came forward, carrying a small traveling satchel in her right hand. She sat down next to the girl and then placed the bag on the step between them. "I've brought you some more things I thought you might like."

Grace opened the bag and pulled out another dress, this time one that was a pretty pale blue like the ocean in early morning with the first silvery sunlight glazing over it. She waited as Grace unfolded the garment on her lap, then handed it over and laid it gently into her own.

Even though she'd saved the yellow dress for only the best days, she'd been so hard on it that there were tiny tears along the hemline, a pink watermelon juice stain on the collar, and dirt smudges on the cuffs.

The blue dress was an even finer piece of clothing, a dress meant for parties or dances. The girl thought it much too fine for her; she'd have no place to wear such a thing.

"Try it on if you'd like," said Grace with a touch of a smile. "The yellow dress fit you quite well. I'm certain this one will, too, but if not, I'll have a seamstress make the necessary adjustments."

The girl looked at Grace and searched her eyes. Grace smiled again. "Go on and try it. I'll wait for you here."

The girl stood, crept inside Reena's door into the empty room that comprised the home's kitchen, living, and dining space, and she slipped out of the shirt and knickers and into the pale-blue dress. The neckline was much lower than she'd expected, baring the tops of her breasts, but the waist was a perfect fit, and she loved the way the gathering below the waistline made the skirt swirl and then settle with each of her movements, as if it were dancing. The material was shiny, silky, lightweight, and smooth on her skin. It smelled of that wonderful combination of lavender and vanilla, a scent she would always associate with the woman called Grace.

When she stepped back outside onto the porch, Grace turned to meet her eyes. "Why, it's lovely. Just lovely." She patted her gloved hand on the step beside her, and the girl sat down again. "I knew it would suit you. Now," she said and reached into the bag again. "I've some other things, too."

She thrust into the girl's lap a pair of pantalets, a camisole, a corset, a straw hat with blue flowers on the brim, and a new pair of stockings. The girl watched until the parade of finery ended. Then she touched each of the items with her fingertips and wished she could thank the woman with words.

"The only thing remaining is to get you a pair of good street shoes." Grace scooted closer and placed her own polished black boot next to the girl's foot. "I'm trying to gauge your size, if I might." She leaned so close that the girl could catch that scent again, that wonderful, sweet, womanly smell.

Grace straightened. "We're in luck. You look to be about my size in shoes as well. Next time we see each other, I'll bring you a pair or two. Would you like that?"

The girl nodded.

"Now for the really good part," Grace said. "I heard that you received the art supplies. Do you have them here?"

The girl understood that Grace wanted her art things back, got up, and retrieved the satchel from underneath the house. She returned to Grace's side and handed it over.

"Oh no," said Grace. "I don't want to take them back. I just wanted to see you with them."

This was too much, too much generosity. And yet the girl did want the art sticks and the paper pad. She opened the satchel and pulled out the art sticks, then lifted her palms as if to say, *I don't know how to use these things.*

"I'll give you lessons. We can draw together if you like. I mean, would you like that?"

The girl's vision momentarily blurred from this kindness.

"These are called pastels." Grace touched the art sticks. "You can create all sorts of colors of your own."

Knowing that her seascape was not good, the girl pulled out the sketchbook and opened it to her drawing anyway. Grace smiled when she saw it. "Very nice!" she exclaimed.

The girl pointed to the place where sea met sky and frowned, then followed with a questioning look into the woman's face.

"I see," said Grace. "You've been working to create light on the page. It's not easy, but it can be done. We'll work on that." The girl nodded. "Now," said Grace, "I've something else. I know you can write, because I've seen your handwriting. I assume you're able to read?"

The girl nodded again before she'd really thought about it.

"The poems you've been writing, why, I recognized them immediately. You're a fan of Emily Brontë." The girl didn't move. "Were you aware that you wrote lines of hers?"

The girl nodded.

"Here. I've a book for you." Out of the bag she pulled a small book bound in dark-brown leather. "It contains the works of Emily Brontë." She handed it over. "And might I ask, where did you hear of her?"

The girl looked up, wanting to shout, *From my mother!* Instead, she ran her hands over that smooth old leather and felt its warmth.

"Ah, but I've thought of that as well." Grace retrieved the last item from the bag, a board of slate with a piece of chalk tied to it with string.

"Here," Grace said, passing it over. "Now you can answer."

After taking the slate board on her lap, the girl touched it with her right index finger. Not for three years had she tried to communicate so directly with another person. There were those who could understand her by her facial expressions and gestures, but she hadn't tried to use words in all this time. She picked up the chalk, remembered the feel of it in her fingers from her days in school, and then set the chiseled end on the surface of the slate. What harm could come from this? She formed the letter *M* and then wrote the entire word, *Mother*.

Grace looked over. "So your mother was a reader of poetry?"

The girl nodded.

Grace breathed out deeply, smiled broadly now, opening her pretty face. "Now we're getting somewhere. And did she teach you to read and write?"

The girl shook her head and then wrote *School* on the slate board.

"Just as I had suspected. I knew you had been educated. I knew it." She waited for a moment. "But what happened?"

The girl shrugged.

Grace went on: "I must ask you," she said, her voice softening, "I must know. Why are you here?"

The girl didn't move.

"What happened to your family?"

Rolling the piece of chalk in her hand, the girl pondered answering the question truthfully. For years, she'd heard Reena's pat answer. Reena would tell inquisitive people that the white girl was only visiting, that her folks were away and would come back soon to fetch her. She could write out such a lie, and it would probably save her a lot of trouble. But after waiting for a few long moments, she finally wrote *Storm*, because it had been so long since the truth had been expressed. Holding her history inside had been such a lengthy, lingering thing.

Grace looked over and stared at the single word on the slate. Then a short sniff. Straightening her back, Grace darted her eyes away and then gazed back at the girl again. Her voice was a whisper. "Was there no one else who could take you in?"

The girl shook her head.

"I'm so terribly sorry."

The girl gazed away.

Grace said, "Have you never spoken?"

The girl shook her head again, this time with vigor.

"Did you stop speaking because of the storm?"

The girl gave a single nod.

Grace's mood changed from sadness to resignation. "I can help you."

In that long moment, a new sensation was beginning to surge through the girl, a premonition, something coming up in her throat. But there was such sincere determination in Grace's face. "I can. I can find you a home. A better place, a safer place."

The girl thought of asylums. She pictured herself chained to a steel bed in a room without windows, without light or sound, a place worse than death.

Surely this woman Grace wouldn't send her there, but Reena always said not to trust a one of them. She said you could start out with a well-meaning one and have that person overpowered by a mean one. Better not to trust the lot of them, she'd said. The girl shook her head, forgot about the slate she held in her lap, and pointed strenuously to the house behind them.

"I can see that someone has shown you a great deal of kindness. But I can do so much more. I have at my disposal the ability to make a real change, a lasting change, for you."

The girl listened.

"We could see a doctor—"

At that the girl stiffened. She picked up the slate and chalk and thrust it back into Grace's lap, anger firm in her movements and her back, which had gone rigid.

Grace appeared stricken. "I'm sorry," she said.

The girl held still.

Grace didn't move for a long time, either. "I see that I'm pushing you too fast. I regret what I said." She took a deep breath and let it out. "Truly I'm sorry."

The girl blinked.

"For now, let's simply be friends. How about that?"

The girl pursed her lips and then finally nodded.

"Very well. I have only one more question to ask of you. What, pray tell, is your name? I've asked around, and no one seems to know it."

The girl almost took back the slate and wrote it out for her. But Grace said, "Of course, in the newspapers you're known as Miss Girl—"

The girl pulled back again. Newspapers? Reena had mentioned something about newspapers, too, but what did the newspapers know of her? Fear knotted inside her stomach. She would not tell the woman, kind as she was, another thing. The girl stood up and pushed aside the satchel and the other things Grace had given her, this time with even more urgency.

Slowly Grace rose beside her, regret and worry written all over her tensed face. "I'm sorry again, truly I am. It seems I always say too much." She sighed. "But keep the slate, please. It's my gift to you, as are these other things. Nothing is owed in return."

The ocean wind picked up long strands of the girl's hair and sent coils of it flying. Out in the alley, sandy swirls had kicked up like ghosts at play.

Grace looked the girl over. "I'll see you again?"

The girl nodded.

Grace seemed reluctant to leave, but she walked down the steps and into the yard before turning. "Soon, I hope."

Watching Grace walk farther away, the girl would've liked to believe the odds would someday be in her favor, but the knot of fear still lived in her stomach, and she wanted the nice young woman, despite her dresses and her good intentions, to leave, to disappear into those sandy ghosts that blew up out of these alleys. Doctors and newspapers?

Grace reached the gate and let herself out. The wind whipped at her hair, too; long streams of it went flying like ribbons, freed from her hat. She plucked the stray ones off her face, turned back one more time, and said with a smile, "By the way, you look beautiful in the dress. Like any other girl."

Chapter Twenty-Five

GRACE

I walked into the office and told Ira, "You'll never guess what happened this morning. I talked with her."

After I placed a bag of donated clothing on the table, I smiled, remembering. "Well, *I* talked to *her*, actually, and she wrote to me. It was fascinating, and I learned the most tragic thing. All the members of her family died in the storm three years ago. She was left utterly alone."

Ira stood in his usual pose, hands clasped behind his back. His face was freshly sunburned again.

"She took another dress of mine, gladly, in fact, and some other things, too. She didn't seem terribly impressed with the poetry book; much more so with the dress and the art supplies I'd sent her way before, but that's only natural, a girl of her age. Then I pulled out the slate and began asking her some questions. She didn't hesitate to write back to me."

"Congratulations."

"Don't be so quick to congratulate me, however. In only a few moments' time, I managed to somehow frighten her. I'm not sure what I did. I offered her help."

"What sort of help?"

"I mentioned a doctor. She didn't like that."

"Many people are superstitious. They don't trust modern medicine any more than the quackery of the past."

"I realize that now. And another thing, Ira: she is the one the newspapers are writing about. The Miss Girl who runs the wall."

He looked baffled. "I'm sorry, but I haven't taken the time to read the newspapers lately."

I gave him the short version of the story. "It's no matter. Public interest should die down soon. I haven't told anyone else, and as far as I can tell, you and I are the only people who know she is the one."

Now he was wiping off his spectacle lenses, but he gazed my way with a smile. He was much more attractive without the hardening effect of his eyeglasses. I was sorry that he must wear them. "I'm surprised she would call so much attention to herself, or perhaps it was unintentional."

"Most definitely it had to be unintentional. Anyway, I do believe I've started something valuable with her. I do feel we have the beginnings of an open exchange."

"Good for you, then," he said, but he looked troubled.

"Are you well?"

"Yes," he said, then gestured to a letter on the desk. "But I've heard from a colleague of mine who has been working in the Rio Grande Valley, near Brownsville, on the border with Mexico. His father in Houston has taken ill, and therefore he must leave his post and come this way. And he writes of the most deplorable conditions. Most of the poor are immigrants from Mexico: penniless, starving, with sick children, and still they work, picking fruit for the most part, because it is all they can do to earn a living. I think he would like to switch positions with me."

Ira brightened, but it seemed rather forced. "As always, there are so many places in need and not enough of us to go around." He gazed toward the window wistfully, as if he could imagine himself leaving, flying free of complicated feelings. But perhaps I was flattering myself. He had served in many places before Galveston, though it staggered me to think that he would someday leave here as well.

My voice cracked when I said, "Of course." I had to think of something else or I would collapse. "Do you ever wonder, then, why all this suffering? I mean, do you ever question God or your faith?"

His shoulders lowered, and then his entire demeanor softened. "All the time. I question it all the time. But even though I don't understand everything about God's plan, I still must persevere and continue to work. That is how I get past the doubts."

"Such an honest answer."

"Faith can be fragile, even among those of us in the ministry." And then his voice was softer still, and his eyes were more open. "The biggest mistake is to try to go through it alone."

He moved closer, then took another step, which brought him right before me, and before I could breathe, he had wrapped his hand around my wrist, the most considered and caring of gestures. I smelled hair pomade and shaving powder and the scent of him, and in that moment I desperately wanted to cling to him again, to put my arms around him and lay my head on his chest, as one would lay one's head on a feather pillow. Sinking, falling.

My shoe squeaked when I moved my foot, and a floorboard creaked when Ira shifted his weight and moved closer still.

"Hold still," he said and then he touched my hair.

It came out of me too quickly to stop it. "Did I ever tell you that I am engaged?"

Something had been caught in my hair. A piece of a leaf, and Ira was removing it for me. His touch so gentle. He offered it, now on the tip of his finger, for me to see.

But his face fell as my words hit him, and there was an immediate sense of retreat. I was engaged; thus, it was too late for him already.

Too late for me, too. In my world, one did not break an engagement; to agree to marry was a solemn, almost-sacred promise.

Releasing my wrist, he stepped back and said, "No, I wasn't aware of that."

"I'm to be married next year."

He cleared his throat and blinked several times. "Then I give you my best wishes."

"He's a wonderful young man. His name is Jonathan, and we've been friends since childhood."

The walls made short popping and creaking sounds. When Ira said, "I shall pray for you a blessed union," they could have been the sounds of my bones breaking.

"Even our parents were friends."

His face showed the shock of this new information, along with a deep hurt. But there wasn't even a hint of sarcasm in his voice when he said, "How wonderful for you."

That evening I attended a party with Jonathan. After long days at the seawall and our separation from each other and our friends, he was almost desperate to socialize and spend the evening out together, and I was willing to go for his benefit. Additionally my impossible feelings for Ira demanded that I spend more time with my fiancé.

In the carriage on the way to the party, he told me, "Father will not let up. He continues to insist that I spend my days down at the seawall, observing this 'modern engineering miracle,' as he now calls it. But what I do is actually quite simple. I report back everything that I've learned about the wall, even some things I didn't learn . . ." He stopped and gave me a wink. "But he still doesn't find it enough. My education has not been satisfactory."

For me, the first two months of summer had passed quickly. I watched the sky blazing with gold and burgundy as the sun went down.

"Summer is well under way. It will be over before we have time to appreciate it."

Jonathan said, "You sound like my father."

"I'm sorry."

He folded his hands into his lap and kneaded them together. "And what about you and your days? How are you holding up? Are you tiring of the work yet?"

"Surprisingly, no. Even though Mother has released me from my obligation early, I don't want to stop. I find it rewarding. And I feel a sense of duty to the people and to Ira."

Jonathan seemed hurt, but he looked over at me and smiled. "Ira, is it now?"

I remembered why I'd fallen for Jonathan. He rarely took anything too seriously. "We agreed to use our given names on the first day we met."

"Very modern. But is he not a self-righteous bore? I've heard he is."

"Not at all."

"He probably goes to bed with a Bible and wakes up in a bordello."

I was surprised he would say something so crass. "Impossible."

"He's genuine?"

"Yes."

"Well, what do you know?"

"He's truly dedicated, and I find that true dedication is never boring."

Jonathan stared straight ahead, and his voice grew softer. "I'm worried about you."

Smiling, I tried to catch his eye. "Whatever for?"

His focus stayed on the street ahead of us, but his tone became serious. "The other day someone suggested, uh, made me think that . . . Well, since you haven't had a father, you might become attached to older men and their causes . . . more easily than others would."

I released a long breath. It was true that I held on to childishly idealized images of my father, of a man too perfect to stand up to the kind of scrutiny that the rest of us put each other through so regularly. But my work in the alleys was the most authentic thing I'd ever done. Jonathan's concerns were appreciated but unwarranted. "Ira isn't an old man. He's probably only about thirty."

"I didn't know that."

As we rode onward, the night air was warm and heavy around us, comforting as a blanket. "Don't worry about me, Jonathan. I'm fine."

He looked surprised as he turned to me. "Even with Etta . . . ?"

"Yes, even with Etta here, stealing all of the attention. She must need it. I only wish I could know her better. She remains so unknown to me."

"To us all."

"I've tried to regain my footing with her, but to no avail." A new headache began to throb at my temples. I shouldered the blame for the break with Etta, but she was choosing to maintain it. Viola had once called her "Etta the Aloof."

"Perhaps you should do something away from the house, just the two of you."

"Perhaps," I answered and then began to think about it, about the respite we would both feel if we were to finally clear the air. Maybe I would try again with Etta.

At the event, the unexpectedly cool evening floated me from face to face. I mingled and caught up on my friends' activities, enjoyed excellent food and entertainment, and was a bit surprised that I found so much pleasure being among my usual company. In fact, many times during the night my love for them welled up within me. Clearly my work with Ira had not taken away from my enjoyment of this other life. There was room for both inside me.

Later I saw Etta at the party, surrounded by admirers, of course, but it was now a smaller group of admirers. I managed to pull her aside and ask her to lunch with me the following Sunday after church, and she agreed. Then she walked about the grounds with Jonathan and me, and later we watched fireworks rocket over the city and erupt against the bowl of black sky, trailed by their smoky, weblike remains. The evening had been lovely, with Jonathan at my side, and a cleansing sense of relief washed over me, too, as I knew that I would perhaps soon make my peace with Etta.

Over lunch the following Sunday, I wasted little time with small talk, and as soon as the waiters had taken our order, I said to Etta, "I apologized once before when the wound was still fresh. I'm offering you my apologies again."

We were sitting at a table next to a picture window with views of the beach and the gulf beyond. Etta stared that way for a long moment. "It's not necessary for you to apologize again."

"I think it is."

"Your disclosure about my circus man did me no harm."

"Yes. I've noticed that."

"So, again, there's nothing to be sorry about."

"You're too gracious. Despite your protests to the contrary, I was wrong."

The waiter arrived with our first course, a seafood bisque.

I wished I could tell her about Ira. I wished I could tell someone. His hand on my wrist, his eyes when they rested on me. I had no one to talk to about it.

Etta accepted my apology once again but would not open the door. She would not talk to me, really talk to me. We ate the next course in silence.

Over dessert, she spoke of the house, the servants, and my mother's business. She wanted to know about the construction of the house, overseen by my father's father, how long we had lived there and how long Clorinda had been with us—for all of my life.

She always perked up at any mention of my mother. Finally she said, "Bernadette has spent several long days away from the house conducting business by herself, and although I have offered her my assistance, she always turns me down."

I set aside my spoon. Her rebuttal and this meaningless talk were too hard to swallow. I answered her unspoken question as best I could: "I don't know where she goes. She has always done business on her own, and I've always been relieved not to have to share it. Someday, I must learn to handle our affairs, but for now she takes on that chore and always has."

With a look of serious consideration, Etta pondered my answer and then went back to eating. I still did not know her at all, because that was obviously the way Etta wanted it. Etta and I would not recover from my mistake; the damage had been too deep.

Chapter Twenty-Six

The Girl

"Don't you be wearing that one, child," said Reena when she saw it.

The girl clutched the pale-blue skirt in both hands, as if to say, *You'll have to pry it off of me.* She had tried to wear the flowered hat, too, but found that it was too big on her head and the wind kept threatening to blow it away for good. She loved all of her new things, however, and had been familiarizing herself again with the poems of Emily Brontë. So many were sad, many about dying.

Reena shook her head and pointed straight into the girl's face, like an arrow. "Of course you like it, and maybe that nice lady meant to be nice. But it's no good. You be asking for trouble if you wear that one about."

The girl shook her head.

"Mark my word."

Looking down, the girl held still.

"Save it for a dress-up game, but don't you be going anywheres in that frock."

The girl nodded but didn't mean it one bit.

"You best listen to me this time."

She nodded again, hating to lie to Reena, but she had no intention of not wearing that silky blue dress and all of the new undergarments beneath it, too. It was, however, a hot thing to wear when the sun was bearing down, so she saved it for the evening. During the day, she wore her old discards on the boat with Harry, but she wasn't about to give up either of the dresses that had come from Grace. What Reena didn't know wouldn't hurt her.

After Reena had fed her a plate of her famous deep-fried shrimp, and when the air was cooling and the sun was beginning to melt over the Texas mainland, the girl slipped into the pale-blue dress, put the yellow bonnet on her head, and made her rounds about the alleys.

She visited old Madu and gave him some green cattails she'd found in the marsh, where she'd stalked a blue heron until she could see the gleam in his eye, and she also gave Madu a perfect sand dollar she'd found on the beach. Madu would cook the cattails and eat them like corn on the cob, and then he'd crush the roots for flour. He picked up the sand dollar and held it up to the waning light. "Well, this'd be a real fine one, girl."

Madu liked the whitest ones without a single nick or crack or chip. He'd told her once that they were the sea's good-luck charms. And the one she gave him on this day was as unmarked and perfect as any she'd ever found.

After leaving Madu, she took Harry a plate of dinner down on the docks, courtesy of Reena, and while Harry shoveled down Reena's food, he told her about the silver king tarpon some deep-sea man had caught that day out in the gulf. The giant fish had leapt six feet out of the water over and over as it attempted to lose the hook and free itself. She listened to the story until the sun went down and the stars came out.

Later that night, she walked back up Pier 19 toward the city at a slow, easy pace, swatting mosquitoes from her neck with the new white linen handkerchief she'd found in the bottom of the bag from Grace. Under the blue dress, her bare feet were light on the weathered wood planking, and she couldn't stop gazing down at the way the skirt flowed with each step like a series of waves. She tried to imagine the kind of life such a dress had known before and wished she could trust the young woman named Grace. She wished she could get a glimpse into her world.

The girl walked down to the dark end of the dock, where she could gain the alleys. Behind her, a guffaw, a throaty laugh, and a hoarse comment that she couldn't quite understand. She turned and saw three men, apparently dockworkers, but men she didn't know, new ones, not from Galveston, not friends of Harry's. In the moonlight, their faces were as ugly and pinched as crabs, with reddened, veiny, sun-scorched skin tracked with lines. They had sweat circles on their clothing and blackened hands as big as claws.

"How much?" one of them shouted.

Reena had been right. Men such as these three wouldn't have paid her any mind before, but now they were teasing her, asking her how much the dress had cost. Of course they knew she couldn't have bought such a thing. Of course they knew she'd received it through some act of charity. She turned away and walked faster.

"We're takers," said another man. "Don't you be leaving."

She kept walking, head down, her bare toes peeking out from beneath the blue skirt's frilly hem.

She smelled them next. On her heels now, an odor like day-old fish, brackish water, unclean bodies, and whiskey. She picked up her skirt and walked faster. They matched her pace, and she couldn't understand why were they so intent on catching her. She didn't know what they wanted, but she was old enough to sense danger.

Then a claw on her arm, spinning her around. "Like I said, how much?"

The biggest of them was standing there, his breath coming out in snorts like an angry bull with a smell like bitter, rotten milk.

Confused, she shook her head and wrestled free. Obviously they had mixed her up with someone else, but instinct was telling her to get away, and to get away fast. Her heart was hammering as if it would bound out of her chest, and her throat went dry. She darted looks about to see if someone she knew was nearby to help her. No one. Not a soul in sight. She took a step back.

"Don't come down here if'n you don't mean business."

The other two laughed.

Now sensing the wrong in it, the danger in those leering stares, she took another step backward away from their smells and hatefulness. Panic gripping her gut, she recalled a line of Brontë: *I know not how it falls on me.*

"Well, would you look at that? She's playing hard to get."

The men laughed again and glanced at each other.

Another one said, "A tease we have us."

They glanced at each other and chuckled even louder, their coarse laughter and breath stinking of tobacco and spit.

She took that opportunity to spin and run in earnest, the dress now hiked up all the way to her waist, the pantalets below giving her almost as much freedom to move as her old knickers once had. She tore down the first alley, then sought the even darker alleys, where she could find help or at least disappear.

But the men could move fast, too. They were never far behind, and as they gained on her, a kernel of fear exploded in her bowels and pulled into her center with the power of an undertow, then expanded, exploding until she was nothing but it, nothing but the fear of it.

She would not remember the clutch from behind, the jerking, the ripping sensation of being pulled around, the shove to the ground. She would not hear their grunts, their triumph. She would not remember where she was, the time of night, the position of moon or stars in the sky. She would not remember the taste of foul, parched mouths or the touch of calloused, black-nailed hands; she blocked it out by sealing her eyes and cocooning all else, until it was done and left nothing except the excruciating heat, the sizzling, blistering, scorching, suffocating heat and pain. Her breath weak, her silent voice an even more silent cry, and finally only the whine of a distant wind.

While she was held there, while it was done against her, she had thought of the moon snail. Such a lovely name for a creature, but one that drills into the shells of mollusks until it can digest the living creature inside. She darkened into black and then was nothing.

She should have kept that sand dollar, that pure white piece of good luck. She should have kept it.

Chapter Twenty-Seven

ETTA

First she had to think of a lie. It had to be a good lie, too, a plausible story, one that would explain her absence all day. She didn't want to claim she was going on an excursion with someone else, as she didn't want to involve anyone who might later contradict her story. Etta was well practiced at insinuation and avoidance, but she'd had little experience with outright lying.

Innuendo was another matter. For instance, everyone in her social circle now believed she was the famous Miss Girl, who had run the seawall. Etta had playfully let them believe it, but she had never actually claimed to be that person. There was a distinction. If people made mistaken assumptions, she felt no compulsion to correct them, especially if it benefited her to let them believe otherwise.

But concocting stories out of nothingness was more difficult. When she had lied to her mother to meet Philo, for example, she had eventually been caught. Etta decided to tell her aunt that she had been having some cricks in her neck, and that she planned to spend the day at the Galveston Athletic Club getting a massage and a vapor bath to see if the problem could be solved through relaxation. She would claim to have visited the tailor and milliner after that.

"Do you suppose you should see a doctor?" Bernadette asked. Etta was donning her hat and preparing to leave the house. They were standing in the huge marble-tiled foyer, where their voices sounded hollow.

"I despise doctors," Etta replied in a whisper.

"However, do you truly believe that only one day at the club will make a difference?" There was genuine concern in her aunt's eyes, and for a brief moment, but only a brief one, Etta experienced a twinge of remorse. Bernadette said, "Perhaps you should stay home and rest."

Etta tugged on her gloves and leaned forward to kiss her aunt on the cheek. "I need to try something else. Then I'll see how I am."

"I shall worry until you return."

"I'll be fine."

Her aunt looked resigned. "Have a useful day, then."

Useful indeed. If she were successful, then by evening she would return knowing so much more than she did now. She would know the reason for her aunt's mysterious visits to the place she thought of simply as the "plantation," for lack of a real name.

As the train crossed the bay, Etta gazed out over the water, a strange color on this day, a frothy gray green sitting under heavy, overcast skies. The evening before, she had allowed Wallace McKay to visit her, to call on her again, so to speak. Because she had already been in Galveston for over two months and hadn't yet been pursued seriously, perhaps this was going to be more difficult than she'd once believed. She couldn't afford to discourage Wallace now.

And besides, there was a new girl in town by the name of Jewel Ann Jones, whose name suited her well, Etta had been told. Jewel Ann was fabulously wealthy and did indeed wear jewels—rubies, diamonds, and pearls—according to those who knew her, and although Etta hadn't yet met her and assessed her personally, she already feared that this new debutante would turn out to be as bright and brilliant as her name indicated.

Wallace was more tolerable than most, so Etta had allowed him to come over after supper to sit with her again on the portico. But once he was there and once he had begun to make the usual small talk, Etta suddenly felt her clothes tighten, and the neck of her dress became scratchy and suffocating.

They had been sitting and watching the streetcars, the long, lazy evening splayed before them. It was all too quiet, too sedate. She grew fidgety. A ruckus of gulls crossed the vermilion sunset, their wings black slashes against the vibrant color.

Etta thought about what she'd be doing the next day, researching her aunt, and she wondered about herself, about where it came from, this desire to walk the edge between what might be considered a healthy curiosity and obsession. Because she loved her aunt—her aunt had made her feel valued and trusted, something her own mother had never done—and because she admired her aunt, she wanted to emulate her. Etta had to know everything.

She bolted from her chair, leaving Wallace sitting alone, and went to stand at the railing. She gazed beyond the lawn and then turned back to face a surprised-looking Wallace. "Oh, couldn't we please go somewhere?"

Wallace lifted himself with effort from his chair and moved to stand silently beside her, apparently too surprised for the moment to answer. He raked his hand through his hair, and his eyebrows hunkered down over his eyes. "I'll take you anywhere. Where do you wish to go?"

"I'm not sure. Perhaps even a ride would help."

"If it pleases you."

"Wallace," Etta said, glancing his way and trying to calm herself. "Please don't be so patronizing."

"Perhaps I should be rude instead."

Etta sighed, exasperated. "Is there nothing in between for you and your sort?"

His face was unmovable. "My sort?"

"All of you. You're so polite, so courteous."

"I didn't know that would offend."

She had hurt his feelings and alarmed him, too. His normally round face was more drawn than ever before. She was going out of bounds, and for no other reason than she was tense about the following day. "I'm sorry. I've had a dreadful day and I'm taking it out on you."

"I'm sorry to hear that you've had a bad day. You may confide in me if you'd like."

"There's nothing to confide." But Etta gulped. "Nothing in particular happened today. I'm becoming a little homesick, perhaps. I'm truly sorry, Wallace. You're being so kind, and here I am acting the beast."

Relief flooded Wallace's face. "Apology accepted."

Etta moved closer and looped her arm through his. "Shall we go somewhere, then? I'd be much happier in another spot."

"Of course."

They took a carriage to the Garten Verein and then strolled the groomed lawns among riotous flowers, but the place said to kindle romance didn't, and all Etta could think about was what she would be doing the next day. Visions of the plantation house drifted into her head from every direction.

Later they sat on a bench as the sun lost itself behind the trees and the cool of evening finally appeared to be seeping in. Yet again Etta dwelled on her secret journey of the next day, so deeply that she almost forgot Wallace beside her.

When he reached for her hand, Etta had pulled it away before realizing it.

He appeared stunned. He sat still for a long tedious moment and then clasped his hands together and leaned forward over his knees. His voice was barely above a whisper, and Etta did truly feel deplorable at that moment. "Why, then, did you allow me to call on you?"

She searched for an answer.

Wallace went on: "No doubt you've taken a look at most of what Galveston has to offer, and I thought you'd chosen me."

Etta finally found some words but hated them when she spoke. He so desperately needed her compliments, but his vulnerability had the opposite effect on her. Contempt instead of compassion. "You are more pleasing than most."

Wallace hung his head but managed a smile. "Sounds like true love."

And she had nothing left to say except "I'm sorry."

On the train the next day, Etta chastised herself for not doing more to keep Wallace in play. She had to remain in favor. She couldn't do anything to risk being sent back. Would her aunt be disappointed because she wasn't succumbing to Wallace? What would she advise? Etta remembered Bernadette had once said something about making everyone a favorite. Another brilliant piece of advice.

Crossing the bay gave her the feeling of leaving something large behind, and her remorse at acting so badly was an ache as big as these waters. When she stepped on mainland soil, it had the flat feel of going back home, and she didn't enjoy the association. She would need to be more careful, more prudent. She needed to find just the correct balance of encouragement, enough to keep Wallace interested, but not enough to keep others at bay.

Etta disembarked in Houston and wove her way among the random throes of humanity to hire a carriage. She had the sensation of being pulled in a specific direction, as if a rope were tied about her waist.

When the driver stopped on the road in front of the plantation, she told him to take the long drive to the house. He did so, and Etta sat waiting in the carriage, fanning herself with her hat.

Soon, a densely boned, wiry-haired woman, who looked so efficient she must have been the one in charge, descended the steps and peered into the carriage. She inquired of Etta's business, but this one was not the one she wanted.

Etta told her, "I was traveling by and was overcome by the heat. I asked my driver to pull under the shade of your lovely trees until I feel able to go on."

The woman straightened. "I see. You may stay as long as you require."

"Thank you," said Etta, still fanning herself.

The driver glanced back at her and then swiveled forward again.

Etta waited in the carriage until she saw a nurse pushing one of the patients out into a small garden area on the side of the property, not far from where Etta waited. But this one was too young and pretty. Etta had to wait for one who looked hungry.

She spotted the type she wanted in a half hour's time. A young woman dressed in a stained white dress emerged from the back of the house and pushed a different man in a wheelchair. This man's head lolled on his chest, and Etta thought she saw spittle dripping from his mouth. The nurse had brown hair with braids knotted at the back of her head, long loose hairs drooping around her face, and she was as lean as a coatrack, no color in her face. She was perfect.

A breeze gusted every now and then, and Etta released her handkerchief out of the window for the wind to float it away. Then she let herself out of the carriage and went after it. After retrieving the handkerchief, she checked for the gray-haired matron and then, with no sight of her, Etta walked straight to the nurse with the braided hair.

Up close, she appeared even hungrier. Etta tucked the handkerchief into her pocket and retrieved a small roll of one-dollar bills, some of the spending money her aunt was accustomed to giving her. "See here," said Etta to the young woman, whose eyes were etched around the corners in early lines.

No need for introductions. "You may have this money," she said, extending her hand so that the young woman could see it, "in return for some simple information."

The girl glanced at the money, and then she looked up at Etta with lifeless eyes. "I'll give it."

Etta went on to ask the nurse her questions, and in only a matter of minutes she had learned what was huge enough to shatter the sky above. It was more than she had ever expected, or guessed, or thought to imagine, more deceptive than even the schemes she used to read about in dime novels. If she had heard about such a secret, she would have proclaimed it unbelievable, but here it had been done. The powers of the very wealthy to do as they please with whomever and for whatever purpose were enormous. And the bigger the secret, the more effort required to hide it.

Slowly the wind scattered through the trees again, the sun broke through the clouds, and a cat prowled through a garden patch nearby. Etta studied the light. She now held a key that even Grace didn't have.

But as Etta retraced her steps back to Galveston, she thought hard. She had no plans to tell anyone; instead, the power came in holding the secret and keeping it deep inside her. Yes, the power came in the secrecy.

On the journey back, Etta couldn't help smiling, even though she wasn't heartless. She did recognize the inherent sadness in the situation. She remembered her aunt's earlier comment: *Living is costly.*

◆ ◆ ◆

Over the next week, Etta was tempted to share her newfound knowledge, to observe the silent shock on others' faces, but she held herself in check. She needed to woo Wallace back with her charms. Wouldn't it be fun to tell him what she knew? To confide in him? He would be honored, and it would draw them closer. The sharing of it could have fit nicely into her plans, but she resisted. This secret, after all, could keep her in Galveston for as long as she wished, and now that looked as though it could be forever.

Chapter Twenty-Eight
THE GIRL

Reena found her the next morning in Maurice's bed, curled up and shivering, even though the night had been warm. She thought the girl must have taken sick, and after she finished her morning duties in the front house, she sneaked away from the missus, made the girl some warm broth, and brought it to her in bed.

First Reena wiped the girl's forehead with a cool, damp cloth while she sat on the edge of the bed, her weight slumping the mattress down toward the floor. The girl was awake, Reena could tell, but she wasn't opening her eyes.

"Come on and look at me, now. Let me see what ails you." She touched the girl's forehead with a fleshy palm and gently stroked away loose hairs into long red strings on the pillow.

"Come on. Open up and let me see what's wrong with you."

The girl shut her eyes even tighter.

"I can't give you no soup with your eyes closed. We'll make us a mess here on this bed. Come on now. Open up."

The girl shifted her weight and finally did as she was told. Pushing herself back on her elbows, she lifted her body, then slowly opened her eyes to the hazy light. Peering into Reena's glossy black eyes, she felt the warmth from Reena's body, but there was a fog in her head.

Sunlight came through the window as if demanding some answer from her, but she didn't know the question. She had no clear memory of the previous night, only a vague sense of running, a noxious smell, rough skin. Perhaps she'd had a bad dream, a nightmare, one of those intense ones that seemed so real before she awakened with her heart pounding out of every pore in her body. Maybe it had only been that, just a terrible, terrible dream.

But she was changed, different. Her skin felt charged with something hot and itchy, as if she'd been sunburned. She crossed her arms and ran her hands over them, and there was an unpleasant prickling heat, blistering, as if the inner substance of her had been burnt. An awful ache pulsed in the place between her legs. She had a sense of heightened irritability, of being on edge, a sense of invasion she could never explain, even if she could speak.

I know not how it falls on me.

She looked into Reena's eyes, into those kind eyes, into the face of the woman who'd untangled her hair and bathed her face, who had tried to shelter her as best she could, and then came a moment of purest sadness and surrender. For some unknown reason, something was wrong with her, inside her. How futile had been all the effort and the faith that others had in her.

And then her heart beat rapidly in clear resolution of something she could never name. Despite the kind ones who'd done so much for her, it would not be enough. Even this good woman would not be able to protect her.

The night is darkening round me.

Nothing to do but wait until it ended, until it closed around her. She sat with that realization, with that clarity, which wasn't all sadness. Not all sadness. But she nodded to Reena, as if to say, *I'm all right.*

"Well, that's better." Reena's face relaxed, and she looked the girl over again. "You got a scratch on your face. How'd you get it?"

The girl shrugged.

"Probably you was up to no good." Reena leaned in closer. "It's not deep; it's not the thing making you sick. Maybe it was just a little ole bug you caught, and now you is mostly over it. Here," she said, offering up a spoonful of the soup.

The girl let Reena feed her the entire bowl. It was nice to be babied. She would've been embarrassed for Reena's boys to see her being fed in this way, but alone with just Reena, she let it play out long and slow.

Try as she might, the girl couldn't rouse herself for all of the day. Exhaustion would overtake her and lure her to nap, but then she would jolt awake with strange feelings of repulsion and nausea that she couldn't explain. When night finally fell, she wept for no reason. She had lost something; something had been taken from her, but what? It lurked before her like a shadow, but when she reached out to grab it, she pulled back with empty hands.

It had been but a dream. A bad, bad dream.

Finally she slept.

In the morning, Reena brought her food and fed her again, then told her stories of Maurice's antics at school. Finally the girl could go on living. Her skin was still hot, with the kind of heat that seared your heart and boiled your blood. But she could deal with the heat; the pain was easing.

When the bowl was empty, Reena asked, "Now, what else would make you feel better today?"

The girl gestured in the direction of the beach.

"No you don't. You can't go in the water right after you took sick. You be getting sick all over again. Mark my word."

How else could she rinse this heat off her body? The next best thing after surf bathing on the gulf side would be getting on top of that seawall again and looking out to her favorite place. She wanted it more than ever before.

"You best be staying off that wall, too. What you did before, outrunning those boys, why, it was all the front-house people done talked about for days after. They was all wondering who you were, what you looked like without your bonnet covering you up. No," she scoffed. "Now, you don't need to be calling all that attention onto yourself. No, ma'am."

The girl tried to argue with her eyes.

"That there's a fool's game, but you gonna go and do it anyways, isn't you?"

Making a pinched gesture between her thumb and forefinger, she communicated, *Only a little bit.*

"Well, at least you be telling the truth, now. Praise the Lord for that."

The girl looked down.

"I mean it. You must be growing up."

After diving into Reena's soft folds and holding still, she finally let go. Reena got off the bed, and the girl followed suit. She'd slept all day yesterday and two nights in the pale-blue dress. She shimmied out of it.

"Good," said Reena. "That dress has got dirty. You go on and wash it today, but don't you be wearing it outside the yard, you hear me?"

Something told her to agree with Reena's advice, to really agree with it, and so she nodded with conviction.

"Good," said Reena again.

After folding the dress and setting it aside, the girl donned her old shirt and knickers, which Reena had recently laundered and ironed.

"You been seeing that rich white lady still?"

She nodded.

"Good."

Reena had always wanted to keep her in hiding from everyone except a few trusted souls. The girl shot her a questioning look.

"That lady seem nice, better than the others. She help people, and she got soft eyes. And something has got to change 'round here. You can't be living down here in secret forever, girl. Someday you is gonna have to do something with yourself. Maybe that there nice lady can help."

The girl shrugged.

"I'd sure like to believe something good could come out of all this." She gestured around, but her face showed doubt.

It was almost as though Reena knew something, too, something she couldn't say aloud. Reena seemed lost in thought but then finally said, "Sure as shooting, nothing better has come up." Then she left the room and robustly went back to her work.

The girl walked down to the docks, sure that she was probably late and sure, too, that Harry would be waiting for her on the boat. She found him not out in the stern but down inside the boat's small cabin, sitting on the edge of the berth, his back curled over like a shrimp. He looked up, acknowledged the girl, and started to speak, but then a coughing spell began, one much worse than usual; one that bulged out his eyes, turned his face a strange color of bluish red, and brutally went on. Harry had been coughing for as long as the girl knew him, but she'd never observed such a lengthy spell that coughed out all the air from his lungs and left him gasping and ashy colored.

The girl sat down gently next to him on the berth. He'd stopped coughing for now, but he was gravely ill; she knew it from seeing two of her grandparents when they'd had the pneumonia in their lungs. But she didn't know what to do to help Harry. She should have brought some of Reena's broth to spoon into his mouth. Instead, she stood and poured him water from a brown jug he kept in the galley. Just as she tried to pass it to him, Harry started coughing again, a long stream of hacks and gasps and raspy, crackling, wheezing sounds that made her own chest ache to hear them. Harry was only nineteen years old—too young to be so sick.

She stood over Harry until it passed. Harry finally finished coughing and then ran an old stained handkerchief over his mouth. When he pulled it away and slowly set it on his lap, the girl saw fresh blood and stringy fibers that she could only imagine were bits of his lungs. She didn't know what it meant, but she knew with surety that people weren't supposed to cough up blood and pieces of their lungs.

She should have brought that slate Grace had given her. She would write out in bold dark letters, *hospital!*

"If you're thinking a doctor could help, you're wrong," said Harry in a hoarse voice, as if even the effort to talk was straining. "There's no help for it. I've had consumption since I was a boy, but it only got real bad lately." He nodded toward the rolls of tobacco lined up on the galley stove. "Light me one of those, will you? It'll stop me coughing."

The girl picked up one of the rolled cigarettes, put it in between Harry's colorless lips, and struck a match. When the flame reached the end of the rolled tobacco, Harry inhaled weakly, then held the smoke inside, and finally let it out in a narrow gray stream. "Thank you," he said.

The girl lifted her hands, as if to ask, *What else can I do?*

"I won't be going out on the bay today, if that's what you're thinking. I cain't do it. Got to wait for a better day."

She slumped back down on the berth beside him, disappointed not so much because she'd miss being over the water today but because now she was worried about Harry's ability to work.

"I'm going to lie me back down now, after I finish up smoking. You best go on and do something else today."

She sat for a few minutes longer and wished she could say, *I'll be back to check on you later*, but nodded instead, which he seemed to understand. Harry nodded back, and she climbed out of the cabin and then out of the boat.

The day was near perfect, with bright, unbroken sunlight and a cool wind that wound her hair into knots. She retrieved the bonnet from her pocket and put it on her head, tied it down low, and then headed in the direction of the gulf side of the island. She dropped by Reena's and changed into the yellow dress. It felt warm and soft against her skin, like something sunny.

Then she headed toward the stretch of beach that she favored for swimming, a stretch of beach she believed was where her father had built his souvenir shack before it washed away in the storm.

By the time she reached the sea, it was midmorning, and the gulf side was busy with bathers in surf higher than usual. It made rhythmic crashing sounds that sounded like a large animal breathing in and out. It was the kind of surf that redfish like—rough sandy water that comes after storms and quickly leaves. There was reassurance in that surging continuous sound, as if the ocean were saying, *All will go on.*

She wanted to hike up her dress and wade to her knees but decided to heed Reena's warning and not go into the water so soon after her illness of the day before. Instead, she walked the beach and found another sand dollar. It wasn't a perfect one, but it was large. She decided to give it to Madu, and then she found a spiraled whelk shell to give to Reena. But it was Harry who stayed on her mind throughout her long stroll.

No matter how hard she tried to part with the worry, she couldn't let go of the sight of that blood and fibrous stuff on the handkerchief; she couldn't set it free into the wind. She couldn't shake his pale, drawn face and that racking, frightening cough that stayed with her and weighed down her steps. The ring of a ship's bell sounded like a death knell.

At the seawall, a larger group of strollers than usual had taken to the top. The fine weather had no doubt drawn people out. In fact, there were so many of them, along with a few people on bicycles, weaving in and out and dodging the pedestrians, that she figured she wouldn't be noticed among such a throng. She wanted to look out to her favorite place again. After seeing Harry in such a state, she thought it might be the only thing to make her feel better. And she might be able to figure out how to create light with her pastels, as Grace had said, and then she could finish her drawing and give it to Harry.

She went in search of the same old ladder she'd used before and found it tossed aside in the riprap below the wall, out of sight of the people on top, obviously put there by someone else who didn't want to pay the boys to get up and down. She carried the ladder over to the wall. Again she climbed as high as she could, and then she used her strong arms to hoist her body up the rest of the way until she could gain the top.

Once up high, she stood and gazed out to the deep ocean, found her spot of soft, quiet brilliance, and managed to smile. She thought she saw the fin of a whale lift up and then recede back into the depths. There was a whole cloud of Franklin's gulls, hundreds of black-tipped wings cutting into sky. She set her eyes back out to sea. The searing heat beneath her skin cooled in the breeze. Something had changed her, but she didn't have the words, even if speech were possible, to verbalize it.

She turned to stroll for a while and then stopped dead in her tracks. Loud shouts came in her direction.

"There she is!" someone called. "There's Miss Girl!"

Another voice. "She's back!"

A tall man approached her and leaned down close to peer underneath her bonnet. She turned away and faced the blinding sunlight.

"Don't be scared," the man said in a voice that sounded smooth but not trustworthy. "Are you going to run away again?"

It took a minute to settle into her head—the gossip Harry had told her about, Reena's warnings, and what Grace had said about some Miss Girl in the newspapers. Her senses sharpened, and her skin tightened. What a mistake she had made to come up here again. Another mistake! She should've listened. She shook her head and tried to walk away, but others were coming toward her. She ducked her head and turned to her side so they couldn't see her face. But more people came, streams of them following in her wake, calling out to her, laughing, talking, and pointing.

She had no choice but to run again. She picked up her yellow skirt and darted in the direction where she saw less people, which turned out to be the same way she'd run before, down the length of the completed wall. The people in their fine clothes and pomaded hair all passed by in a blur.

Shouts of encouragement, commands for her to stop, cheers, and laughter, and soon it became not exactly fear but the sound of chaos too close and large in the world, all the energy too bright and anxious and compressing, trying to squeeze her through a slit. She ran all the way to the end of the seawall again, jumped off into the same pile of soft sand, once again absorbed the stunning landing, then caught her breath and vanished into the city, into the alleys, leaving a stream of joyous, pushing, pulling, and cheering humanity behind in her wake.

After running down the alleys for several blocks, she stopped and leaned against a wall to catch her breath. She didn't know what this all had to do with her. She, who had only tried to hide for the past three years, had now become the center of so much unwanted attention.

Minutes later she glanced up and into the eyes of the only outsider who could follow her into this world, the young pretty woman called Grace, who was sure to ask her questions. Still, when the girl gazed into Grace's kind face, her eyes so wide and elated and open, she couldn't be angry with the woman for following her. The girl kept breathing deeply and then shook her head and gave a look of defiance.

Grace's face fell. "I won't tell anyone. I've known from the beginning you were the one, and I haven't told anyone. Well, I told Ira—I mean the minister. But you have nothing to fear. Please, don't be concerned."

The girl shook her head again.

"But for someone who wants to be left alone, you certainly aren't behaving as such. If you run the wall like that, people are bound to be curious. Probably every woman I know is a little envious of your running like that and getting away. But people mean you no harm, I'm certain of it. They simply want to know who you are. You've piqued their curiosity. In truth, I think you've charmed them."

Wanting to cry. Suddenly so tired. Wanting to take the woman by the shoulders and shake her. Instead, she turned away. She walked in the direction of Reena's house. She no longer cared if the woman followed her. She hadn't been able to do anything to stop her. On this island, where people should never have tried to put down roots in the first place, on this flattened, sea-beaten, stretched-out strip of sand, there was just no place else for her to run.

Chapter Twenty-Nine

GRACE

Jonathan and I were hosting a small dinner party to include our closest friends: Larke, Wallace, and Viola. Summer was coming to a close; we were taking advantage of Jonathan's waning time among us. Of course Etta was to be included. It would have been difficult to leave her out, and I didn't want to slight her on top of all the damage I'd already done. She had at first responded favorably, but then at the last minute, as Dolly was curling my hair with hot irons at my dressing table, she rapped on my door.

Dolly stepped back when she caught sight of Etta, and I found it such a strange reaction, totally involuntary, as though Dolly had seen something that unnerved her.

"Come in," I said to Etta and smiled. She hadn't joined me in my room since the very beginning, and I imagined she wished to discuss the evening ahead. Informal as it was meant to be, it could still prove to be lively. I hadn't spent time with my dearest friends for almost all of the summer, and I missed it.

Etta said, "I regret it, Grace, but I do believe I'm going to have to miss your evening."

Stung, I said, "I'm so sorry."

"I'm not feeling well. There's a pounding in my temples I can't rid myself of."

But her dark eyes were dancing, as though she enjoyed giving me this news. Her voice was as brittle as ice, and her chin was slightly lifted.

Perhaps I deserved such treatment. I supposed an apology wasn't always accepted. "I'm sorry you're not feeling well. We'll miss you but will hope for your speedy recovery."

"Thank you," said Etta and turned to leave.

But I didn't want the conversation to end so quickly. "Shall I make my apologies to the guests? Or would you be able to see them, even briefly?"

Etta smiled in a halfhearted manner. "I'm not planning to dress for guests tonight. I'm certain you can handle anything that needs doing, Grace."

"Very well," I said, stung once again.

"But you may give my best to Wallace," Etta said in a lilting voice. And then she gave me a knowing little nod, her eyes certainly dancing now in light of this revelation.

"Wallace. Really?" I asked, so pleased that she had in some small way confided in me.

She didn't answer, but not answering seemed like a confirmation. Wallace indeed. Etta said only, "Do have a nice evening."

"Do take care and get well."

Etta smiled and left my room.

Over dinner, Etta's place at the dining table, which had already been set by the servants, remained empty, a glaring constant reminder of her absence. But my closest friends were as entertaining as ever, and I'd missed them. Jonathan was his usual charming self, and he directed the conversation, taking over what should have been my duty.

Wallace, the student of architecture, was speaking about his ideas for more brick houses on the island. "Buildings made of stronger materials fared better during the storm. And I find it ridiculous—ludicrous, truly—that so many flimsily constructed buildings and homes are to be lifted and then set back down in their original condition during the grade-raising." He shook his head. "Why not take this opportunity for improvements?"

And no one, not even Viola, who often had an opinion on everything, could offer a reasonable explanation. Wallace shrugged it off, and I admired his relaxed manner.

Until Etta's name was mentioned.

Over our fruit dish before dinner was served, Viola said, "I see that Etta has been unable to join us."

"She isn't feeling well."

"Ah," said Viola with skepticism in her eyes, and Wallace had stopped eating. His face had paled. Clearly he was infatuated with Etta and didn't want us to see it. But he was ever so obvious, the poor boy.

"She suffers from headaches," I said. "But she sends her best." And I tried to single out Wallace with my gaze. Maybe that would make him feel better.

"I see," said Viola, who looked around at the others. "Perhaps we aren't interesting enough. I get the impression that Etta is easily disengaged."

Larke giggled, as she always did.

Then Jonathan touched the pox scar on his cheek and said, "Perhaps it isn't boredom but intimidation. She's still new here."

How kind of Jonathan to say so. It was the sort of thing he would say even if he weren't so taken with my cousin. And how fond I was of these traits in my dear friends, whom I'd almost forgotten. A little ache entered my chest.

Viola said, "Come now." There was strength in that unfortunate pointed chin of hers. "I doubt that Etta is ever intimidated by anything."

"I agree," said Larke. "And besides, she's probably exhausted. She ran the wall again today. Have you heard?"

I stopped eating.

Jonathan answered, "Yes, it was the talk of the town once again. Miss Girl ran the wall and eluded the boys—all of us, in fact."

Larke picked at the fruit. "It must be tiring."

Viola harrumphed.

"Wait a minute," I said, confused. "What are you saying about Etta and the so-called Miss Girl?"

Larke pushed aside her fruit dish and tossed back her long curls. "Why, they are one and the same, didn't you know? Everyone believes it's your cousin, although she never altogether admits it. I think she likes to keep us guessing."

"Naturally," said Viola.

"But Etta is not Miss Girl," I said before I'd thought it through.

Everyone had stopped eating now. Perhaps this assumption had been a part of Etta's continued allure, and I immediately wished I hadn't said it. But now their interest was piqued.

"Why do you say this, Grace?" asked Jonathan.

"What do you know?" asked Larke, and Viola and Wallace were both holding still, listening.

I sat back and silently put my fruit spoon down. How easily I had almost revealed the real Miss Girl. "I suppose it doesn't matter. Let people believe as they want."

"Of course it matters," insisted Viola, who had never trusted Etta anyway.

"Tell us, Grace," said Wallace, finally joining in.

How was I to get out of this without saying too much? "I can't tell you who the real girl is, but I know her from my work in the alleys. I know for certain who it is because she wears a yellow dress I gave her, one that used to be mine. It isn't Etta, but the real Miss Girl doesn't want to be revealed, so let's let the matter drop. What harm could come from Etta allowing others to believe she's the one?"

Viola made a snorting sound. "I would have predicted no less of Etta."

Larke laughed, and then I looked up to see disappointment in Jonathan's eyes. Here I had said yet another thing about Etta that I shouldn't have. If only I had kept the information to myself.

The only person to whom I could talk about it was Ira. "I saw her again," I told him the next morning in our office.

"Did you?" he said.

But I couldn't return his smile.

"She ran on the seawall again, and just as before, there was much commotion and excitement. She eluded everyone and ran this way, into the alleys. I had already taken the children back and sent them home. So I was able to follow her this time."

I remembered how she had disappeared down the crowded alleys, weaving soundlessly through all the wagons, horses, and running children, how she moved with ease like a fish in water. My body had seemed large and cumbersome compared to hers as I struggled to keep up.

But the worst shock had come when I finally caught up with her and saw the look on her face. Even in remembering it, I experienced the sensation again, of being stabbed, my breath hard to find. "She looked angry with me. She didn't want to see me. I fear I've done something wrong again."

"Grace," he said and studied my face. "I'm remembering the boy I tried so hard to help. His name was Quinn."

"But it isn't the same situation. This is different. It will turn out well."

"It's worrisome, the fierceness with which she is resisting. Perhaps you should heed her wishes, Grace. But you made a fine effort. That's what matters."

"It matters to me that I do more."

"But perhaps you've done all you can."

I glanced away. There was something there, something special in what I felt for the girl. But could I be doing her wrong? Ira had cautioned me to be cautious, advice I had not heeded. I experienced something like a premonition then, a sense of foreboding.

"I was wondering . . ." said Ira.

I looked his way, not really hearing, until he said, "Do you know anyone who might wish to join us here in this work?"

I gulped, taken aback, completely unprepared for such a request. I'd had no idea he meant to add to our numbers.

"There are so many needs, as you know," he said. "And perhaps one of your lady friends would be interested in assisting me, too."

"Of course," I said automatically. Of course, and why hadn't I thought of it myself? Viola came instantly to mind. Viola, with her sensible nature and wisdom, would be perfect. But I didn't want to share this experience; I didn't want to share Ira. But he was suggesting just the opposite, seeming to hint that we not spend our time alone anymore. And why wouldn't he? I was engaged, and things had transpired between us that shouldn't have.

Viola was not attractive, but her lack of beauty wouldn't discourage a man such as Ira. He would recognize her fine qualities. But the walls were crumbling around me. Everything was being reduced to rubble, and I saw myself standing in the center of it, empty-handed and alone.

The evening before, after our guests had left, I had mentioned to Jonathan that Wallace McKay was finally Etta's choice, that perhaps she hadn't joined us because she was toying with him a bit. He wouldn't look at me. He didn't respond. We were sitting on the front portico, and after I told him I thought they would enter a courtship, he stared bluntly ahead. He was crushed by my news.

I had never doubted Etta's appeal. But I hadn't expected the pure pain on Jonathan's face when he learned that she had finally accepted another young man's advances or was preparing to do so. Jonathan had fallen even more deeply under the spell of her charms than I had imagined. His obvious care for Etta was piercing, humbling. I sat back and said in a whisper, "You're in love with her, too."

He shook his head, and I watched him fight off his feelings. "No, you're mistaken. I'm not in love with her, but perhaps I should tell you something. Recently my mind has played some tricks on me."

I sat still. "What do you mean by tricks? Unexpected feelings?" I, after all, knew only too well about such tricks.

Jonathan didn't answer me directly. "This summer, spending so much time at the wall, under my father's direction for these long months—well, it has made me feel helpless. I feel as if I'm being pushed backward instead of forward."

"Etta won't settle. Nor should you."

His voice broke as he whispered, "What do you mean?"

"Etta most likely wants money and love, and you could provide her with both."

The loud *chack* of a mockingbird called out in the night. "She doesn't love me. And besides"—he turned to look at me now, much of the hurt on his face already forced away—"I love you. I always have."

He wasn't exactly cold, but I couldn't say that his words struck me as warm and truly loving, either. He leaned forward to kiss me, but even that moment of tenderness felt forced.

When the kiss was over, I asked him, "What if we were not engaged?"

He looked away and wouldn't answer.

"What if we've made a mistake? What if we've mistaken friendship for more than that?"

Staring ahead again, he shook his head. "I can't even consider it."

I wondered what truly mattered to Jonathan; probably the same things that mattered to all the young men we knew—pleasing his parents, graduation, then settling down and becoming successful. Maybe those things were more important to him than true love. "Perhaps we should reconsider."

He shook his head again. "I've failed at other things, but not this."

"Loving or not loving a person should not be viewed as failing or not failing."

Jonathan sighed. "We made promises to each other."

The night was as dark as the sea depths. All shade and definition were gone. I said softly, "But promises sometimes need to be broken."

I touched his hand. We sat without talking, and when he left me, he didn't kiss me again. He asked me to promise that I would attend a dinner upcoming on Saturday, hosted by friends of his parents, the most pretentious people, who had invited a group over to hear about their latest jaunt to North Africa. It seemed to mean a great deal to Jonathan that I go with him, so I would accept my invitation when it arrived.

"What is it, Grace?" Ira was now asking me in such a quiet voice I almost didn't hear him. Sunlight was pouring into the window and spotlighting a large rectangle on the floor. I couldn't take my gaze off it.

Finally I looked his way. "What? Oh, nothing." I shrugged. "At least, nothing that won't work itself out."

His eyes clouded over, and he forced a tone of levity. "Darkness on this bright island?"

My smile quickly faded. Ira and I were lost, too. "You of all people know there is."

He paused. "Of course. I meant within you."

"Some darkness is inevitable."

"Perhaps."

I wished I could talk to him, but once we spoke of it, there would be no stopping. I couldn't even hold his gaze for long. I couldn't face his eyes, couldn't face these feelings that could launch me into his arms. I could slip with one word.

Outside, low clouds were moving in, and a distant boom of thunder rattled the windows. Clearly it was a good thing that Jonathan and I had had another year to decide if we were right for each other. I had not gone looking for uncertainty, but it had crept up on me with the cunning of a cougar and then ensnared me in its claws.

Chapter Thirty

ETTA

Tilly and Matthias Christiansen lived in an enormous Victorian house on Fourteenth Street, complete with filigree trim and several octagonal windows, where they were hosting a dinner party. When Etta accepted her invitation, she sent a note to Tilly asking to be seated next to Wallace at dinner. She planned to use the opportunity to regain his interest, and that task, in turn, would help break the monotony of hearing about the Christiansens' North African journey.

Tilly wore a bun like a knitting ball and a preposterous hat topped with papery fruit that seemed half the size of her torso. Despite her finery, she managed to float the scent of something musty in her wake.

Matthias was much easier to swallow, with his large head, quiet methodical movements, and dark pomaded hair striped with silvery bands. But his hands were gnarled from arthritis into odd nutlike formations that Etta was strangely drawn to studying.

The evening began with champagne and finger sandwiches on the back terrace, where the guests had a chance to look through the Christiansens' photographs and treasures brought back from abroad. Before the group moved inside for dinner, Tilly had already begun to describe the weeklong trip across the Atlantic aboard the *Celtic*, with its splendid meals and informative lectures.

In the dining hall, Etta noted that Tilly had obliged her request. Etta was seated next to Wallace, and on this evening he looked particularly dapper. His hair had recently been trimmed, and Etta had the strange urge to touch the newly revealed white skin behind his ears. In the warm light given off by the candles, his skin appeared particularly supple.

While Tilly went on to describe the first stop on their journey, Funchal, the capital of Madeira, an island off the African coast, the salads were served. Grace and Jonathan had both attended this little gathering, an unusual outing. They sat across the table, only a few chairs down on her right.

Tilly was raving about Funchal's clean stone streets and the Catholic cathedral where it was rumored that Christopher Columbus had married. Next, she said, they went onward to Gibraltar, Algiers, and Malta. Tilly paused to eat her salad before moving on to talk about what she said were her favorite spots: Athens and Egypt.

Etta finally had a chance to converse with Wallace. "Do you enjoy going overseas?" she asked him.

Wallace was dressed in what appeared to be a new suit tailored just so, and that, combined with the effects of the new haircut, made him look perhaps even a bit handsome. "With friends, yes. With my family, no."

"Why not with your family?"

"They move too slowly for me. My father wants to linger for days in one museum, and my mother will stare for hours at a single painting, whereas I want to see it all, everything a new city or a new place has to offer."

Etta smiled and leaned closer. "I prefer your way. I think I would enjoy traveling with you."

He barely glanced at her as he lifted the fork to his mouth, chewed thoughtfully, and swallowed. He said rather flatly, "You flatter me."

"Not at all," said Etta. "If I had to choose a companion for a jaunt overseas, I would want it to be you."

"You don't say."

"Oh, but I do." Etta lowered her voice and said, "Perhaps just the two of us."

Wallace put down his fork, and his face colored. "Your aunt would never allow you to go without a chaperone."

Etta cocked her head to one side and moved closer. "But I'm speaking of wishes, dear Wallace, of desires that have little to do with what my aunt would want for me."

Wallace kept his eyes averted, and Etta realized something that startled her off her game. Acting the temptress was not working. She watched Wallace gulp and sensed him pulling away. Something had changed between them. She had been too harsh that day at the Garten Verein. Now he was acting politely and nothing more.

So, this would be more work than she had anticipated. A sharp edge of panic entered her chest, and she drank her champagne with determination to dispel it. Then she whispered near his ear, "Tell me something no one knows, Wallace."

He let out a short laugh.

She made her voice breathy. "Tell me of your desires."

He grimaced. "You toy with me."

"I want to know."

"No. You must have heard about Jewel Ann."

Etta's breath caught in her chest, and she sat back. "Jewel Ann Jones? I've heard nothing about her and you."

"We are on our way to courting, one could say."

A shiver rode up her arms, and her heart hammered in a frenzy of panic and fear. If she could lose Wallace, she could lose everything. Her appeal, her aunt's admiration, and even her life here. She could never go back to mediocrity. Never!

"Why, Wallace, didn't your affections make quite the sharp turn? Wasn't it only a week or two ago that you were showing feelings for another? Namely me?"

"Ah yes, but I don't take rebuff so well, I'm afraid. And the girl caught my fancy before I knew what was happening to me. The turns of the heart can be ever so fickle."

Etta fought to keep her composure. She didn't take rebuff so well, either. She lowered her voice, and all the play had left it. "You should have told me."

"I thought you would have heard by now."

Fickle indeed. The bite of rejection was a new intense sensation under Etta's breastbone. Even though she had never been in love with Wallace, the fact that his attentions had turned elsewhere was a cruel blow.

Etta accepted an offer of more champagne. During the main course, although Matthias took over most of the travel oration, describing the Acropolis and the Parthenon, the Olympic Stadium, and then onward to Constantinople, Etta couldn't listen. The words drifted in the air like a funeral toll. All she wanted was more champagne. That fluid full of bittersweet bubbles was the appropriate flavor for the moment.

She was having difficulty eating, too. The light in the room looked cheerless, and then even more panic crept into her chest, constricting her breathing. If she could so easily be replaced in Wallace's affections, then what of the others?

Later, small groups at the table aborted the endless talk of the Christiansens' journey and delved their way into separate conversations. Down the table, more talk of this Jewel Ann, who was said to be so rich and so wild that she ran her carriage during the day with only white stallions, then had them changed to black stallions for the night. Always she wore bright colors and enormous hats.

Etta drank more champagne. The light in the room took on a muted quality, as if a layer of smoke had filtered in. She eavesdropped on other conversations and felt herself growing distanced, the voices slurred together. Smiling faces appeared clown-like.

On her right, the conversation was centered on Grace and her charity work. Grace was saying how interesting poor people were. Etta let out a loud sigh. Wallace glanced her way and cleared his throat.

More boring and pointless chatter. She found herself listening not to the words but instead studying the way each one was formed. Some people smiled between their words, others paused, and still others curved their mouths around the words. Strange inflections and different kinds of laughter left a sour aftertaste in her mouth.

Some fool had asked Grace to elaborate on the personalities of the poor. It wasn't Wallace but the young man whose graduation party she'd once attended. She remembered now. He smoked a pipe, and his name was Neil. He asked Grace, "Interesting in what way?"

Grace was basking in her moment. "Each is unique. They are less concerned with protocol and manners and more concerned with each other."

"Truly?" asked another person.

Etta stared at her cousin. Saint Grace was looking a bit desperate. She was working to hold the others' waning interest and to counter their disbelief that the poor could be interesting. "There's an old voodoo man, and women who make stuffed crabs and hawk them, and children who make do with so little."

Someone responded, but it sounded like a murmur to Etta. There wasn't an interesting conversation at this entire enormous table, covered with nauseating food. Instead, she sat still and gulped more champagne.

She didn't listen again until the conversation had turned to Miss Girl, and many eyes turned her way. Finally she would get some attention during this dreadful evening.

"How do you do it? The jump is so . . . far down," someone was asking her.

Etta perked up and immediately played coy, so natural and so easy for her. Back to the way she should always be, in the center of attention. "I've no idea what you're talking about."

The faces turned her way, and people smiled and gave little nods.

But then Wallace said, "Etta is telling the truth. She truly has no idea what you're talking about."

A moment of silence then, and Etta stopped breathing. Wallace went on for all to hear. "She, in truth, is not the real Miss Girl. It's someone else, and in fact Grace knows her."

"Then who is she?" asked Neil as he turned in Grace's direction.

Etta closed her mouth as even more eyes turned away from her. Yet another insult. Another slight. She wouldn't claim to be the true Miss Girl; she had never claimed it, but it had been promising to let people believe it. It had buoyed interest in her. And what had Wallace said? Something about Grace?

Grace was trying to act as if this were nothing serious. She said, "It's of no consequence." But in fact she shot Wallace a darted glance that silenced him. She seemed panicked. Etta gazed at her cousin's face and saw its disingenuous naïveté. Apparently Grace was going to pretend that it was the most innocent thing in the world to correct the assumption that Etta was Miss Girl.

"But is it true?" someone had asked again. "Do you know the real girl?"

"I do," said Grace dimly, looking down. "But that's all I can say on the matter."

Here was another thing meant to harm her. Grace had done it again! Just when she needed this attention, Grace stole it away. Etta took another long gulp of the champagne.

"Who is she?" someone asked Grace.

"What is her name?" asked another.

"I'll say no more. She's a reserved person. She likes to keep to herself."

Etta felt a cold distance from all of them. The child no longer asked to play, who sat on the sidelines and watched, only watched. Etta's anger was thumping up inside her mouth by then, forcing out the words that she had sworn to herself not to say, words that under any other circumstance she would have kept to herself. But spite won a big battle inside her. Etta said, "Grace knows nothing."

All heads turned her way. She must have spoken much louder than intended. Her scalp was numb, and her own voice had a gruff and slurred quality. "She doesn't even know the whereabouts of her own father."

Time stopped. A cold, quickening silence hung in the air.

Etta's head spun. The light in the room was charged and dense. A little laugh sneaked out of her.

Someone said in a shocked whisper, "He's dead"; it must have been Jonathan, coming to Grace's defense.

"No," said Etta. "That's the most interesting part. In fact, he's alive in an asylum. What everyone else doesn't know, but what I have managed to find out, is that my long-lost uncle is a madman."

Chapter Thirty-One

GRACE

Everyone was staring at me.

At first, Etta's words floated past me, unreadable. What preposterous thing had Etta said? Later I would think of the careful expression I had put on my face. My reserve was so well practiced. My mother couldn't have done it better herself.

But inside my head thoughts whirled like a tornado, and a small secret space that was tailor-made for shame and fear and disbelief was suddenly packed with too much turmoil to hold. My face never released its false appearance of calm, however—that mask I had been trained to wear.

Jonathan stood up beside me and tossed down his napkin. "What a ridiculous thing to say, Miss Etta Rahn. I fear you've had too much to drink." Then sweet, kind Jonathan turned to me. Thank God he was there.

I could've coolly accused Etta of lying, but instead I rose from the table, excused myself, and found my way to the empty foyer. All sorts of confusing thoughts and memories built pressure in my face, behind my eyes, and there was something noxious in the air of that house.

Jonathan was close behind me. "Do you want to leave?" he whispered to me when we were out of the others' hearing range and alone. I nodded to him instead of speaking, and he went in search of the butler to fetch our wraps and summon the carriage.

We rode back to my house in a kind of stunned stupor; the only comments I remember Jonathan making one-word expressions of his dismay at Etta's behavior, such as "Shocking" and "Unbelievable." The skin on his face was stretched as taut as a drum.

Above us, the night sky was dark and cold. I shivered against the upholstery although it was warm. We passed brittle grass and weeds, listing in the moonlight, trembling in the fragile, dark air. I asked the driver to go past the gulf, and I got a glimpse of the ocean. The light of a soft-edged, nearly full moon caught on swells in a line that went straight toward the dark horizon, a quicksilver path showing me the way.

I don't remember sorting through what I'd heard by any rational means. But as preposterous as Etta's accusations had sounded to others, they didn't sound so to me. A stunned quiet filled me, a complicated truth that I could feel in rising, hushed memories. And I was certain of one thing: shame this deep and fear this gripping had to have some root in truth.

In fact, he's alive, in an asylum.

The few memories I'd had of my father contained an element of the unusual, of distance, of dreaminess, of tripping on the stairs and laughing about it, of studying ants and leaves. And the more I remembered, the more what Etta had said terrified me. Perhaps when Clorinda had said my mother was "too soft for dis here world," which never fit my mother, she had been talking about my father instead.

The shudders continued to rise and arrive on the surface of my skin. And then other memories began flooding me, washing over me in cold, clear waves, young memories that had easily been suppressed, memories of a gentle man who didn't seem of this world. Now the few things I remembered cast a new light.

How had Etta come up with this? How could she know that which I did not? She could only have learned through her mother; the secret must have been shared between her and my mother. They must have held on to a sisterly connection I knew nothing about.

When we arrived at the house, a thin layer of condensation coated the windows of the carriage like a veil of deceit. I told Jonathan, "Leave me, please."

"Grace."

"I mean it. Please. I must talk to my mother alone."

He looked overcome. "Grace, I must tell you something. I've always heard rumors of something mysterious about your father's death. Not what Etta put forth, but people have always wondered. Apparently it was all very sudden and unlikely."

I took his hand and squeezed it. "Thank you. But for now it is Mother who must answer my questions."

I stormed my way up the stairs, fully aware that the coming moments were most likely going to disintegrate all I'd known as true. I charged directly to her room after entering the house, past everything we owned, now seeming stained and tainted, while the servants stood about, stilled by my early return from a party that was supposed to last the evening and by my obvious rage.

I must have looked miserable, because when I took one last glance behind me, both Clorinda and Dolly stood on the landing below, gazing up at me. Clorinda appeared fraught, and Dolly was wringing her hands.

I found my mother upstairs on the settee with a book on her lap. This was the place she had painted herself into, her secret corner.

I concentrated on putting one foot before the other. Mother glanced up as I entered the room, and the expression on my face must have been telling, disastrously telling, for she dropped her book, and her face fell in shocked anticipation.

"Etta says that my father is alive and in an asylum. Is it true, Mother? Is my father alive?"

She looked stricken, which scared me, and then just as quickly she recovered. She straightened herself and then patted the edge of the settee, requesting me to sit. "Of course it isn't true. Let's talk."

"No, Mother, I won't sit down. Just tell me now, because I don't believe you. I'll find out if you mean to deceive me on this. Don't let me find out you've lied to me again."

"Lower your voice, Grace. I'll explain."

"Explain away," I said but refused to sit.

She forced a resigned, sensible expression on her face. "You've been the recipient of malicious gossip. Something like it circulated long ago, and I had thought it was over. Who said this to you?"

"Etta, but it doesn't matter who told me. I know *you're* lying. I can tell by the way you're avoiding my eyes and becoming tense."

Mother appeared stunned but said calmly, "You're upset and taking it out on me."

"Mother, I swear if you don't tell me the truth now, I'll walk away from you and never look back."

"Don't be ridiculous."

"Tell me the truth, Mother."

I had never talked to my mother in such a tone, and her face reflected disbelief. I stood, waiting, as the clock ticked, and for long moments we remained locked with equal amounts of determination. Then something odd flashed across my mother's face, perhaps the first realization that she was going to lose this fight. I watched as she moved through denial, fear, and finally arrived at some point of resignation. She'd hidden her deception for so long, perhaps she'd never imagined herself in this moment, when all would be inexorably revealed. But here she was; the truth was written all over her.

She slumped back, her face pale. Mother looked about the room, as if gathering strength from her possessions, and then she closed her eyes in a way that appeared like prayer. Finally she opened them and gazed up at me directly, her eyes pained but steady. "I wanted to spare you."

She was a stranger to me. Completely unknown. "Spare me?"

"What I did, I did out of love for you."

There was too much desperation in her voice for that to be true. Truth was apparently something my mother could enter and leave at will, like walking through a door. "You told me he was dead when he's not, and that was for love?"

"In my position, you would have done the same. I was in a terrible spot. Listen to me . . ." Her fingers were white-knuckled and gripping the arms of her settee. "He was fine, perfectly fine, when we married. I envisioned nothing but a glorious wedded life ahead of me, and then he began to slip. Nothing monumental in the beginning, but as the years went by he became more and more confused and incapacitated. Soon I was handling everything, and he rarely went out anymore. I couldn't trust him to run a simple errand. When he did go out in public, he would act strangely, either mired in silence or starting all kinds of talk with anyone he met, and I didn't know what to do. Oh, Grace, do forgive me. You don't know what torment I've been through."

"You?"

"And you, too. I was thinking of you, of your safety. I remember once he was letting you handle an oleander leaf. Of course you know that oleander is poisonous. But he couldn't make the simplest judgments."

"Where is he? Locked away someplace?"

"I found the best care possible. He's looked after and kept well, and no one has been hurt for it."

My voice rose, shrill. "I have been hurt. I grew up without a father."

"He couldn't have been a father to you. He can't even take care of himself. And I didn't want you to be humiliated, shunned by others, and thought of as lacking."

It all made sense to me now. My mother had always talked more about her courtship with my father than the marriage. "I'll be the judge of whether or not he can be a father to me. You sent him away not because you couldn't take care of him here, but because you wanted to hide him."

New lines were etched beneath her eyes like commas, and the corners sagged as she looked at the truth. "I'll grant you that. It was some of both."

"But more so because you wanted to hide him."

At first she seemed surprised at my insistence, but then her face crumpled. Two tears streaked down her face and shimmered in the lamplight. I was glad for the moment that I had hurt her. Every inch of me quivered with my right to be justifiably cruel after what she had done. So elaborate a deception. So carefully plotted.

"I guess I deserve that. You're right. It was primarily because it was so, so"—she searched for the right word, her voice sounding hollow in the room—"humiliating."

And so the truth at last. Easier for my mother to arrange the world to her liking than to accept something so powerfully *less*.

"Would you have wanted to grow up with a child for a father?"

"I don't know, but I wasn't given that choice. How did you do it? How do you fake someone's death?"

She sniffed. "I took him to New Orleans to see a specialist; that much is true. But the doctor said he was beyond help, and I couldn't just bring him back here. People were beginning to talk. The doctor suggested the home outside Houston, where I took him for care and safety, and then as I was taking the train back to Galveston by myself, the idea struck me. I could simply say he'd fallen ill in New Orleans and had died. It solved everything. I did nothing illegal, Grace. I never executed his will; I had been handling things for years, so I simply continued doing so. I told people he didn't have a will. His parents were dead and he had no siblings. No one questioned me. I've always visited him and made sure he was treated well. And no one has been able to spurn you because of it." After her explanation, she sat quietly, crying.

I lingered, not sure if I was supposed to comfort her or leave, and in a few minutes, as the enormity of this news sunk in, as this new truth fully struck me, I didn't want to watch another moment of her pain unfolding. My pain was a huge teeming bay that left no room to float hers. I couldn't stay another moment in a home where appearances were more important than the truth.

I left the room and flew back down the main staircase, whisking past Clorinda and Dolly, past their frozen faces, but then I stopped. They deserved to know, or perhaps they already did, but I said it anyway, in recognition of their loyalty and steadfastness and years of devotion to us.

"My father is alive."

Dolly's face reflected shock, but Clorinda's did not. Clorinda of course had probably helped my mother. She had probably been more my mother's partner than ever I'd realized before; I could see it in her eyes. But her look back at me, although kind, was not apologetic.

Dolly reached out her hand to me as we stood there face-to-face. I took it in mine and squeezed. Then I turned away from them, and my body filled again with a hot rage.

I ran down the stairs to the front door. I paused, then strode into the main parlor and stared down at my mother's collection of china figurines.

Ugly, ugly, their cold glassy stares. They made my stomach turn. I fell to my knees before the display table and grasped the one that most resembled a family—a triple figure of a woman and a man dressed in finery, pushing a baby carriage—falsely colored, falsely poised. I held it in my hand and tried to scratch at it with my nails, but the material was too hard and slick for me to ruin it. Nothing mattered as much to me as damaging that figurine, so I stood and smashed the family to the polished wood floor, where it crashed apart in flaky white shards and floating powder.

I left my mother's home while the fine chalky dust of that broken china still drifted in the air. I heard Clorinda say in my wake, "Lord God Almighty."

Walking away, I could hear the other maids calling for me, calling for a carriage for me, but I would be long gone before the driver could be summoned. They had known me during all those years when my world revolved only around me, and still their concern for me was sincere. But I needed to share this sorrow with only one person.

I took long steps, heading in the direction of the Methodist church, where Ira slept at night. I knew this because it had been posted on the board outside our office for all the time we'd worked together, there so anyone could find him if in need. And there had never been a soul as much in need of him as I was at that moment.

I don't remember my thoughts, only my feelings of such deep betrayal that tore me apart, and I needed to see the only person in the world who could calm me, the only person who could help me find a place for this new truth. My father alive. Not dead. But insane. Hidden because he no longer suited. The stars overhead pulled me, my footsteps pounding out his name.

On the church grounds, I found his quarters easily, and when he opened the door, an expression I can't describe—fear, concern, gratitude, and love—shone back when he saw me. I touched him. I had been waiting, knowing it was inevitable, and then I was sinking into his chest, my face on his shoulder, my body encircled in his arms, the solid length of him against me, and that awful urge to cry that had always lived inside me broke free. I cried until every single cell inside was drained and all that was left was the horrible empty husk of humanity I was.

The next day, Ira accompanied me on the train to Houston and then onward to the address I had demanded from my mother. He sat next to me, his warmth comforting me on my quest to see the man I hadn't seen since I was five, the man I barely remembered but whom I hoped I could still love.

"When we arrive, do you wish to go in by yourself?" Ira asked me in the kindest voice I'd ever heard.

I was putting off an inevitable decision. In some ways, coming to grips with what Ira and I had meant to each other was more frightening than seeing my father for the first time in fourteen years. I said, "Would you follow behind me?"

"Of course."

"In case I can't hold up."

"But you will, Grace. I know it. You will hold up. Your fortitude is greater than you know."

I couldn't think of the future. Ira took my hand and lifted it toward his face, as if he intended to kiss it, and then suddenly he seemed not to know what to do, and he laid my hand back down on the seat between us. He smiled at me, I suppose apologizing. But had it not been for his caring, his sincerity, his presence, I believe I would not have been able to go on with my life.

What was to happen next? Where would I be had not Etta come, had I not been sent to work with Ira, had I never known the truth? One tiny word or event could mold our lives into very different shapes. Mine had assumed a complicated form, but it was larger, so much larger, as a result.

The journey passed heavily. The heat was alive and wavering and gave a deep dreamy quality to the air and sunshine. On the mainland, the train took us past cornfields, empty farm roads, and green cotton patches, scenes of pastoral tranquility so at odds with the turmoil that lived inside me.

And yet, sitting there beside Ira, I could hear each new moment coming to life, each breath and each heartbeat.

"Ira," I said to him, "you are the finest man I've ever known."

At the institution, they led us to my father, who was kept in a private room near the back of the huge old house, where people such as my mother were able to hide away their disgraces. As we walked down a center hallway, a woman cried out, and then a childlike voice called, "Help me, oh please, help me," and I wondered if I could do this, but Ira seemed to believe I could, so I kept placing one foot down before the other.

The nurse opened his door, and I saw his back, curved and ridged with spiny protrusions. So much older than I had expected, but when he turned to face me, I saw a face I remembered, older now, but the same long, straight nose that my mother had once described as "aristocratic," soft gray-blue eyes, narrow cheeks, and prominent chin. His face appeared peaceful and soft, ivory in color, and his eyes settled not exactly on mine. His hair was thin and pale and combed away, so light and wispy it looked like nothing, blonder than mine, like part of the sunlight streaming in from the window.

His room was made up like a regular bedroom, not as an infirmary room or ward, and the private nurse who attended him left us alone. My father gazed up and said, "Hello," as if I could have been one of the nurses who worked there. Ira stood behind me as I sat beside my father and took his hand.

"I'm Grace, your daughter, Grace."

"Oh yes," he said, smiling, then laughed. "So nice to meet you."

He didn't know me.

And yet I stayed with him for much of the afternoon. Except for a few moments when his face changed expression, a kind of distant alertness momentarily taking over at the lilt of my voice, or when his eyes drifted to some unknown or perhaps remembered place as I spoke of myself, he showed no change in recognition or mental faculties.

Outside the most sorrowful rainfall began to patter the packed dirt, dropping large, glossy tears on the leaves of rosebushes. He was like a child, just as my mother had said. But my heart rushed to the surface. I would not abandon him, childlike as he was. He was still my father, and knowing that he was alive had already begun to fill that place left empty inside me all those years ago. Perhaps a God-given gift, my intuition had told me that there was no last chapter at the end of his tale, and I'd never recovered because of it.

As we returned to the island, Ira beside me, his hands next to mine, I felt the island's pull and the slow rise and fall of the sea. It tugged at the soft spots between my ribs. What had transpired in my family was no stranger than the fact that people lived and thrived despite all the sad things that happened. And Ira and I were but a man and a woman in a carriage surrounded by a world filled with unexpected wonders and wounds.

The trajectory of my life had been forever altered, and there was only one person to credit. Etta had provided this devastating gift, this knowledge, both excruciating and enlightening. That morning I had learned that her infatuation and curiosity about Mother had driven her to uncover it. She had released the secret, and in many ways I was thankful she had, but I would never allow her or anyone else to again describe my father in such a way. I never wanted to hear that word *madman* ever again.

And what of my mother? Keeping the secret must have consumed her. I did believe she had thought she was protecting me. How hard she must have worked to keep me from knowing! I had an image of my mother staring down a distant storm, rumbling ever closer, her fists raised in silent defiance, insisting it not come, still standing there even as the sky cracked open and the first hard pings of rain hit her.

At least she had made sure that my father wasn't locked up in a cage or tortured, as I'd heard was often done in other asylums. She had found probably the best and kindest care for the afflicted as was possible. My mother took care of everything so well, especially herself.

The floodwaters again poured down my face. Ira held me and whispered in my ear, "You'll withstand this, Grace. You will." I turned my face to say something, and then his lips were on mine and I was kissing him back, our mouths salty from so many tears and sweet from so many words we had yet to say.

Chapter Thirty-Two

THE GIRL

The girl rubbed her eyes awake and thought of Harry. Not since he'd first taken bad sick had they been out on the bay again. Every day Harry had stayed huddled in his berth in the boat, the boat rocking lifelessly with the will of the waves, straining against the ropes. Harry stayed inside, coughing and choking and hacking up blood and mucus and suffering, suffering as the girl had never seen a person suffer before.

She visited every morning, took him breakfasts and suppers from Reena he barely touched, and often sat with him until he'd garnered the strength to shoo her away, saying, "Be gone with you now" in his broken voice.

She returned every morning, always holding on to the hope that she'd arrive to find him out in the sunlight, working on some little thing that needed fixing, back to his old self again, miraculously healed. But each day brought more weakness, and one day the girl got a glimpse of his leg. It was chicken-bone thin with pale, plucked flesh drawn tightly over it. If only he would go to the hospital.

◆ ◆ ◆

One day he lifted himself up on one elbow, stretching out his side to get enough air into his lungs to form words. He pointed at her to make sure he had her attention. "Visitor I had. Told me that girl was in the newspaper again."

He stopped for a minute, his labored breathing accompanied by a rattling sound. "No good, no good."

She nodded.

"There's people trying to find you. Like it's some kind of a game. But once they gets a hold of you . . ." He stopped and shook his head. "No telling."

The girl lowered her eyes. She should never have gotten up there again. People would be all over her like Grace was, maybe asking to help but really doing nothing of the sort, further complicating her already complicated existence.

Still, as she sat there on the edge of Harry's bed, listening to him fight for every breath, she remembering the running, jumping off the wall, escaping, and she had a feeling of something else, too, something beyond memory. There was a fire in her gut like undigested food, voices rumbling down deep inside her, something incomplete, other dangers more threatening than this misunderstood running on the wall, and somewhere in her center the other danger lived and grew behind a closed door, the unspeakable thing that she couldn't express even if she were able to express anything.

"What's wrong?" he finally asked.

She lifted a hand and pointed a chapped finger in his direction.

"No," he said, "what's wrong with *you?*"

She shook her head.

The rain came down the next day in panels that looked like glass under a layer of dew. The girl had stayed indoors at Reena's for all of the daylight hours until Reena sent Maurice for her. He shook her awake and then passed on the message that Reena wanted her company in the big house kitchen. The girl put on her blue dress for such an occasion as going into the big house, something she'd done only twice before.

Reena scolded her unfairly, telling her not to be "lazing around no more," "moping around never did no one any good," and that she needed help fixing supper. And then Reena fixed her gaze on the blue dress. She frowned in disapproval but handed over an apron and told the girl to slice onions and chop peppers for the evening supper, a jambalaya she often made for her white family. It was Reena's favorite meal to cook on a Saturday, and as the girl watched her put it all together, she helped herself to stray pieces of boiled sausage and shrimp as Reena was cutting and tossing them into a pot.

"Someday you is gonna have to learn something else besides getting yourself into trouble."

The girl tried to smile, but it came out as a grimace.

"You don't need a whole lotta words in your mouth to be able to cook," said Reena. "It's just some knowing about seasoning, and what goes together with what, and how long to let things simmer." She looked up. "I be teaching you shortly. That's how I learnt—from a good cook, my own mama, God rest her soul."

The girl leaned against the working table and watched the pot begin to fill. Cooking wasn't such a bad idea, but she would've preferred to have become an artist.

"You best start watching me every day." Reena waved a big arm at the nice white house they were standing in. "And then maybe I can get you a job someday in one of these here houses."

The girl kept on watching. The jambalaya was finally put together and set to simmer, and then someone called out in the backyard for Reena. Reena wiped her hands on her apron front and strode to the back door, which swung open on its oiled hinges without a sound. The girl was right behind her.

A fisherman from the docks, and a friend of Harry's, was standing there. The girl wondered why he was seeking Reena, and then in her gut she knew he wasn't looking for Reena, that he was probably looking for her.

"I'm a-coming for that girl there," said the man, gazing at them. "Harry has gotten real sick, and he's a-asking for her."

"Lord have mercy," Reena said softly. She let out a heavy sigh. "Take that apron off yourself, and you best head on down there."

The girl passed over the apron, then started down the steps, hitching up the silky blue skirt in both fists. She joined the man as Reena called out from behind them, "Don't stay too long, you hear?"

The rain had stopped, but everywhere the leaves glistened and pools reflected the ceiling of dark clouds overhead. The girl wished she could run down to the docks. She could jump the low-water spots easily, but the man who'd come for her walked along at a regular pace, as if to say that rushing would serve no purpose.

She stayed with him as they walked all the way to Harry's boat. On the planks at the back of the boat, the man left her.

As she stepped into the stern, a sour, musty smell that she remembered hit her nose, something not nearly as bad as the smell on the day she and Harry had returned after the storm, but there was still something familiar about it from that time.

He was stretched out in the berth, with heavy quilts pulled up to his neck, his face pale as linen and his lips bluish and chafed, a clammy dullness on his skin, his cheeks sunken, as if scraped out with a knife, his eyes weary and blurred, his breath and body foul. And there was a feeling of slipping, of bone-white finality and cold.

He motioned her over. "Now listen," he said with effort.

After drawing breath, he held it and then said in a raspy wheeze, "This'll be the last time we talk, and I want you to know I'm leaving this boat to you. It ain't much. But it's all I have. Your pa and your brother would have wanted me to take care of you. And I done the best I could.

Work the boat or sell it. Don't matter to me either way." He lifted his head from the pillow and hacked for a minute, then laid his head back down resignedly. "That's all. You can go on now. Leave me be."

She shook her head. She didn't want the boat. She wanted him.

"This ain't nothing. For a young girl. To see. Go on."

But she stayed.

The girl sat until long past nightfall, until the docks grew silent; until she could hear the splash of jumping fish in the quiet waters of the wharves; until she could hear gull wings in the warm night breezes over the port; until she could hear waves colliding with sandy shelves on the other side of the island; until she heard him draw one long, last wheezing breath, and then nothing at all.

Reena would have said that he'd passed on, but passed on to where, the girl didn't know. She could only hope for Heaven. The girl lifted the quilts to cover his face and head, as that was what she'd seen her mother do to her grandmother's body years before, and then she left the boat where it sat in the brackish port water. She walked down the docks, surprised that there could still be stars overhead, that there could still be this cool night breeze.

Why did the best people die? Why did they leave her?

She wasn't aware of them until they'd crept up on her again, silent and stealthy.

"You're back," one of them said.

"Back for more?" another one said and laughed.

She spun around and stared. Then the lock on the door in her head labeled "Don't Ever Look in Here Again" flew open, releasing a rogue wave that slammed her down. She remembered. That which she had been able to hide away now stood right before her eyes. The same beginning, the same men, the same raucous comments, the same laughter and smells. It was as in the dream, in the nightmare, but it hadn't been a dream after all. Instead, it was real, all too real. Yes, it had happened. She had been taken. She had been used. She had been wronged in the worst way one could be wronged.

But it would never happen again.

Her body became fluid. She moved like water, flowed like water—silky, smooth. She poured away, her feet striking the planks soundlessly, her heart beating in her chest silently, her feet crossing the boardwalk on The Strand and then over sand and gravel and oyster-shell alleys noiselessly, running for so long she thought she'd lost them, but no. When she turned, they were still there, chasing her like a pack of hungry animals, teeth bared, hair stiff like razorbacks, and she kept floating over the earth, running for her soul, for her very life, because she would not let this thing happen to her again. If only she could scream for help.

She ran from memory. No moon tonight because of the cloud cover. Utter darkness except for an occasional flickering candle or lantern behind gently waving curtains meant that she had to move by instinct. She could no longer hear them behind her, only the cooing of mourning doves, the hoots of owls, and mice scratching in the trash piles.

She had outrun them for now and turned right once, then again, changing course and heading back toward the docks on different alleys and streets. They would always track her. She could still feel their nearness reaching out for her with long, tentacle-like arms. While she was running, it came to her—an image, a sketch she had to compose—and it twisted her and wrenched her out. But it was the idea she needed. Otherwise, she would end up like those minnows she and Harry had seen on the dock, those tiny fish dropped on solid land and left to die. Staying would spell her death. By the time her feet hit the planks on Dock 19 again, the wind was wild in her hair and she was already tearing herself out of the blue dress, out of these things that didn't belong to her.

Her story here would be short, but it would be hers and hers alone. Despite all the running and hiding, her life here had included some wonderful things. Big things—a father, mother, and brother. Little things—a perfect sand dollar, a day over the shoals with Harry, a drawing of a fish filled with vibrant colors.

Wearing only her petticoat and underthings, she reached the boat, unmoored it quickly, and jumped on board. Harry's body remained where she had left it. He would have wanted a sea burial anyway.

No longer earthbound, no longer looking back. Life on the island wouldn't leave her; she would leave it. She sailed away until there was nothing else, only the quiet of an underwater world below her, and there she managed to return Harry to the sea.

Yes, holy be thy resting place—a line from Brontë. She wept for him and would always remember . . . *sweet, kind Harry.*

Gripping the tiller hard, she let her breath out in a tremulous stream. Sweat swam down her spine and moonlight planed into her eyes. She stared into the receding lights of the island. She would never have recovered back there. The island had not protected her family; it couldn't save her, it couldn't even heal her. She had only been passing through that place. Fleeing over dunes, marshes, docks, and alleys, along a wall and through to the sea.

Remaining awake and alert until Galveston was barely visible, she kept watching until it receded into a speck and then drowned. She knew nothing of what awaited her ahead; she had never even imagined owning a boat. The stars sparkled and nudged ever so slightly overhead, and the sea parted before her.

Harry had saved her life once and had now done it again, this time by allowing her to leave.

Chapter Thirty-Three

ETTA

And so came the aftermath. Because of her aunt's grand sweeping gesture, Etta learned about the tenacity of a mother's love.

The morning after Etta had blurted out what she knew, her aunt marched into Etta's room and stood rooted there, framed by a large beam of light coming through an open window, making her look resplendent and not of this world. She held her hands high and clasped before her, her back was long and straight, and the muscles along her jawline were clenched.

Etta had never seen her aunt quite so animated. Her thoughts must have been spinning like an eddy, but her eyes showed a dreadful, raw pain.

She had expected rage. She had expected "How could you? How could you?" screamed at high pitch. But this pain, this solitary pain in her aunt's eyes, was almost unbearable.

She had already lain awake during the night, planning her recovery from such a serious error in judgment and admonishing herself for her outrageous loss of control. Regaining acceptance into the circle of friends she had offended would be easy enough given time and a few graciously placed apologies and explanations. Even Grace would forgive her; she had that nature. Already this morning her cousin had gone to see the man who had been hidden from her for years, and Etta had the feeling that her cousin would embrace her father despite his condition.

But her aunt was another matter. She would be the one most disgraced, most betrayed, and the most vengeful. No matter how many times Etta tried to replay the evening in her mind, no matter how many times she rewrote the story more to her liking, the facts remained, and she had said it.

"How did you know?" Bernadette asked.

Etta had decided on honesty. "I followed you."

"Why?"

Etta looked at her aunt with open eyes. "Because I was curious. I wanted to know everything about you."

"You followed me? All the way there? Why didn't you simply ask me?"

"You were avoiding me. You lied to me about doing business in town."

Her aunt's back caved in. She suddenly seemed weary and sad. "I thought I could keep that one thing private." Her age was apparent for the first time, the fine lines chiseled into her face made more visible by the white morning sunlight. "But if you had come to me with what you knew . . ."

"Would you have told me?" asked Etta, working to remain calm. "Even I would never have dreamed what you were hiding. And hiding it from Grace . . ."

"It's hidden no longer, thanks to you."

"Would you have told me?"

Bernadette didn't move a muscle. For once she appeared to be at a loss for words, and Etta sensed her weakening.

Etta said, "I am truly sorry. I was distraught. The evening wasn't going as planned, and I lost my temper. I said it before I had realized it."

"So you aren't responsible for the words that came out of your mouth."

"Of course I'm responsible. That's why I'm apologizing."

"That apology will never be accepted."

Etta began to panic, and then came the blow.

"You have two days to gather your belongings and say your good-byes."

Etta gasped. So this would be her punishment, the thing she most dreaded. Back to normalcy, back to mediocrity, back to Nacogdoches. "You're sending me away."

"Yes," said her aunt, "back to where you came from."

Etta looked down. She had been bettered. Rejection sliced through her as though she were made of grease. All her doing. All her undoing.

Hot tears formed in her eyes, and bitter regret cut farther inside her. She stole a glance out of the window at turbid, churning clouds that reminded her of curdled milk. A sour truth in her gut, she finally opened herself, her voice a plaintive whisper. "I'll do anything to remain. I'll do anything to make it up to you. Please."

Bernadette shook her head. "It's not what you've done to me. It's that you did it to Grace. That is what I cannot abide. The betrayal will always remain. I can't have you in my house any longer."

Later, when Etta remembered back to this morning, she would be appalled by the speed of it. Everything had been destroyed by only a few words. One minute, one deed, one word had the power to tilt the world in another direction. "But Galveston is my home now."

"No," said Bernadette. She had a handkerchief folded in her hand and she dabbed at her neck. "It isn't and probably never should have been. I agreed to help my sister with you, and this is how I am repaid."

"But I'm truly sorry. I'll make it up to you. If I'm forced to leave, what shall I do?"

"Do whatever you like. But you must go."

Etta's throat constricted. "I'll beg."

"Oh no," said Bernadette. "It won't do you a bit of good."

After her aunt left her alone, Etta sat before her dressing table, her face in the mirror a chilled icy-white and lifeless thing, her hair the color of bitter bark, her breath dry and ragged. She picked up a comb and began raking it through her long locks repeatedly, from her scalp all the way down to the coiled ends, as if by doing so she could rid herself of the events of the previous day. Of course Grace would mean more to her aunt than a favored niece. But how huge the punishment for only a few words. Simple words.

Outside, the gulls screeched for her as if in pain. Sitting in her skin was difficult. She had no alternative but to do what her aunt insisted. She hadn't planned well enough, and she hadn't been in Galveston long enough to secure a secondary option. Like Philo, Etta had performed with no safety net below her. Impulsiveness had always been her downfall, and once again it had leveled her and overtaken her carefully contained plans. It had won.

Two days later, Grace accompanied her to the train. During the carriage ride to Union Station, Etta looked out of her window. What match in marriage, what home filled with fine things, what beautiful children and travels could she have had? In front of her, a ripple passed down the horse's flank, and the horse's head lifted in defiance of something, smelling the wind.

The sun was too bright. The horse whinnied in protest, and Etta wondered if there was something she could say to change her fate, some last plea, but as they drew nearer to the station, the air emptied from her lungs.

They arrived early at the station and had to wait for the train to begin boarding passengers. While Seamus delivered her trunks to the station, Grace stood with her in the shade, out of the sun's sharply fanged rays. Occasionally Grace gazed out at the pulsing sun, as if she'd never seen it quite that shape before. Grace was good at heart. Even the recent turn of events hadn't ruined her, but of course she hadn't experienced the same degree of failure that Etta had. And she didn't possess the wrath her aunt did, either.

Etta finally turned to Grace and asked, "So, will you marry Jonathan?"

A small furrow made its way down Grace's forehead. "I honestly don't know."

"Will you write and let me know?"

Grace looked down at the ground, as if searching for answers. "I don't know."

"Please."

"Well"—Grace hesitated—"I'll think about it."

"You're right. Perhaps we shouldn't write."

Grace smiled in a way that was both kind and regretful. "Mother says the two of us together were always trouble."

Etta nodded. "We're too different."

Grace seemed pensive, and then her voice changed. "Oh, I don't know about that."

Etta watched the air around her quickly fill with dust motes and fragments of flowers and other tiny particles, capturing a quavering light. All floating, drifting, and so haphazard. At the beginning of the summer, their relationship had begun in such a hopeful manner—that unspoken pact made at the sea, when they believed they were more enlightened than their elders.

Etta said in a whisper, unable to meet her cousin's eyes, "We didn't end up any better, did we?"

"Better than our mothers?" said Grace. "Oh, I don't know. We still have time."

"You're too kind."

"No," said Grace, "I'm not kind. I'm still reeling, if you want the truth."

Etta managed to speak. "I'm sorry. Honestly, Grace . . ."

Grace looked at Etta with glistening eyes. "You opened my mind. It's the most confusing mix of emotions. I hate your tactics, but I wouldn't have known had it not been for you. You came here and changed everything."

Etta's eyes filled with tears that she made no attempt to bat away. Two streams floated down her face, unchecked. "I changed everything except myself."

Grace moved closer and took Etta's hand. "There's hope for us . . ."

Then Etta did what she never expected to do. She held her cousin close, felt her body against hers, and embraced her. As the surge of their related blood coursed through them, Etta's lungs refilled with life-giving oxygen. They stayed there, entwined, even as streams of people rushed past them to board the train.

If only she could go back in time; if only the future could be destined differently. Then something like love filled her, something like that old family history written within the seams of their skin, but she finally let Grace go. In the end, she hadn't fared well in the world of her cousin. Would these moments in her life, this fog that was Galveston, eventually blow away, leaving behind only a faint memory?

"Take care of yourself," said Grace.

Etta couldn't pull her gaze away. She had never been the recipient of such kindness. "I've never trusted anyone, you see."

"I understand."

Etta gulped. "No one at all."

"So find a way to trust, and also find happiness," Grace said.

"And I will wish it for you, too."

As she walked to the station house to purchase her ticket to Nacogdoches, the sense of finality dragged her down with enormous weight, each step pulling her onward into the deep bowels of Texas, the bowels of hell.

She had lived in two worlds now. One full of hope, one hopeless. One light, one dark. One full of the future, one full of the past. She had almost successfully made the hop from one to the other. Almost.

A cloud passed across the sun; then the sunlight returned like a spear in her eyes. Around her, it brightened the world. Her head cleared, and she swallowed the first taste of real freedom.

Lord Almighty, this was her life, her moment, her decision. There had to be more out there than just these two worlds. She reeled even as she stopped walking, holding completely still. People peered at her curiously as they wove around her, but she went blind to them. Why was she letting others snatch away her free will and send her down a path of their making, not hers? What was she doing taking directions yet again from someone else, when no one could really force her to board that train to Nacogdoches?

Before, she had thought of herself as a freethinker, even a rebel, but it turned out she had been as disappointing as those old bones and tools found in the Caddo burial mounds. Her moves had been small; now was the moment to take a leap.

She walked again, her gait changing to rock solid as she finally found footing in her own ideas. She had a lot of learning to take with her. Could brutal sorrow be transformed into fierce determination? Her chest filled with something close to joy. Yes, yes—it was all in her. Etta clenched her fists at her sides so hard her nails dug into the skin of her palms.

She had been banished from Galveston, a tiny speck in the sea. So what? In years to come, it would be forgotten and meaningless. There had been life before this, and there would be life after. Now she was truly free—not a shamed daughter sent away or a shunned niece sent away again, but a new woman who could become anyone she wanted. With her trunks full of expensive and fashionable clothes and money she had saved from her aunt's generous allowance, Etta could go anywhere.

New Orleans! The name embedded itself like a sparkling diamond in her brain. She would go to that fabled city. She could take what she had learned in Galveston and turn it to her advantage.

She gazed about. Here, she might have been tempted to marry only for money, to settle for something less than what she'd once felt for Philo. But why should she?

Etta walked onward, the new plan beginning to sing inside her head. She was young and beautiful, there were endless possibilities, and life's potential was not lost, not yet. She would think of her aunt no longer. After all, Bernadette was a woman of the old order. Her time was over, but Etta's was just beginning.

Chapter Thirty-Four

GRACE

My friends Viola and Larke stood by me throughout those early dark days of scandalous gossip. And Jonathan, too, dear Jonathan.

Viola spent hours on my porch, in the gardens, in the library, talking everything over. Once she said, "You've lost your father all over again. First you lost him to death, now the death of what you thought he was."

Yes, it had been difficult to accept that my father was not of sound mind. Had this revelation about my father been made earlier in my life, I might have taken the same course as my mother had and placed it in hiding. Ours was a society that did not accept what it saw as lesser souls.

I said, "But he lives."

Viola shook her head. "And your mother? Will the two of you ever be the same?"

"I'm not sure I want things to be the same."

"But will you ever make amends?"

"I hope so."

"You could put it behind you?"

"I hope to."

Viola considered me.

I shrugged. "Nothing can change what's already been done. What good could possibly come from not putting it behind us? I'm thinking about forgiveness."

My words could've come from Ira's mouth.

On the beach three days later, the children dipped, blew, bounced in imaginary boats, and spun like eddies. I walked with Joseph down the strip of packed sand. A church volunteer who was helping me stayed with the children, who were playing in the gentle surf of that day.

Joseph was now ready to venture all the way to the water's edge. On the hard sand, he even allowed the lips of low, transparent, sliding waves to reach his toes. Still he was fearful, and I would not let him go. In fact, I squeezed his hand tighter than he squeezed mine. I would not let him go under. I would not let it happen again, as we had allowed Etta to go under so long ago.

Later we strolled down to the docks in search of the girl. I had been told that she'd been missing for days, and although I had searched, I'd come up with nothing. I told myself she had simply gone into hiding again. And I tried hard to believe it.

We headed toward a boat slip where some fishermen had directed us to look, but it was empty. Another fisherman told me that boat had been gone for a few days.

As I stood before the empty slip looking into the murky water, something shiny drew my eye. It caught on the piling beneath the planks, mostly submerged, but some of it dry and out of the water, hanging on the splintered wood. It reflected the light of the throbbing afternoon sun. Joseph and I located a stick, and I used it to lift the thing from the water.

My blue dress now lay crumpled on the dock in front of me. I recognized it, although the sun and salt water had bleached its color. My old dress, abandoned there, most of it drenched and stuck on the rough splintery wood planks, the dry part flapping in the wind. It had not floated away; instead, it had remained despite the water and wind, kept here as if by some omnipotent being who knew I needed to see it. That dress lit by the sunlight, no girl in sight. As I stared down, somehow knowing that this abandoned dress contained a message, that it meant something, a hollow pit opened inside me. I could imagine her tearing out of this garment and the reach of those like me, who had perhaps prodded and pried too much.

I couldn't look at the dress, not at what this meant. Instead, I gazed out to the bay, an emptiness inside that could've contained all that water. I had played a role in this, my dress the confirmation of that fact. But knowing nothing more than that, I stood until the sun sank lower against the blank, cloudless sky, all the while willing that light not to leave me.

Joseph did nothing to snap me back into composure. The sweet, uncanny wisdom of the very young kept him nearby, playing quietly, while my mind ran through all the possibilities. Why had she gone? Where had she gone? Would she survive?

Then it was sunset, and the bay turned to sheets of liquid silver sprinkled with gold. Joseph took my hand. The sky was a burnished red, the water beneath our feet an iridescent burnt pink. This was the color I used to try to capture on canvas, this burned and brilliant sunlight at the end of day that made everything, even the rawest, ugliest thing, look soft like a baby's velvety cheek.

Where was she?

I didn't know, and the others who knew her didn't either. So I suppose no story is complete without its tragedies. I had failed her.

From time to time, accounts of Miss Girl appeared in the newspapers, and she became the talk of the town once again. Apparently there were impersonators on the seawall. Everyone in Galveston believed she was very much alive and well, and that she ran the wall for unknown reasons and at unexpected times, mysteriously preferring to remain anonymous, her story untold. I liked to think that she might be back, having simply played a frivolous trick on those of us who cared, that she had hidden herself better this time, and then ran the wall just to tease us. I liked wishing it. And when that hope faded, I imagined her along another shore or on another island much sweeter than Galveston had been to her.

Over breakfast one morning, when the servants were out of the room, my mother said, "I wish I could've been different for you, Grace. You have a right to be angry at me for the rest of my life."

My mother's hair had turned completely silver by then. Overnight the youthful dark streaks had bleached themselves away. Her eyes were more delicately set, her gaze diffused, and she rarely wore rouge anymore. Her face had taken on a softened, muted quality.

This was her way of asking for my forgiveness, a step forward in her view. At the beginning of our newfound relationship, even her gaze had been like porcupine quills. Her presence darkened a room. How sharp was the edge, the ragged break between love and hate. But I didn't want to hate her or hurt her any longer. Nothing was as desperate as a bitter woman, and I would not become one.

I said, "I hope not to hold on to grudges and bad feelings forever."

"But your father . . ." she said, her voice trailing away.

True, my father's existence was one that others would find of little value, but for lack of other options, I would take it. I also knew by then that people came into one's life, and sometimes they stayed, but staying couldn't be taken for granted. Other times they slipped away. All one could do was hold on to what was learned and try to paint with the purest and truest colors.

There were times when I would venture that my father knew me. Sometimes I saw a soft U-shaped smile or a changed light in his eyes when I walked into the room. Other times he would lift his eyebrows and put his lips together, as if he were going to say something important, something revealing, and always a surge of hope then rose in my chest, but just as quickly he looked lost again. Sometimes he spoke of old memories: his mother, an old family dog, yellow flowers in a garden, a blue jay he once tried to catch. Sometimes I saw my own face in his expressions. Other times I saw my fingers in his hands.

I had already consulted an alienist from England, a doctor who specialized in the treatment of people such as my father, but he came up with no new recommendations. He gave me hope, however, by describing some possible treatments under review, including an experimental electric shock therapy that we might try in the future. I'd even considered bringing my father to Galveston until I was told how difficult it was for people like him to leave a familiar place. The nurses at the home told me that often a change of location brought on hallucinations, rages, and crying. I couldn't have borne it.

My mother had said, "Bring him here? Are you trying to punish me in front of everyone?"

But the idea of bringing him closer was not in any way an attempt at punishment. I had never considered it that way. That was her world, not mine.

Jonathan dined with us the last evening before leaving to return to Yale. He arrived dressed in more casual attire than usual, no jacket, and he needed to see the barber. He had aged, too. The summer had not turned out to be anything like we had expected.

He hadn't abandoned a sinking ship, so to speak, even though I was poor company in those days. Jonathan had never asked for any details about my father's condition and had not asked to join me on a visit to see him. Gossip had made its rounds, and everyone now knew that I had chosen Ira to accompany me the first time. I had tried to imagine taking Jonathan along. I tried to imagine him sitting quietly in the room while my father gazed out of the window or picked at the buttons on his shirt.

Would Jonathan understand my urge to be near him?

We had canceled the gala to celebrate our engagement, and the new pink silk gown hung in my wardrobe, a glistening arrogant reminder, awaiting our decision.

When we ate dinner with my mother, it was difficult for me to make light conversation. Those days were over. Tension hung in the room as heavy as the humidity in the air. But he and my mother were better than me at such things. They managed to make small talk despite it all. Jonathan sat with me throughout long tepid meals with my mother.

One night after dinner, on the portico he said, "I lost myself for a while, Grace."

I nodded.

"I-I . . ." He paused. "I'm talking about Etta. Even though I despise her now."

I couldn't help but feel sorry for her, someone who had defeated herself. "It was never about Etta."

"What was it about then?"

We had both turned to another, but there was no reason to hurt Jonathan any further by reminding him. "It's about whether or not we're a good match."

He looked at me in the way I'd always loved—full of adoration and tenderness.

"We endured physical separation for three school years, and then during our most important summer together a distance emerged."

"Distances are meant to be crossed. We can find each other again, Grace. I know it. I still love you."

I meant it when I said, "And I love you." I loved Jonathan, but not in the way I should've.

"Isn't that enough?" he asked pleadingly.

"I used to think so."

He took my hands. "Look, our love has been tested. Brutally tested, in fact. But many wise people would say that tests can strengthen a couple. It can become, in fact, an advantage."

I appreciated his effort, but now I was in love, really in love for the first time in my life.

He said softly while still holding my hands, "Your life has changed in so many ways. I believe you should let things settle for a while. Let's wait the year out before making any decision. We have that much time, at least."

His sweet blue gaze reminded me of the boy I'd known, but the tension along his jawline made it obvious that our youth was over and both of us had to face adult truths. I answered chokingly, "In truth, Jonathan . . . I feel we should break our engagement now." I made myself face his pleading eyes. "Things happened this summer that should not have happened had we been right for each other."

He looked saddened but not crushed. "Are you sure, Grace? I mean, the scandal of a broken engagement . . ."

I smiled wryly. "In view of recent scandals, this one will pale in comparison."

He almost laughed, and I was filled with warmth for Jonathan. We had started as friends, and friends we would remain.

In the end, he agreed.

After Jonathan left for school, I continued to work with the man who had opened my heart and mind. With all the complications surrounding me at the time, I thought that perhaps he might want to back away graciously from a woman whom he thought was still promised to another.

But I was wrong. Standing close to the same spot where only months before I had met him for the first time, he took my hand in his and spoke in his familiar soft voice. His eyes were imploring and shiny. "You could end your engagement. We could make our partnership both professional and marital. It wouldn't be an easy life, and I probably shouldn't even ask . . ."

I wanted to touch the fine hairs that drifted onto his collar. We had never even found the time to have that talk about Darwin.

He went on: "You don't have to answer right away. Think about it, and let me know your answer when you're ready." He swallowed. "Should your answer be yes, I would be the happiest man . . ."

"I have already broken my engagement, but I must ask: Why do you believe in me?"

He stepped forward and put his hands on either side of my waist, and that tender weight had the effect of lifting me to the vast blue sky with a wind composed of both fear and desire.

He whispered, "Because you don't yet. But you will."

When I think of that time with Ira and Etta, when the memories are so strong they bore into me like beetles, I always return to this special moment, when I wished for order and sensibility and shape in the world, even though I knew it wasn't possible; when I knew that our path would not be easy, but should we take it, we would walk together side by side as equals.

But my life had begun on this island, and it would end here, too. I looked away and breathed in. Viewed from afar, as if by a creator, Galveston Island must have seemed the most unlikely place to settle, given all the solid land where we might have laid claim and grown surer and more solid roots.

I focused on his face again and said, "Your life requires moving from place to place, following the greatest need. And my life must remain here, now more than ever. Someday my mother will be gone, and perhaps my father will outlive her. I must remain here, Ira, to look after both of them. I couldn't go with you when you leave. I simply couldn't."

"I would never leave you . . ."

"But your work . . . the needs down on the border?"

He said in a whisper, "Please don't assume that I can't find happiness in one place. I have and I will."

"But the needs on the border?"

"I'll find someone else to go."

My eyes stung, but I did not blink. His face was sunburned again. Soon I would be the one to take care of that. I would rub cream into the burn and insist that he wear a hat in the sun. Ira, the wealthiest man I'd ever known in terms of humanity, was too considerate to press me for a decision on that day.

Looking back later, I found it curious that I didn't accept his proposal then and there. Perhaps the conventions of the day still affected me more than they should have, and I lacked the courage to slip quickly from one engagement to another and therefore slap society so alarmingly in its face.

"Grace," he told me one day as I was leaving.

I spun around.

"Hold your head high. Always hold your head high."

I smiled a good-bye and turned to leave again. Then I did as he said. I walked straight and tall, in the posture that I imagined had once been my father's, to wait for this man who said he would also wait for me.

Chapter Thirty-Five

The Girl

At dawn, she woke up out at sea, having let the wind take her where it wanted. She rubbed her eyes awake and donned an old shirt and some pants of Harry's. Miraculously she had sailed through the pass from the bay into open ocean, and in the broad circle of water surrounding her, there was nothing but sea and sky, no land in sight. All around her she faced her special place along the horizon. She sat taller and peered closer, a sudden excitement building. She had found it, that place she'd always sought—that glistening meeting of the water and the heavens, no land to be seen, not even an island.

All along she had been drawn here; all along it had been calling her to leave, to abandon the island that had not been able to protect her family's lives, nor in the end hers, either. Back there, her plight had been but one small droplet in the deluge of a great human tragedy, a massive drama of loss and suffering and searching, her plight only one among thousands. And now she was here, crossing empty sea to be born again, she hoped, to land in a new life.

Would this be a new beginning, or would she meet an untimely death? Would she meet other kind souls like Reena and Madu? Or would she be hunted again? Would she hit a sandbar and capsize, sail into starvation, or would she slide upon a seaside town that welcomed her? Away from Galveston, that place of death, would she someday recover her voice? There was no way to know and nothing to do except sail onward. A clear directive sped through her brain like a whip of cool air. *Sail west. Put the morning sun on your back.*

She plowed into the unknown, the sea below her and the open sky above.

My life will begin again.

It tasted sweet; it tasted true.

Epilogue

GRACE

I started painting again, at first in a futile attempt to recapture that end-of-day light, and when I still couldn't get it right, I started to paint the girl as I remembered her on the seawall, wearing my old yellow dress, silhouetted against the island sky, the sea below her. I preferred to remember her in this way, above the rest of us.

Galveston continued to believe in Miss Girl simply for the joy of it, and more for the absence of a breathing, heart-beating, imperfect person than if she had been discovered and found to be all too humanly flawed. She became more colorful than an average person, not unlike the way I remembered my father, deeply tucked into a past that I could never quite reclaim.

I didn't talk about her again. My declaration to have known Miss Girl was quickly forgotten in the aftermath of that fateful evening. Better anyway to let the invented stories supplant the real girl, who belonged to no one.

At first, I didn't know what colors to use. I began with gray seawall and brown sea and painted her dress a pale, bleached yellow, the sky barely lavender. But as I worked longer, I devised a gust of cerulean sky, a swath of emerald-green wave, a tendril of red hair trailing from beneath the edge of her bonnet, a flame that still burned.

Her dress changed to sunny yellow, and her arms became the color of ripe peaches. Her cheeks were soon flushed into a different shade of warm pink. I finished one painting and then another, and it gave me comfort to put her form on canvas, to keep her image alive in a changing beauty, to in some way mark her presence and remember her. One day I could finally stand back and smile at her image without crying.

My mother disapproved, but I sold those paintings in a gallery and then donated the proceeds to my causes in the alleys. Over the years to come, she became my most popular subject, and my paintings of the girl appeared everywhere, in homes and restaurants and hotel lobbies, but never far from the water.

Each small stroke I blended with care, bright colors and deep ones, a combination of light and dark equally necessary for contrast and fullness. I brushed the strokes into small dense patterns, into joy and despair and all shades in between, into life before my eyes. Perhaps I would paint her for weeks, perhaps for months, maybe for years, but most likely for decades, until I could no longer pick up a brush.

ACKNOWLEDGMENTS

Much appreciation to my fabulous agent, Lisa Erbach Vance, who believes in me and is always helpful and honest about my work. And to Amara Holstein, Jodi Warshaw, and the team at Lake Union: this book would not be if it weren't for your wisdom, guidance, and support. A special thanks to Jami Durham of the Galveston Historical Foundation for her reading and historical critique of the manuscript, as well as finding the original source of the "Miss Girl" story.

I utilized many fine resources while researching this book, among them *Galveston: A History* by David McComb; *The Alleys and Back Buildings of Galveston: An Architectural and Social History* by Ellen Beasley; *Isaac's Storm: A Man, a Time, and the Deadliest Hurricane in History* by Erik Larson; and *Daughter of Fortune: The Bettie Brown Story* by Sherrie S. McLeRoy.

And finally, I want to thank the special people of Kentucky, who have taken me in as their own. Being here has been an unexpected and ongoing blessing.

ABOUT THE AUTHOR

Photo © 2015 Whitney Raines Photography

Ann Howard Creel was born in Austin, Texas, and worked as a registered nurse before becoming a full-time writer. She is the author of seven books for children and young adults, as well as four adult novels, including *The Whiskey Sea* and *While You Were Mine*. Her children's books have won several awards, and her novel *The Magic of Ordinary Days* was made into a Hallmark Hall of Fame movie for CBS. Creel currently lives and writes in Paris, Kentucky, where she is renovating a vintage house. Follow her at www.annhowardcreel.com.